The Centaur in the Garden

The Centaur in the Garden

MOACYR SCLIAR

The University of Wisconsin Press

The University of Wisconsin Press
1930 Monroe Street
Madison, Wisconsin 53711

www.wisc.edu/wisconsinpress/

3 Henrietta Street
London WC2E 8LU, England

Originally published in Portuguese as *O Centauro no jardin* by Editora Nova Fronteira S.A., Brazil.
Copyright © 1980 by Moacyr Scliar
Translation copyright © 1984 by Margaret A. Neves
Introduction copyright © 2003 by Ilan Stavans

5   4   3   2

Printed in the United States of America

Library of Congress Cataloging-in-Publication Data
Scliar, Moacyr.
  [Centauro no jardim. English]
  The centaur in the garden / Moacyr Scliar
  p. cm.—(The Americas)
  ISBN 0-299-18784-5 (pbk. : alk. paper)
  I. Title. II. Americas (Madison, Wis.)
PQ 9698.29.C54 C4313   2003
869.3'42—dc21   2003040186

Only the horse can cry for man. This is because in the centaur the nature of the man and the nature of the horse are combined.

—12TH-CENTURY BESTIARY

Let us not rejoice too much in the face of these human victories over nature.

—FRIEDRICH ENGELS

They say that for the Indians, the soldiers of Pizarro or Hernándo Cortes were centaurs too. When a soldier fell from his mount, the Indians saw what they had thought was a single animal divide itself into two parts, and were terrified. . . . Had it not been for this, it is thought, the Indians would have killed all the Christians.

—JORGE LUIS BORGES

It is always agreeable to see a destroyer of fables become the victim of a fable.

—GASTON BACHELARD

Never before had I seen
someone look at a horse
so tenderly, as it coursed
deep into his eyes, bearing
him inwardly, where everything
was sea—and the sea, horse.

—CARLOS NEJAR

Since when do Jews ride horses?

—JOSEPH HELLER

"The Unicorn in the Garden"

—JAMES THURBER (story title).

INTRODUCTION
ILAN STAVANS

It was on a flight from Dublin to the United States that I read the novel *Life of Pi.* In retrospect, it seems to me to be appropriate that it was in transition—"on the move," as the expression goes—where I first encountered it, for it is, at its core, a book about transitions that, suspiciously perhaps, also wants to erase its origins.

By chance, I had been introduced to its author, the Canadian Yann Martel, in Germany, a few days prior. Martel had just won the Man Booker Prize in England for this novel and was traveling around the continent to fulfill teaching stints and to promote its various European translations. Shortly after our meeting, I read the author's note, with which Martel introduces *Life of Pi.* In that notice he sets in motion the adventure of one Piscine Molitor Patel, an Indian boy left alone on a Japanese lifeboat with a set of companions: a zebra, a hyena, an orangutan, and a 450-pound Royal Bengal tiger named Richard Parker. In the end, he survives the last of his 227 days at sea with Parker. Everything in the volume is global: the nationalities of the characters, their journey, the cosmopolitan education of Martel himself (he was born in Spain and has lived in Mexico, India, Brazil, Canada, Germany . . .). Also in the notice he thanks Moacyr Scliar for "the spark of life." I had asked the Canadian via e-mail where he had met Scliar, who, as it happens, is a dear friend of mine and also one of the contemporary novelists

I admire the most. Before Martel had a chance to answer my question, the exposé was all over the globe: Martel was accused of unfairly borrowing for *Life of Pi* the plot of a novel by Scliar, *Max and the Cats,* published in Brazil in 1981 and translated into English by Eloah F. Giacomelli in 1990. In it a boy survives a shipwreck with, yes, a jaguar, and is almost devoured by a shark.

Newspapers these days—oh but has it ever been different?—are ready to do anything to sell copies, and a bit of twisting of truth appears not to conflict any one. Larry Rother, whose story in the *New York Times* first denounced Martel's excess, obviously never bothered to read either one of the books. Had he done that, he would have realized, rather quickly, that beyond the similarities in the premise, there appears to be no lifting of sentences and passages. The question, then: Has Martel crossed the dangerous line? When it comes to plot, the answer is evasive. How often a film about an illicit affair set in Rome feels like another film about an illicit affair that takes place in Buenos Aires that feels like another film . . . ? In our inauthentic culture, so much is dé jà vu.

This is not to say that Martel is guiltless. The set of *Max and the Cats* is during and after World War II. It links Germany and Brazil and, as always in Scliar, it parades a cast of outlandish characters. Marked by the style of magic realism, it questions the voice of the protagonist by doubting if the events chronicled took place or not. It rotates around the shipment of zoo animals from the Old World to the New. *Life of Pi* is also about a zoo in transition. It takes place in the seventies and unites India with Canada. The surrealist quality of the narrative is also accentuated. But Martel is more interested in psychology than in allegory. His boy is a savant able to cope with the death of his parents, sibling, and the rest of the sailors and passengers, and survive aloof on the sea, with a biting sense of direction. There is a sequence in which he hallucinates an oasis in the middle of the ocean full with magical creatures. In the end, he arrives to Mexican shores and is rescued by natives. Superficially, then, the novels by Martel and Scliar are quite similar, but dramatically they are diametrically different: their denouement, the roundness of their protagonist, their message . . . each dances to another rhythm.

To aggravate the situation, Rother included in his tall-tale a number of inaccuracies and errors not worth wasting print on again. The short cut is that many and more obscene cases of actual plagiarism—by the *New York Times* itself, for instance—are worth our consideration.

Martel no doubt offered a series of improper comments to the media, among them the suggestion that Scliar is "a lesser writer." He also articulated various subterfuges to his borrowing that ring untrue, such as having heard of—but never read—Scliar's novel through a review by John Updike. Updike, as it happens, has never written on Scliar. In any case, Scliar was offended and the affair went from the ugly to the outrageous. The Canadian has tarnished his sudden success with a controversy that, in and of itself, might have preempted his future career. Will he ever get beyond the accusations? Is the media, in particular the printed press, able to allow him a second chance? And does he deserve it? He certainly didn't credit Scliar appropriately in the author's note and has paid the price for the mistake.

To me, the controversy is less interesting than the fact that it has brought more attention to the sixty-five-year-old Scliar than ever before. This, I think, is the only welcome twist of events in the entire mess. He is a world-class fabulist with a solid and distinguished oeuvre waiting to be discovered by a larger audience. About a dozen books of his have appeared in English and while the attention they have received by reviewers is invariably enthusiastic, they have failed to catch on. *Max and the Cats,* as far as I'm concerned, emerges from an enchanting proposition but is a minor work. *The Gods of Raquel* and *The Strange Nation of Rafael Mendes,* which were published in English in 1986 and 1987 respectively, are memorable studies of the crossroads at which Judaism has found itself in Brazil from the colonial period to the present. Even more mesmerizing are Scliar's hundred-plus fabulous stories. In 1999 they were gathered in a single volume titled *Collected Stories,* in the Jewish Latin America series published by the University of New Mexico Press. There is an ethereal, almost mythical quality to his imagination, and his stories, invariably brief, only tangentially allegorical, are a superb introduction to his canon.

Scliar was born in Porto Alegre, in southern Brazil, in 1937. By profession he is a physician. For a while he was director of Rio Grande do Sul's department of public health. The neighborhood where he grew up was distinctly Jewish and he belonged to a series of youth organizations that oriented him toward Zionism. As an intellectual, he came of age during the years of the Salazar dictatorship. His strategy to cope with repression was to use fables, as he does in *The Carnival of the Animals* (1985). But like Aesop, Lafontaine, and Augusto Monterroso, his choice of animals as leads in his tales doesn't preclude him from commenting on the folly of human nature. People are at once selfish and foolish, he suggests mordantly, and fate plays dirty tricks on us. What should be our response? Scliar's answer is sharp: approach the contradictions of life with a sense of humor, but don't let humor preclude you from appreciating the complications that makes us tick.

His best performance as a novelist, though, and the book that is dearest to his global followers, is *The Centaur in the Garden,* originally published in 1980 in Rio de Janeiro by Nova Fronteira and translated into English by Margaret A. Neves in 1984. I am thrilled that it is available again in the United States. (By the way, this was, to my knowledge, Scliar's first book available in Shakespeare's tongue and the one that has captured the attention of American audiences in a more sustained fashion. At home, it is not only a runaway bestseller but also, considered by critics and the public alike, a classic that has introduced the nation to the dilemma of modern Jews in Brazil.) I've seen this novel compared to works by Franz Kafka (*The Metamorphosis*), Nikolai Gogol (*The Nose*), Philip Roth (*The Breast*), Mordecai Richler (*The Apprenticeship of Judy Kravitz*), and even Updike himself (*The Centaur* and, indirectly, the Rabbit saga). These equations are neither unfair nor improbable. One could add other names to the list: Isaac Babel, for instance, and perhaps Sholem Aleichem, at least in so far as angst—the angst that came as a result of the Emancipation—is presented through the prism of laughter.

This is a picaresque book in the ancient Iberian tradition that juxtaposes realistic descriptions with outright fantasy. At its center is Guedali Tartakowsky, a Jewish centaur born into a family of Russian immigrants in Rio Grande do Sul. Scliar captures like no one else the perplexity of Jewishness in Latin America. In his tale, Scliar presents Jewishness as a physical deformity that Tartakowsky spends his life trying to correct. But before that happens he needs to run away from home, misunderstood as a result of his stigmatized identity. Not only is he Jewish and an immigrant, but he is also half human and half animal. This inbetweenness follows him from one misadventure to another (as he looks into reconstructive surgery, for instance) as he searches for the possibility of redemption. Scliar isn't an alarmist, and he doesn't deliver the plot in pathetic fashion. Instead, he pushes the tragic destiny of Tartakowsky through an infusion of comedy. Its style is vintage Scliar: crisp, speedy, cinematic, succinct. There is nothing "lesser" in it. On the contrary, it stands as a towering piece of existential art.

It is obviously impossible to know what the future will rescue from our vociferous present, but if I may take the opportunity to voice a suggestion, it would be to appreciate, in universal terms, the vulnerable stance of minorities south of the border through the prism of this novel. For, while it is undeniably about Eastern European *shtetl* dwellers in the Pampa, it is also about the universal quest for acceptance and assimilation. Tartakowsky is an alienated soul of the type Kafka and Babel exposed to us. What he wants the most in life is to be accepted, but how? His appearance makes him different. His heart is cut in two. Can the division that defines him ever disappear? And if it did, what would remain of this enigmatic creature, at once insider and outsider? If the trials and tribulations of Latin America's Jewry might be found in a nutshell, it is in *The Centaur in the Garden*. But any intelligent reader is likely to substitute the Brazilian landscape with his own, for Tartakowsky lurks in our own midsts, no matter how much American Jews struggle to erase their ethnic difference in order to fully belong to the mainstream. Justifiably, the National Yiddish Book Center selected the novel as one of the hundred most important modern Jewish books.

Such importance is ultimately in the hands of readers. They are the only ones holding the measuring stick that validates a work of literature. Once a work of art is released in the universe, it no longer belongs to its author. It is now the property of that never-ending river we call "the human heritage." This is not to say that plagiarism is welcome. Ours is a capitalist society based on the concept of private property. That concept not only refers to money, real estate, and purchasable items, but to the brainchildren of talent and the imagination too. With the exception of Scliar's *Collected Stories,* his English-language titles are currently out of print in the United States, which saddens me. Surely a visit to the library is a recourse, but this Brazilian master deserves better. By borrowing the plot of *Max and the Cats* for *Life of Pi,* Martel has emphasized the indirect origin of his novel. It might be a novel about transitions, but now it also about the inadequate crossing of limits. Inadvertently, Martel has paid tribute to a first-rate Jewish-Brazilian imagination. Scliar, of course, deserves an even higher tribute: our belated consideration.

The Centaur in the Garden

SÃO PAULO:
A TUNISIAN RESTAURANT,
THE GARDEN OF DELIGHTS
SEPTEMBER 21, 1973

NOW THERE'S NO MORE GALLOPING. NOW EVERYTHING'S ALL RIGHT.

Now we're just like everybody else; we no longer attract any attention at all. The time when we were considered strange is past—why didn't we ever go to the beach, and why did my wife, Tita, always wear slacks? Us, strange? No. Last week the Indian medicine man, Peri, came to visit Tita and he was strange—a skinny little man with a sparse beard, wearing rings and necklaces, holding a staff and speaking a funny language. It might seem unusual for such an odd-looking fellow to come calling on us; still, anyone is free to ring doorbells. And besides, he was the one who was dressed oddly, not us. Us? No. Our appearance is absolutely normal.

Here we are, with our children, our friends, and our friends' children, having dinner in the Tunisian restaurant. We used to come here more often. After Tita and I moved to Pôrto Alegre the dinners became rarer, but they are still a good way of getting the old group together. As a matter of fact, today we have a special reason to celebrate: It's my birthday. Thirty-eight years old. Thirty-eight—the caliber of the revolvers used by the security men in our condominium, if I remember correctly. A splendid age. An age of maturity, but also of

1

vigor; of comprehension, of valuing the things that are good,
such as the excellent food here in The Garden of Delights, a
pleasant place where we feel at home. It's true that just a
minute ago, I had a disagreeable sensation as I glanced at the
Arab waiter. I remembered our first trip to Morocco, the
nauseating smell of the ship. I grew upset, I actually shuddered.
Paulo, seated beside me at the long table, saw it: Why, Guedali,
you're pale! It's nothing, I said, just a slight stomach pain, it's
gone already, I'm fine. He takes advantage of the situation to
ask me if I've been exercising, if I continue jogging as we used
to do together. Slightly ashamed, I confess I haven't. It's been a
long time since I did any jogging, or practice any other sports.
I've been to soccer games with my kids, who are great fans of
the International team from Pôrto Alegre, but that's about all.
Ah, says Paulo triumphantly, that's why you've got that belly on
you, that's why you're having these pains. Look at me,
Guedali, I'm in perfect shape. I still run every night, regularly.
You shouldn't give it up, Guedali. Run, man, make the effort.
Not for the sake of the Cooper method, but for the sake of the
challenge. Life without challenges isn't worth living. Listen to
your old friend Paulo.

Paulo is right. I should go jogging. I thought about starting
up again on the farm I have near Quatro Irmãos, in the interior of
Rio Grande do Sul. But now the land is all under cultivation;
there's nowhere to run. As a matter of fact, I have a beautiful
soybean farm out there. My own brother, Bernardo, manages
it for me. Everyone said it was madness to get involved in
farming, let alone farming with Bernardo for a partner. He
used to be unstable, quitting things he had started and wandering
around all over Brazil. But when he came knocking on my door
one day asking for help, I decided to risk it. And it worked out
fine; Bernardo revealed himself to be a first-class farm manager.
He mechanized the farm and got the advice of an agronomist
on how to use fertilizers and weed killers. He keeps the
workers on a tight rein—in short, he makes things operate well.

Good old Paulo. A good friend, a good business partner.
Thanks to his sense and foresight we got into the export line.

A great idea. It was what saved us when business was going badly during the time I lived in São Paulo. We've exported tons of merchandise, especially to Morocco, where I have good contacts.

A fine friend, Paulo. Paulo and Fernanda, Júlio and Bela, Armando and Beatrice, Joel and Tânia ... all fine friends. It's good to be among friends, enjoying the wine—strong but tasty—in a picturesque, cozy atmosphere. Yes, it's very good to be here in the Tunisian restaurant.

The only thing that bothers me slightly just now is the Arabian music—strident, played at a very high volume. But even this has its advantages: if wings should rustle outside, above the high palm tree that one can see through the window, I won't know, I won't hear them. I think the sound I hear is the wind, a hot wind that has been blowing since this afternoon. Probably it's going to rain.

Tita, sitting across from me, smiles. She is prettier than ever. The times of suffering she went through are written in the lines of her face, making her beauty all the more mature, deeper, softer. Dear Tita, my dear wife.

To my left are our sons, the twins. For half an hour they've been whispering to each other, the little devils. Undoubtedly up to some monkey business, as usual. They are two good boys, intelligent and studious. And how they grow! Soon they'll be taller than I am—and I'm very tall. They're already asking me for a car; one of these days they'll be bringing home their girlfriends. Someday they'll be getting married. Someday I'll be a grandfather. Things are fine.

That is, things are almost fine. There are still things that bother me. My insomnia, my restless sleep. Every so often I awake at night with the sensation of having heard a funny sound (the rustling of the winged horse's feathers?), but it's only my imagination. Tita, who has remarkably sharp ears, never hears anything; she sleeps soundly. And dreams. I don't need to lift her eyelids or spy into her pupils as if through a window to know she is dreaming. Sleeping side by side for such a long time results in a transfusion of dreams. The horse

that I saw slipping through the clouds a little while ago now
gallops across the pampas of her dreams. And it doesn't upset
her. My dreams are the ones I need to correct. It is my horse I
must catch and dispossess of all its strange appendages. Or else
eliminate it entirely from my dreams. There are sleeping pills
produced specifically for this.

Certain odd things happen to me too, which add up to
disquieting messages. For example:

Just a few minutes ago I was scribbling on my paper
napkin with the gold ballpoint pen I received from my
friends—a beautiful imported pen—and to my surprise I was
scribbling this sentence: *Everything is all right now.* An absolutely
banal sentence, but in grotesque, angular letters. What force,
what magnetism, had guided my hand to trace those letters? I
don't know. I confess I don't know, in spite of my thirty-eight
years, in spite of all the extraordinary experiences I have been
through. There are many unknown things inside me, many
secrets. Isn't it time to open the floodgates, to let the torrents
flow? Yesterday I saw scenes of a flood on TV. Animals were
swimming in the muddy waters, looking for refuge in the tops
of trees that were still above the surface. The wet face of a
monkey, shown in a close-up shot, particularly impressed me:
helpless innocence. Isn't it time to tell these friends of mine
everything? Now that everything is all right, shouldn't I tell
them? There is nothing to be afraid of. No tail will swish to
shoo away the flies that buzz around me.

Speaking of flies, there are certainly plenty of them here.
This restaurant serves good food, but it isn't the cleanest place,
they must throw the garbage out back. Still, one has to close
one's eyes and not complain. These people get irritated easily,
and retaliate: only yesterday they were riding camels across the
desert dunes, their long headdresses flapping in the wind. If
betrayed, they would swear vengeance, and stab even a friend
at the first opportunity. They are Berbers. Of course they don't
ride camels anymore; When they close up the restaurant they go
home in a car, but I still see a sinister gleam in their eyes.
Maybe it's only my Jewish paranoia.

*   *   *

Yes, I can tell everything. Modest but high toned. Dignified, without falling into cheap humor or permitting plays on words. No allusions to Cavalleria Rusticana or to Buridan's ass. If Indians come into my story—and there were still Indians in the Quatro Irmãos region back in 1935—they won't come on horseback like the valiant settlers, but on foot, humble in spite of their air of mystery, looking for jobs.

I won't speak of the private horses that gallop within us—I don't know if they exist. Nor of cavalcades, meaning history's ceaseless progress toward an unknown destiny. I don't see why one should call the incessant march of history anything else except the incessant march of history—one might add, to satisfy some, that it never slows down or goes in reverse.

So why don't I stand up? Why don't I tap my pen against my wineglass, calling for everyone's attention, and announce that a secret is about to be revealed?

Why? I don't know. I feel insecure. I am afraid of standing up. I fear that my legs won't sustain me; the truth is that I still haven't learned to trust them. Bipeds don't have the same firmness as quadrupeds. Besides, I'm drunk. One toast after another—to the man celebrating his birthday, to the man's wife, to his son, to his friends, to his parents and brothers and sisters, to his export firm, to his farm, to his favorite soccer team—and the wine has gone to my head. Tita, seated facing me, makes a sign to me to stop drinking. She is conversing with a girl who is sitting beside her, a very pretty girl as a matter of fact. Her beauty is of an unusual kind: long copper-colored hair, dark glasses (at night? why?) that almost hide her enigmatic face. A striped masculine shirt, half-open, shows off necklaces and the contour of well-formed breasts. I don't know her. I only know she is a friend of Tânia's who recently got divorced. I lift my glass to her: your health! Tita shoots me a warning glance. It isn't jealousy. She knows I'm drunk, and fears I'll talk nonsense, tell absurd stories. Before the operation I was more sensible, she's always saying.

Tita is right. It's better to stay quiet. Better to scribble,
Now everything is all right. In spite of the grotesque handwriting,
in spite of the rustling of wings. In spite of the scenes that I
am now remembering.

A SMALL FARM IN THE INTERIOR,
QUATRO IRMÃOS DISTRICT, RIO GRANDE DO SUL
SEPTEMBER 24, 1935–SEPTEMBER 23, 1947

ONE'S FIRST MEMORIES, NATURALLY, CANNOT BE DESCRIBED IN conventional words. They are visceral, archaic. Larvae in the heart of the fruit, worms wriggling in the mud. Remote sensations, vague pains. Confused visions: a stormy sky above a tempestuous sea; from between dark clouds, a winged horse majestically descending. It advances quickly over ocean and continent, leaving behind beaches and cities, forests and mountains. Little by little its speed diminishes, and now it glides, describing large circles, its mane rippling in the wind.

Below, bathed in the moonlight, is a rustic wooden house, isolated and still. From its windows a weak yellow light shines out into the mist. A short distance away is the stable. Farther on lies a small patch of woods, and beyond them the wide fields. Among the thickets of the trees, small animals fly, run, leap, and crawl, hiding themselves, chasing and devouring each other. Chirps, squeaks, trills.

A woman's sharp scream echoes through the valley. Everything grows hushed, motion arrested. The winged horse glides through the air, its wings outstretched. Another scream, and another. A series of screams—and then silence again. The

winged horse circles the house again and disappears without a
sound into the clouds.

It's my mother who is screaming; she is having a baby. Her
two daughters and an old midwife from the vicinity attend
her. She has been in labor for hours, but the baby shows no
signs of coming. Her strength is drained; she is almost
fainting. I can't stand it anymore, she murmurs. The midwife
and the girls exchange anxious glances. Should they call the
doctor? But the doctor lives forty kilometers away—is there
time?

In the neighboring room are my father and brother. My
father paces back and forth as my brother, sitting on the bed,
stares at the wall before him. The screams come more and more
frequently, one after another, and between them are curses in
Yiddish that make my father shudder: "That criminal! He took
us from our home and brought us to this hell, to this place at
the ends of the earth! I'm dying, and it's his fault, the
murderer! Oh, my God, I'm lost, help me!" The midwife tries
to calm her; everything's all right, Dona Rosa, don't panic. But
her voice betrays her anxiety: by the light of the lantern the
midwife looks in alarm at the tensed, enormous belly. What was
inside it?

My father sits down, burying his head in his hands. His
wife is right, he is to blame for what is happening. All the
Jewish colonizers of the region, who had come from Russia
along with him, had already gone to the cities—Santa Maria,
Passo Fundo, Erechim, or Pôrto Alegre. The revolution of 1923
had expelled the last remnants of the colonization.

My father insisted on staying. Why, Leon? my mother asks.
Why this stubbornness? Because Baron Hirsch placed his trust
in us, he answers. The baron didn't bring us here from Europe
for nothing. He wants us to stay here, working the land,
planting and harvesting, showing the goyim that Jews are just
like everybody else.

A good man, the baron. In 1906 Russia had been defeated
in the war against Japan, and the poor Jews—tailors, carpenters,

small businessmen—lived in miserable hovels in the small
villages, terrorized by the threat of the pogroms.

(A pogrom: drunken Cossacks would invade the village,
charging on their crazed horses against children and old
people, flailing their sabers in all directions. They would kill the
citizenry, loot and burn the village, and then disappear,
leaving the echoes of screams and neighing behind them in the
tormented night.)

In his mansion in Paris, Baron Hirsch would awaken in the
middle of the night in great alarm, hearing the sound of
hoofbeats. His sleepy wife would say, it's nothing, Hirsch, go
back to sleep, it was just a nightmare. But sleep would not
come for the baron. The vision of black horses trampling lifeless
bodies would not leave him. Two million pounds, he murmured
to himself. With two million pounds I could solve the problem.

He saw the Russian Jews living happily in faraway
regions in South America; he saw cultivated fields, modest but
comfortable homes, agricultural schools. He saw children
playing among the trees. He saw the iron tracks of the railroad
company (in which he owned a great deal of stock) advancing
into the virgin forest.

The baron was very good to us, my father repeats
constantly. A rich man like him wouldn't have needed to worry
himself about poor people. But no, he didn't forget his fellow
Jews. Now we have to work very hard so as not to disappoint
such a charitable, saintly man.

My parents do work very hard. It is a thankless existence:
clearing the land, planting crops, treating the livestock for
parasites, carrying water from the well, cooking. They live in
fear of everything: drought, flood, frost, hail, insect plagues.
Everything is difficult, they have no money, and they live
isolated from other people. Their nearest neighbors live five
kilometers away.

But my children will have a better life, my father consoles
himself. They'll study, become well-educated. And one day
they'll thank me for the sacrifices I made. For them and for
Baron Hirsch.

*   *   *

The screams cease. There is a moment of silence—my father raises his head—and then the crying of a newborn baby. His face lights up. "It's a boy! I'm sure it's a boy! From the way it cries, it has to be!"

Another scream, this time a savage cry of horror. My father jumps up, standing immobile for a second in confusion. Then he runs to the next room.

The midwife meets him in the doorway, her face splattered with blood, her eyes popping out: "Oh, Mr. Leon, I don't know what happened, I've never seen anything like it, it isn't my fault! I guarantee you that I did everything just as it should be done!"

My father looks around, not understanding. The daughters are huddled together in a corner, sobbing in fear. My mother lies on the bed in a stupor. What's happening here? yells my father, and then he sees me.

I am lying on the table. A robust, pink baby, crying and moving its little hands—a normal child from the waist up. From the waist down: the hair of a horse. The feet of a horse— hooves. A horse's tail, still soaked with amniotic fluid. From the waist down, I am a horse. I am—and my father doesn't even know the word exists—a *centaur*. A centaur.

My father approaches the table.

My father, the colonist Leon Tartakovsky. A rough, hard man who has seen many things in his lifetime, horrible things. Once a peasant man got stabbed in an argument and my father stuffed his entrails back inside him. Another time he found a scorpion in his boot and killed it with his great fist. Yet another time he put his hand into a cow's uterus to deliver a calf that was wedged crosswise. But what he sees now is by far the worst. He shrinks back, leaning against the wall for support. He bites his fist; no, he must not scream. His scream would break all the windows of the house, would carry across the fields, would reach the slopes of the Serra do Mar, the ocean, the very gates of heaven.

He can't scream, but he can sob. Sobs wrack his large body. Poor man. Poor family.

Once the initial shock is past, the midwife assumes control of the situation. She cuts the umbilical cord and wraps me in a towel—the biggest one in the house—and puts me in the cradle. Here she encounters the first difficulty: I am very large. My feet—that is, my hooves—hang out. The midwife finds a crate, lines it with blankets (Did you think of straw, midwife? Confess, did straw cross your mind?) and settles me there. In the days that follow the brave woman takes care of the house and the family: she cleans, washes, and cooks, taking food to each person in turn. She insists that they eat and keep their strength up. They have suffered a severe shock, these poor Jews, and they need to recuperate from it.

Most important, she takes care of me, the centaur. She gives me my bottle, because my mother only cries and can't stand to look at me, much less nurse me. She gives me baths and keeps me clean—not an easy job, for my feces are those of an herbaceous creature and give off a fetid odor. Then the midwife understands that I need green stuff, and mixes finely chopped lettuce leaves in with the milk.

(Many a time, she is to confess in later years, she ponders suffocating me to death with a pillow. It would end the family's torment. Nor would it be the first time. She had once strangled a one-eyed child born without arms or legs, squeezing the delicate neck until the single eye became glazed in death.)

He really isn't bad looking, she sighs, as she places me in the crate to sleep. His features are agreeable, and he has pretty brown hair and eyes. But from the waist down ... awful! She has heard of monsters, creatures half chicken, half rat, or half pig, half cow; or half bird, half snake; lambs with five legs, werewolves; she knows all these creatures exist, but never dreamed she would someday be taking care of one. Go to sleep, little one, she murmurs. In spite of everything, she likes me, this woman embittered by the deaths of her own four children.

My sisters cry all the time. My brother, who always was quiet and strange, becomes quieter and stranger. As for my

father, he has work to do, so he works. He clears land, mows
hay. Chopping down trees with his ax, attacking the ground
with his hoe, he gradually rediscovers his self-control. Already
he is able to think without falling into the depths of despair.
Painfully, he seeks explanations, formulates hypotheses.

He is a man of few insights. Though descended from a
family of rabbis and learned men, he himself is very limited.
Even back in the Russian village, he had gone to work in the
fields because of his lamentable mistakes in interpreting the
Talmud. God didn't give me a very good head, he always says.
Still, he trusts his instinctual good sense; he knows how to
interpret his own reactions, like the hair on his arms standing
up, the pounding of his heart, or the heat of his face. All these
things are communications. Sometimes he has the impression
that God speaks to him from inside, from a point situated
between his navel and the top of his stomach. He is searching
for a certainty of this kind. He wants the truth, no matter
how sad it may be.

Why has this happened to him? Why?

Why was he chosen for this, and not a Russian Cossack?
Why he and not a peasant, or another farmer of the region?
What crime had he committed? What had he done wrong that
God must punish him in this way? No matter how he
cross-examines himself, he cannot manage to pinpoint any sins.
Not serious ones, at any rate. Smaller faults, perhaps. He once
milked a cow on the Sabbath, the sacred day of rest, but the
cow's udder was full; he couldn't leave her lowing in pain.
And he didn't even use the milk, he threw it away. Sins? No.

As he convinces himself of his innocence, a doubt
emerges: Is the centaur really his child?

(Centaur. I am to teach him this word someday. At this
point he is not much versed in mythology.)

But immediately he is stung with remorse. How can he
think such a thing? Rosa is absolutely faithful to him. And even
if she weren't, what sort of father could sire such an exotic
creature? There are strange people in the region; grim, surly
half-breeds, bandits, even Indians. However, he has never seen
anyone with horses' hooves.

There are lots of horses in the area, even wild horses, skittish beasts whose whinnying he sometimes hears in the distance. But—a horse! There are perverted women, capable of making love with all sorts of creatures, he knows. Even with a horse—but his Rosa isn't one of these. She is a good, simple woman, who lives only for her husband and children. A tireless worker, an excellent housekeeper. And faithful, very faithful. A little irritable, a bit sharp at times, but kindhearted, wise. And true to him.

Poor woman. Now she lies motionless on the bed, wide-eyed and apathetic. The midwife and her daughters offer her soup, rich broths; she shows no reaction, says nothing, and does not accept the food. They try to force her mouth open with a spoon, but she refuses to open it, keeping her teeth stubbornly clenched shut. Nevertheless, a few drops of liquid, a few particles of egg, a few chicken fibers enter her mouth, and she involuntarily swallows them. No doubt this is what keeps her alive.

Alive, but quiet. Mute. Her silence is an accusation to her husband: It's your fault, Leon. You brought me to this place at the ends of the earth, this place where there are no people, only animals. My son was born this way because I looked at so many horses. (She could supply other examples: women who laughed at monkeys and whose children were born hairy; women who looked at cats—their babies mewed for months.) Or perhaps she would cast doubts on his family history: you have lots of disease and deformity among your relatives, your uncle who was born with a harelip, your cousin who has six fingers on each hand, your diabetic sister. In short, it's your fault! she might scream. But she doesn't. She hasn't the strength.

Besides, he is her husband. She has never been attracted to any other man, nor indeed even thought of another. Her father said to her: You will marry Tartakovsky's son, he's a good boy. And thus her destiny had been decided. Who was she to argue? As a matter of fact, the choice of young Leon didn't displease her. He was one of the handsomest boys in the village, strong and cheerful. She was lucky.

They were married. At first it wasn't so good . . . sex, that is. He was rough and clumsy; he hurt her. But soon she grew accustomed to him, and actually enjoyed lovemaking. Everything went well—until they were awakened one night by the trampling of horses' hooves and the savage yells of the Cossacks. They ran and hid in the forest near the river and remained there, trembling with fear and cold, watching the light cast by the burning village. The next morning they went back to find the main street full of mutilated bodies, and the houses in smoking ruin. Let's get out of here, said Leon gravely. I want nothing more to do with this accursed place.

Rosa didn't want to leave Russia. Pogroms or no pogroms, she liked the village. It was where she belonged. But Leon's mind was made up. When the emissaries sent by Baron Hirsch arrived, he was the first to volunteer for the Jewish colony in South America. South America! The terrified Rosa imagined naked savages, tigers, gigantic snakes. She would take the Cossacks anytime! But her husband would not discuss it. Pack the bags, he ordered. Pregnant and panting for breath from her exertions, she obeyed. They embarked from Odessa on a cargo ship.

(Many years later she would still remember that voyage with horror: the cold, and afterward the suffocating heat, the nausea and the odor of vomit and sweat, the decks crowded with hundreds of Jews, the men in berets, the women with scarves tied over their hair, the children who never stopped crying.)

My mother arrived in Pôrto Alegre sick and feverish. But her odyssey was not yet finished. They had to travel to the interior, first by train, then in horse-drawn wagons over a trail cut through dense forests, to get to the colony. A representative of the baron was awaiting them. Each family received a section of land—my father's was the most distant—a house, tools, and livestock.

My father awoke singing every day. He was very happy. My mother wasn't. She found life in the colony worse—a thousand times worse—than in the Russian village. Days of backbreaking work, nights inhabited by mysterious sounds: chirps, squeaks, rustlings. Above all, the invisible presence of the

Indians watching the house. My father made fun of her. What Indians, woman! There aren't any Indians anywhere near here! She would grow quiet. But at night, when they sat beside the stove drinking tea, she would see the Indians' eyes in the burning coals. In her nightmares the Indians would break into the house, mounted on black horses like those of the Cossacks. She would wake up screaming, and my father would have to calm her.

Still, little by little she became more accustomed to the place. The birth of her children, in spite of the difficult deliveries, was a consolation. And the thought that her children were being brought up in a new country, with a real future, actually was a source of enthusiasm to her. She began to feel quite happy. But Leon was never satisfied—three children weren't enough for him. He had to insist on a fourth. He wanted another son. She resisted the idea strongly, but in the end gave in. It was a difficult pregnancy; she vomited constantly and could hardly move about with her enormous belly. I think I'm going to have four or five, she would groan. Moreover, she was bothered by hallucinations: she would hear the sound of gigantic wings rustling above the house. Finally, the long painful labor—and the monster.

Maybe it's something temporary, thinks my father hopefully. Like his wife, he too has heard of children who were born hairy like monkeys—but after a few days they lost their hair. Who could tell, maybe this was the same sort of thing. What they must do was wait a bit. Perhaps the hooves would fall off and the hide come loose in large pieces, letting the belly and normal legs appear, a little atrophied from having stayed inside the dark cavity so long. As soon as they were freed, however, they would begin to move, the quick little legs. He would give his son a good bath and burn the repulsive leftover parts in the stove. As the flames consumed them, everything would be forgotten like a bad dream, and they would be happy again.

The days pass, my hooves don't fall off, my hide shows no cracks whatsoever. Another idea occurs to my father: it's a disease. And perhaps curable. What do you think? he asks the midwife. Could it be a disease, this thing my son has?

The midwife can't say with any certainty. She has seen some strange cases: a child that was born with fish scales, another that had a tail—only ten centimeters long, if that, but indisputably a tail. Is there a treatment? Ah, that she doesn't know. Only a doctor could say.

A doctor. My father knows that Dr. Oliveira is competent. Perhaps he will have an answer, perhaps he can solve the problem of the horse-baby by means of an operation, or even some injections that, when given in the hindquarters, might cause the hooves to dry up and fall off like broken branches, and make the hide peel away to reveal the beginnings of normal legs. Or with drops, pills, tonics—Dr. Oliveira is acquainted with a wide variety of medicines, one of them would surely work.

But one thing torments my father: Would Dr. Oliveira keep the baby's existence a secret? The anti-Semites could very well use what had happened as proof of the Jews' connection with the Evil One. My father knows that for much less than this, his ancestors were roasted in ovens during the Middle Ages.

But he can hesitate no longer. A son's life is more important than any risk involved. My father hitches the mare to the wagon and goes to town to speak to the doctor.

Two days later Dr. Oliveira appears, mounted on his beautiful roan. A tall, elegant man with a carefully trimmed beard, he wears a long cape to protect his English tweed suit from the dust of the road.

"Good day, what a pleasure to see you!"

He is a jovial, talkative fellow. He pats my sisters' heads affectionately as he comes in, greets my mother, who doesn't answer him—she still hasn't recovered from the shock. Here is the child, says my father, pointing to my crate.

Dr. Oliveira's smile disappears, and he actually draws back a step. The truth is that he didn't believe my father's story; he made no hurry to respond to his summons. Now, however, he is seeing the thing with his own eyes, and what he sees leaves him stunned. Stunned and horrified. A seasoned professional, he has seen many upsetting things, many ugly diseases. But he had never seen a centaur. A centaur takes him beyond the limits of his imagination. Centaurs are not listed in medical texts. Which of his colleagues has ever seen a centaur? None of them. Neither have his professors, nor the luminaries of Brazilian medical science. This case was without doubt unique.

He sits down on the chair that my father offers him, removes his gloves and regards the little centaur in silence. My father anxiously tries to read his face. But the doctor says nothing. From his suit pocket he takes a fountain pen and a leather-bound notebook and begins to write:

A strange creature. Probably a congenital malformation. Impressive resemblance of the inferior-posterior members with equine parts. As far down as the umbilical scar, a normal, well-built child. Below this point, body is mulelike. Face, neck, and trunk show smooth pink skin; there follows a small transitional zone of thick, wrinkled tegument heralding what is to come farther down. The blond hairs that cover the skin in this zone become darker and darker, and there appears, cruelly, horsehide of a bay color. Also haunches, shanks, pasterns, hooves, tail, everything resembling a horse. Penis particularly notable, being monstrously large for a newborn baby. A complex case. Radical surgery? Impossible.

My father cannot contain himself. "Well, Doctor?"
The startled doctor looks at him with hostility.
"Well, what, Tartakovsky?"
"What is it? This sickness my son has."
It isn't a sickness, says the doctor, putting away his notebook. So what is it? asks my father insistently. It's not a disease, the doctor repeats. And what is to be done? My father strains to control his voice.
"Unfortunately, nothing," replied Dr. Oliveira, getting up. "There is no treatment possible for a case of this type."
"No treatment possible?" My father cannot take it in. "Aren't there medicines for this?"

"No. There are no medicines."

"Or any type of operation?" My poor father is ever more anguished.

"No. No operation."

My father is silent a moment, then makes another attempt. "Maybe if we were to take him to Argentina . . ."

Dr. Oliveira puts his hand on my father's shoulder.

"No, Tartakovsky. I don't think they would have any treatment in Argentina for a case of this type. In fact, I doubt that any doctor has ever seen a thing like this, a creature so . . . unusual." He looks at the little centaur moving inside the crate and says in a low voice:

"I'll be frank, Tartakovsky. There are only two things to do: let him die, or accept him as he is. You must choose."

"I've already chosen, Doctor," murmurs my father. "You know the choice is already made."

"I admire your courage, Tartakovsky. And I am at your disposal. There isn't much I can do, but you can count on me."

He takes up his medical kit. "How much is it, Doctor?" asks my father. The doctor smiles. "Oh, please, there's no charge."

He starts toward the door. But then an idea occurs to him, an idea that makes him turn around sharply.

"Tartakovsky . . . Would you mind if I photographed your son?"

"What for?" My father is surprised and suspicious. "For the papers?"

"Of course not," the doctor assures him, smiling. "It's for a medical journal. I want to publish an article about this case."

"Article?"

"Yes. When a doctor comes across a case as rare as this one, he should publish the things he observes."

My father looks at him, then looks at the little centaur. I don't think it's a good idea, he mutters. The doctor insists: I'll cover his face, nobody will know he's your son. I don't think it's a good idea, repeats my father. Dr. Oliveira won't be dissuaded: it's a journal that is widely read by doctors,

Tartakovsky. It could even be that one of them would have a suggestion for treating the problem.

"But you yourself just said that there is no treatment!" shouts my father.

Dr. Oliveira realizes he has committed an error. He clarifies himself: What I said was that there is no treatment available yet for cases of this type. But in the near future a medical colleague might discover some new drug, some operation. And then he'll remember what he read in the journal, get in touch with me—and who knows but what something can be done for your son?

My father ends up agreeing. How can he do otherwise? But he imposes conditions: Dr. Oliveira has to bring his own photographic equipment—a large camera on a tripod—because my father will not hear of photographers. Strangers here, no.

The preparations for the photos are complicated. They shackle my hands and feet, but even so I switch my tail nervously and they have to tie it down too. When they put a black cloth over my head I begin to cry. Stop this, for the love of God! screams one of my sisters. Shut up, growls the doctor, struggling with the old camera. Now that I've started this, I'm going to finish it. The magnesium flare explodes, causing my sisters to scream in fright. Get them out of here, Tartakovsky, orders Dr. Oliveira. My father orders them out of the room, and the midwife as well. The doctor continues taking pictures, frame after frame.

"Enough!" yells my father, beside himself. "That's enough!"

The doctor perceives that the man has reached the limit of tolerance. Without a word, he bundles up his camera and other paraphernalia and takes himself off.

(He sends the photographs to Pôrto Alegre to be developed. A total failure, they are dark and blurry, and worst of all, do not show the lower part of my body clearly. One can discern that below the waist there is something different, but one cannot distinguish exactly what it is. To his great disappointment the doctor realizes that he cannot use the photographs. They are inconclusive and don't really prove anything. If he published an article with illustrations of that kind he would be accused of lying. He ends up throwing the photographs away, but he keeps the negatives.)

Little by little the household returns to normal. The family begins to accept the presence of the centaur.

The two girls—sensitive, sweet-tempered Deborah, twelve, and spirited, intelligent Mina, ten—take care of me. They like to play with my fingers and make me laugh; they even forget the grotesque body—not for long, of course, because the nervous movements of my hooves bring them back to reality. Poor little thing, they sigh, it isn't his fault.

Bernardo also recognizes me as a brother, but for different reasons. He is jealous; he feels that I monopolize everyone's attention in spite of being a monster. He actually envies me: he would like to have four hooves too, if that's what it takes to win our sisters' affection.

The midwife continues to help the family, and my father does his work in the fields, but my mother remains supine, immobile, her gaze fixed on the ceiling. My father, worried, fears she may have gone mad. But he doesn't do anything; he doesn't call Dr. Oliveira. He avoids upsetting her. He wants to give her time; he waits for the fearful scar to heal. At night, he leaves a lamp lighted in the room, for he knows that terrors multiply in the dark. In the dark, the plant of madness puts down roots, stretches out runners, grows luxuriant. In the dark hideous visions proliferate like worms in rotting meat. It is by lantern light that my father removes his clothes (not his underwear; one shouldn't be seen naked.) He lies down softly. He doesn't touch her, because he can feel her pain as if in his own living flesh.

His wise, patient conduct begins to yield results. My mother shows small signs of recuperation: at times a moan, at times a sigh.

One night, as though sleepwalking, she gets up and goes to the crate where I lie. My father anxiously watches her from behind the door—what might she be doing?

For a few seconds she stares at me. Then, with a

cry—"My son!"—she throws herself upon me. Startled out of my slumber, I begin to cry. But my father smiles, murmuring, "Thank God! Thank God!" as he wipes his eyes.

Now that the family is reunited once again around the table, now that everything is all right, my father decides that it's time to circumcise the child. A religious man, he has to fulfill his obligations. It is necessary to introduce the boy to Judaism.

Cautiously, fearing her reaction, he presents the matter to my mother. She limits herself to a sigh (from that time on she is to sigh a lot) and says, "Very well, Leon. Call the mohel, do what has to be done."

My father hitches the mare to the wagon, which is used only on special occasions such as these, and goes to town in search of the mohel. He tells him he had a son and without going into details (without saying the boy is a centaur) asks him to come and perform the circumcision that very day: the time prescribed by the Law has already run out. And the ceremony would have to take place on the farm, because the child's mother was ill and couldn't travel.

The mohel, a small hunchbacked man who blinks his eyes constantly, hears the story with growing distrust. The whole thing smells fishy to him. My father insists: let's go right away, Mohel, it's a long trip. And the witnesses? the mohel asks. Unfortunately I couldn't find any witnesses, says my father, we'll have to perform the circumcision without them. No witnesses? The mohel likes this less and less all the time. But he has been acquainted with my father for some time, and knows he is a man to be trusted. Besides, he is used to the oddities of country people. He gets his bag of instruments, his prayer book and prayer shawl, and climbs into the wagon.

On the way my father begins to prepare him. The boy was born with a defect, he says, trying to affect nonchalance. The mohel grows alarmed: is it serious? I don't want to have the child dying of the circumcision! No, no, not at all, my father calms him, the child is deformed but very strong, you'll see.

They arrive at sunset, the mohel complaining about the

difficulties of working by lamplight. He gets out of the wagon muttering and cursing.

The family is gathered in the dining room. The mohel greets my mother, pays my sisters compliments, recalls that he performed Bernardo's circumcision: that one there gave me a lot of work! He puts on his prayer shawl, asking where the baby is.

My father takes me out of the crate and places me on the table.

"Good God!" cries the mohel, dropping his bag and cringing backward. He turns and runs for the door. My father runs after him, grabs him. Don't run away, Mohel! Do what has to be done! But he's a horse! screams the mohel, trying to get loose from my father's strong hands, I have no obligation to circumcise horses! He's not a horse, yells my father, he is a defective child, a Jewish son!

My mother and sisters weep softly. Seeing that the mohel has stopped fighting, my father lets go of him, locks the door. Staggering, the little man leans against the wall with his eyes shut and body trembling. My father brings him his bag of instruments: come on, Mohel. I can't, the man groans, I'm too nervous. My father goes out to the kitchen and comes back with a glass of cognac.

"Drink this. It'll help you feel better."

"But it's not my custom—"

"Drink!"

The mohel empties the glass in one swallow. He chokes, coughs. "Better?" asks my father. Better, moans the mohel. He instructs my father to hold me on his lap, and takes his ritual knife from the bag. But again he hesitates. Have you got a good hold on him? he asks, looking over his spectacle rims. Yes, says my father, go ahead, you don't need to be afraid. Won't he kick me? asks the mohel. There's no danger, my father assures him, come on.

The mohel draws near, and my father separates my hind feet. And there they are, face to face, the penis and the mohel, the huge penis and the little mohel, the small fascinated mohel. Mohel Rachmiel has never seen such a penis, he who has performed so many circumcisions. He senses that this will be a transcendent experience, the greatest circumcision of his life, the memory of which will go with him to his grave. Horse or not, it matters little. There is a foreskin, and he will do what the Law prescribes for Jewish foreskins. He takes up the knife, drawing a deep breath ...

The mohel is an expert. In a very few minutes the deed is accomplished, and he drops back into the chair exhausted as my father tries to sooth my howling, wrapping me up and walking back and forth with me. Finally I grow quiet, and he places me in my crate. My mother feels ill; Deborah and Mina have to help her to bed.

More cognac, says the mohel in an almost inaudible voice. My father serves him a glass and pours another for himself. In spite of everything, he is pleased; the Law has been fulfilled. He invites the mohel to stay overnight with the family: we have a bed for you, sir. The mohel jumps up. No! I don't want to! Take me back! As you like, my father answers, surprised and confused—why all this shouting, now that the worst is over? He puts on his coat: I am at your disposal. The mohel gathers up his instruments, stuffs them back in the bag, and without taking leave of anyone, opens the door and gets into the wagon.

The return trip is made in silence. They arrive at the mohel's house in the wee hours of the morning, the roosters already beginning to crow. How much do I owe you? asks my father, helping the old man out of the wagon. Nothing, the mohel mutters, you don't owe me anything, I don't want anything. Very well, says my father, holding him, but there is one thing. This matter will stay between us, do you hear? The mohel looks at him with loathing, jerks himself loose, goes inside his house and slams the door. My father settles himself again on the wagon seat, clucks to the mare. The tired animal begins to move. He is returning to the farm, to his family, to little Guedali.

A few weeks later I take my first steps. The equine portion of my body develops faster than the human portion. (And will it grow old sooner? Will it die earlier? The following years are to prove that it won't.) My hands still move without definite purpose, uncoordinated; my eyes don't identify images, nor do my ears distinguish between sounds. Yet already my hooves trot about, carrying a body that can't hold itself erect but oscillates grotesquely like that of a doll. They can't help laughing, my parents and sisters (but not my brother) at the baby's obvious surprise: now he's in his crate, now out in the yard—from which they hastily remove him. One thing my father determines immediately: Guedali is not to go outside the limits of the farm. He can run about in the fields nearby, pick wild blackberries, bathe in the stream. But no one must see him. A man of experience, Leon Tartakovsky knows the cruelty of the world. It is necessary to protect his son, who is, after all, a fragile creature. When strangers come to the farm, I am hidden in the cellar or in the barn. Wedged between worn-out tools and old toys (headless dolls, broken cars) or among the cows that silently chew their cuds, I become painfully aware of my shanks, my hooves. I am obliged to think of something called horseshoes. I become conscious of my thick, beautiful tail, of my enormous penis with its circumcision mark. I become aware of my belly (huge, how could my poor little hands scratch such a big belly?) and my long intestines that digest and assimilate my food, often inadequate for a horse's organism, although for humans—and especially for Jews, tasty: beet soup, fried fish, the unleavened bread of Passover.

(Of course, before this, I had already formed a vague notion of my monstrous body. Imagine this example. Lying in my crate when I was a few months old, I must have brought a hoof up to my mouth, as babies always do with their feet; the hoof would have cut my lip, and from that sharp pain, from that hurt, there must have remained the notion of conflict between hardness and softness, between the brutal and the delicate, between the equine and the human. Doubtless I vomited that night.)

Little by little, a sense of my own oddity germinates within me, incorporating itself to my very being, even before I ask the inevitable question dreaded by my parents: Why am I like this? What happened for me to be born this way?

To this inquiry my parents respond evasively. Their
answers only increase the anguish that is to permeate my whole
being—an anguish going back to my most remote beginnings;
back, I believe, to the image of the winged horse. This anguish
is to crystallize, deposited permanently as it were in the marrow,
of my bones, in the buds of my teeth, in the tissue of my liver.
But my family's love acts as a balm; the wounds heal, the
disparate parts unify, the suffering acquires a meaning. I am a
centaur, a mythological creature, but I am also Guedali
Tartakovsky, the son of Leon and Rosa, the brother of
Bernardo, Deborah, and Mina. I am a little Jewish boy.
Thanks to these realities, I don't lose my mind. I face the fearful
whirlwind, journeying through the blackness of many nights,
and emerge dizzy and weak on the other side. It is a pallid
smile that Mina sees on my face in the morning, but this smile
is enough to make her clap her hands with joy.

"Come on, Guedali! Come on and play!"

Mina loves plants and animals. She knows the name of
every tree, identifies the songs of the regional birds, and can
predict the weather by their flight. She fishes better than
anyone, takes up serpents and spiders in her hands, runs
through the fields barefoot without cutting herself on the thorns,
and climbs trees with amazing agility. Touch him here, she
says to Deborah, see how soft his coat is. The timid Deborah
comes closer. Her fingers caress me, play with my tail. (The
memory of this sensation is to stay with me for many years;
whenever it is evoked my coat stands up, waves of
voluptuousness rippling over my hide.) If I lie on the ground,
they lie down too, leaning their heads against my haunches.
How nice it is to be here, says Deborah, looking at the sky. (A
cloudless sky, without winged figures.) Mina jumps up: let's
play tag! I trot slowly on purpose, letting them catch me. They
double up with laughter.

Bernardo watches us from a distance. As time passes, he
becomes more and more withdrawn. My father loves him; he
is an industrious boy, a great help in the fields. He also has
extraordinary mechanical ability. He improvises farm tools,
makes kitchen utensils that my mother exhibits proudly, and

builds traps for mice and rabbits. But he hardly speaks to me, in spite of Deborah and Mina's insistence. He prefers to ignore me. I might have shared a room with him, but my father, sensing his hostility, decides to build another room for me, an addition to the house. These living quarters are ample, with an independent door through which I can come and go as I like. And really, it's better that I don't walk around inside the house too much. My footsteps make the walls shake, and the crystal wineglasses my mother brought from Europe, her only treasure, tinkle dangerously inside the china cabinet. But meals must be taken together as a family. I stand near the table, holding my plate; my father tells stories from the Bible and my mother watches vigilantly to make sure I eat enough. Little by little they discover the peculiarities of my diet: it must be abundant (I weigh as much as several children my age) and above all, it must contain lots of green, leafy material, as the midwife realized early on. In consequence, my father plants a big garden from which I daily consume heads of lettuce, cabbage, and celery. I grow strong and well developed.

There are other problems: that of clothing, for instance. My mother knits pullover sweaters adapted to my body. They terminate in a sort of blanket to cover my back and hindquarters, for southern Brazil is cold in the wintertime. These jobs are a comfort to her, although she never manages to recover completely from the original shock she had at my birth. Many times she looks at me with an air of hurt surprise, as if asking herself, What is this thing? How did this creature ever come forth from my womb? But she says nothing; she hugs me tightly, although she avoids touching my coat, being allergic to horsehair.

During the Revolution of 1893 tales were told of a mysterious creature, half man and half horse, who would invade the Legalist camps at night, grab a poor young recruit, take him to the riverbank and cut off his head. It wasn't me. I wasn't born until much later.

From a book on the legends of southern Brazil, Deborah teaches me to read. I learn with great facility. Negrinho do

Pastoreio and Salamanca do Jarau are already my friends, part of my everyday life.

I enjoy Deborah's reading to me. I like to watch her writing or drawing. And above all I like to hear her play the violin.

The violin had been in my family for generations. My grandfather, Abraham Tartakovsky, had given it to my father, hoping to transform him into a great virtuoso like the many others who sprang up in Russia during that period: Mischa Elman, Gabrilovitch, Zimbalist—all young Jewish prodigies. But my father didn't like music. He learned to play the instrument unwillingly, and as soon as he got to Brazil he put it away in its case and forgot about it. Deborah discovered the violin and asked my father to teach her how to play it. She had an excellent musical ear, and learned at once. From then on she practiced every day.

A beautiful scene:

Standing in her sunlit bedroom one morning, Deborah plays the violin. Ecstatic with joy, her eyes half shut, she executes pieces that she knows by heart: "Dream of Love No. 5" and others. I watch her through the window. She opens her eyes and notices me, giving a little start. Then she smiles. An idea comes to her: do you want to learn to play too, Guedali?

Do I want to! More than anything else. We go down into the cellar—which from then on becomes our studio—and there she shows me the finger positions, the movements of the bow. I learn quickly.

I wander through the fields playing the violin. The melody mingles with the sighing of the wind, with the birdsongs and the trilling of the locusts; it is all so beautiful that my eyes fill with tears. I forget everything, forget that I have hooves and a tail. I am a violinist, an artist.

"Guedali!" cries my mother from a distance. "Come and eat!"

Eat? I don't want to eat. I want to play the violin. I play it

upon the hillsides, in the marshes with my hooves submerged
in the icy water, in the thickets where the leaves of the trees
drop onto my haunches and cling to my wet coat.

A rainy afternoon in September. High on a bank, I play a
melody I composed myself. Suddenly there is a loud pop: a
string has broken. I stop playing and stare at the violin. Then,
without thinking, without hesitation, I automatically throw it
down into the stream below. The muddy waters carry it slowly
away. Trotting along the bank, I accompany its movement. I
see it catch on a submerged tree trunk, I see it sink. And then I
go back home.

On the way I realize what I have done. Now what? I ask
myself, upset. What will I tell them? I gallop back and forth,
lacking courage to go in.

Finally I open the door. Deborah is sitting in the dining
room, reading by lantern light. I lost the violin, I tell her from
the doorway. She looks at me, incredulous: "You lost the
violin, Guedali? But how?"

I lost it, I repeat, my voice trembling and insecure. My
father comes in: What's all this about, Guedali? You lost the
violin? I lost it, I insist, I left it somewhere, I can't remember
where.

They all go out to look for it, carrying lanterns. For
hours they walk through the fields. Finally they are convinced:
the violin is truly lost. And it will be ruined with the rain that
is now falling in torrents. They go back to the house. Deborah
locks herself in the bedroom, crying, and Mina reprimands me
for being so careless.

Late that night, I try to kill myself.

All alone in the basement, I work a large nail out of an old
rotten board. I plunge it again and again into my back, my
belly, my hooves, biting my lips so as not to cry out. The blood
runs; I don't stop, but keep on wounding myself. At that
moment Bernardo appears, having come in search of a tool. He
sees me: What on earth are you doing? he asks in alarm. As
soon as he realizes the truth he advances toward me, trying to

disarm me. I resist him. We fight, and he ends up getting the nail away from me. He runs to call Deborah and Mina.

They come, they bandage me up. And for the rest of the night they stay with me, telling me stories to entertain me. Stories of dragons and princes, pixies and giants, witches and sorcerers. It's no good, sisters, I say, I wish I could be people, people like Papa, like Bernardo. Confused, they don't know what to say; they recommend that I pray a lot. And so I do, thinking about God until I fall asleep. But the figure that appears to me in my dreams isn't that of Jehovah; it's the sinister winged horse.

In the weeks that follow, I avoid my family. I don't want to talk to anyone. I gallop through the fields, going ever farther away. This is how I meet the Indian boy.

He is coming out of the woods as I walk down the trail. The sudden encounter makes both of us stop short. Surprised and suspicious, we stare at each other. I see a naked bronze boy holding a bow and arrow—a huntsman. I know about the Indians' existence from the stories my sisters tell. But what does he think of me? Do I seem strange to him? Impossible to know. He gazes impassively at me.

I hesitate. I should run away, I should go back home, as my father recommended, but I don't feel any desire to flee. I move closer to the Indian, my right hand raised in a signal of peace, repeating, "Friend, friend," like the white men in my sisters' stories. He remains motionless, looking at me. I should offer him a present, but what? I don't have anything. An idea occurs to me. I take off my pullover sweater and hold it out to him, "Present, friend!" He doesn't say anything, but he smiles. I insist: "Take it, friend! Good pullover! Mother made!" Now we are very close to each other. He takes the pullover, examines it curiously, smells it. Then he ties it around his waist. He gives me one of his arrows and draws slowly backward about twenty steps. Then, turning his back, he disappears into the forest.

I go back home and lock myself in my room. My father comes to call me to dinner; I tell him I won't be there, I'm not hungry. I don't want to talk to anyone. I lie down, but I can't get to sleep, I'm too excited. My life is already changed, for I found a friend. The arrow clutched to my chest, I make plans. I will teach the little Indian boy (I've even guessed his name already: Peri) my language, he will teach me his. We will be great companions, Peri and I. Together we will explore the forest. We will have secret hiding places, pacts, rituals. And we will never leave each other.

I can hardly wait for morning to come. I run to the place where I met him, taking a few precious offerings: toys I got for my birthday, the fruits that were in season, and a necklace of my mother's that I pilfered through the window. She likes this necklace a lot, I know. But one should do anything for a friend, even steal for him.

The little Indian is not there. Why should he be? I don't know. I only know that I was certain I would meet him there, and I can't believe he didn't come. I go for a short walk around the area; I climb a hill and look off into the distance. Nobody. I enter the forest:

"Peri! It's me!"

He doesn't appear. I wait hours for him. Nothing. Disappointed, I go home, lock myself in my room, refuse once again to eat. (My belly, my horse's belly, rumbles, but my dry mouth wants nothing to do with food.)

The next day I go again to the meeting place. And the next day Peri again fails to come. Finally, I am obliged to conclude that the boy has abandoned me. Not even the Indians want anything to do with me, I think bitterly.

Once again it is my sisters' affection that sustains me. They play with me and take my mind off my troubles. Thanks to them, I begin to smile again.

But I don't forget Peri. Maybe something happened to him, I think, maybe he got sick; he might still try to find me. I know Indians are very good at following a trail. Sometimes I wake up in the middle of the night imagining that someone is knocking on the door of my room.

"Peri?"

It isn't Peri. It's only the wind, or our dog Pharaoh. I

sigh, feel for the arrow that I keep under my mattress, and go
back to sleep.

Throwing violins in the river or no, trying to kill myself or
not, finding a friend and losing him, I go on living.

Life is very calm on the farm. Weekdays are full of hard
work, with which I begin to help. Indignantly, my father
opposes my pulling the plow, but now I cultivate my own
garden, and plant corn too; the ripening ears with their golden
grains peeping through the husks give me a deep pleasure.

On Friday nights, everyone dresses up in their best
clothes. We gather around the table, where the crystal goblets
brought from Europe sparkle upon the white tablecloth. My
mother lights the candles, my father blesses the wine, and thus
we celebrate the arrival of the Sabbath. We also celebrate
Passover and the Jewish New Year. We fast on Yom Kippur—
when the rest of the family goes to the synagogue in the town.
On these occasions my father and the mohel exchange pointed
glances without saying a word.

The wheat is planted in season; chickens hatch, lay eggs,
are sacrificed. The cows calve. Once (a terrible time) a cloud of
locusts passes over the farm, fortunately without causing much
damage. The seasons follow one another. According to my
father these are good years, bringing neither too much dry
weather nor excessive rain. From him I learn about the phases
of the moon, and he also teaches me songs in Yiddish. We all
sing together around the great wood-burning stove where a
pleasant fire flickers. We drink tea with cookies, many times
there is popcorn, hot piñon nuts, baked sweet potatoes. The
picture of the united family is a charming one, from which it is
almost possible to conjure away the vision of the half-horse
(lying on the floor and partially covered with a blanket) which is
the other half of the half-boy. It is almost possible to look at
my face—at eleven, I am a good-looking lad, with brown hair,
lively eyes, a strong mouth—and at my upper body, and forget
the rest. I can almost relax in the warmth of the fire and let the
time go by without thinking of anything.

*   *   *

But my parents don't forget, nor relax, nor stop thinking, especially my father. Many times he gets up at night to watch me as I sleep. He looks at me fearfully, full of foreboding: my sleep is agitated, I mumble things, move my hooves. He stares hard at my large penis: a circumcised penis, but still a horse's penis. What woman (Woman: my father doesn't even ponder any other type of female creature. A mare, for example, never crosses his mind. For my father, I am a growing boy, a boy with abnormal appendages, perhaps, but nevertheless a boy.) would accept him, he asks himself, what woman would ever go to bed with him? A prostitute, maybe, a crazy or drunken woman, a degenerate. But a girl from a good Jewish family, like Erechim's daughters, for example? Never! they would faint if they even saw him.

Still, my father knows, someday his son Guedali will feel desire for a woman. Irresistible desire. And what will happen then? My father doesn't even like to think about what might happen on a spring night in September.

The eve of Guedali's twelfth birthday.

A very hot night, even for September. Insupportably hot.

On that night, the boy can't get to sleep. Restless, his face burning, he will roll from one side of the straw mattress to the other. (It's a hard-on; his great penis is erect, throbbing. What to do? Masturbate? Impossible: his fingers refuse to touch the parts of a horse.) Unable to endure any more, Guedali will go out the door and into the open fields. He will rub against trees, dive into the river, but nothing will calm him. He will gallop aimlessly, startling the nocturnal birds.

On a neighboring farm, near a rough fence made of tree trunks, he is to meet the herd of horses. Mares and stallions, motionless beneath the moonlight, staring at him.

The centaur will creep up softly. The centaur will see a mare, a beautiful white mare with a long mane. The centaur will caress her silky neck with trembling hands, the centaur will murmur sweet nothings in her ears. The centaur: mouth dry, eyes wide, the centaur will suddenly mount her. And the whole place goes wild, the animals running up and down,

ome. Startled by the noise, my father comes out of the
Ah, son of a bitch!" he cries, beside himself. He tears
Bento from my back, knocks him over with a blow, and
him until he is out cold on the ground, his face
g.

at night there is a storm. It rains without stopping for
eks. The wheat crop is ruined. The flooding waters
reat chasms in the red earth. Things start to appear:
y shaped pebbles, arrowheads, clay pots. And the
of a horse, a complete skeleton, resting on its side with
etched forward and jaws open, its eye sockets full of

's go away from here, says my father. Let's go to the city.

painful for me to leave the farm. My hooves have
known the pastures, the earth; would they accept the
of the city? I trot through the fields for the last time,
ood-bye to trees, birds, the stream. I murmur farewell to
s and calves. In the place where I met Peri I leave a
a shirt wrapped up in a newspaper.
o back to my room, look around me, and sigh. In spite
thing, it was good living here.

t having a truck nor knowing how to drive, my father
ed two enormous horse-drawn wagons for the move. In
hem, driven by my brother, go a few household things:
e, clothes, the crystal goblets brought from Europe, the
aph of Baron Hirsch. In the other, which my father
o I, well hidden by a canvas cover. My mother and
o by bus.
e midwife comes to say good-bye. Crying, she embraces
pening my coat with her tears. May God protect you,
She gives me a package sent by Dr. Oliveira. It contains
tives of the photographs he took of me. Together is a
ng that I should destroy the negatives myself or else
m as a remembrance if someday, by means of some
t, I become a normal person.

throwing themselves against the fence, as the centaur yells,
"I'm gonna do it! Shit, I don't care, I'm gonna do it!"

Past caring, he will satisfy himself quickly, like someone
who wants to die. Then he will run to the river and take a
purifying bath.

(His hoof will step on something buried in the muddy
bottom. The violin?) He will go back home and sneak into his
room as silently as a thief.

But the story is not to end there. Up to that point my
father can go, at least in hallucinated imaginings. But there is
more.

The mare begins to follow Guedali about.

At night the centaur wakes up, restless, and hears the
supplicating whinny: the mare is there outside the window of
his room.

Guedali hides his head under the pillow. Useless. He can
still hear her. He gets up, tries to chase her away: "Get out of
here! Beat it!" he snarls under his breath, terrified of waking his
parents. But the mare doesn't go away. Guedali throws rocks
at her, hits her with a broom handle. Useless.

She follows him about in the daytime, too. Her owner is
forced to come and get her. Intrigued, he remarks to Leon, "I
don't know what's gotten into Magnolia, she's forever getting
loose and coming over here." He saddles her; she rears, balks,
refuses to leave the place. The man whips her, digs his spurs
into her sides and finally they go off at a gallop, disappearing in
a cloud of dust. From his hiding place in the cellar, Guedali
breathes a sigh of relief. But when night falls—whinnying. In
the wee hours of the morning, a thought occurs to him: could
the mare be pregnant? The possibility terrifies him. The image
of another centaur, of a horse, or worse—of a monster with a
horse's body and a man's head, or a horse with human lips, or
human ears, or a filly with a woman's breasts, or a horse with
human legs—these images will not let Guedali find peace.

Nor will Pasha. Pasha, the great bay stallion, the mare's
erstwhile mate, whom she now despises. Pasha will come after

him, wanting revenge. And Guedali will not be able to avoid the final battle.

One night Pasha might bang on Guedali's door with his hooves. Guedali would yell, "Enough is enough!" and go out to meet his adversary beneath the excited gaze of the white mare.

It would be hooves against hooves, and the fists of the boy against the stallion's teeth, a terrible fight. Physically, the stallion would have the advantage; if Guedali bit him, he would barely scratch his bay hide. The centaur's blows would be strong, but Pasha's jaw is stronger yet. And Guedali's intelligence? Would it be superior to instinct, to the fury of the animal fighting for his life and his mate? Would Guedali have the presence of mind to arm himself with a butcher knife, and use it at an opportune moment?

My father confides his fears to my mother. She doesn't miss her chance: then let's leave here, Leon. I've always told you we should go somewhere where there aren't so many animals, so many horses. Let's move to the city, Leon. There are good doctors there, hospitals—maybe they'll know of some treatment available for our son. We have our savings, you can open a business. And we'll live someplace out-of-the-way, where nobody will discover Guedali.

Leave the farm? my father asks himself, walking through the fields. The idea disturbs him, for he is very attached to the place. He likes to plow, to plant wheat, to feel the ripe heads of grain between his fingers. Besides, wouldn't leaving the land be a betrayal of Baron Hirsch's sainted memory? My father hesitates.

But sudden events force him to make up his mind.

I am discovered.

And by none other than Pedro Bento, the son of the neighboring rancher, a boy of dreadful character. Mounted on the speedy Pasha to pursue a runaway calf, he strays onto our land.

My father and I are far from the house, planting wheat in a distant field. He is irritated: I came along against his will.

And precisely as he is telling me that he
expose myself so much, Pedro Bento ap
screams my father, but it's too late; befo
Bento is beside us. He jumps off his hor
examining me in wonder. He tries to to
back in fear, while my father, anguish s
watches helplessly, not knowing what t

"What animal is this, Mr. Leon?"
me, what is this thing? Where did you
creature?"

My father stutters a confused expl
asking Pedro Bento to keep what he ha
him money. The boy takes it, promisin
anyone, but he imposes a condition: he
every day to look at me. My father has

So Pedro comes back every day. H
with me, and I respond in monosyllabl
him. He is friendly, he tells interesting
first friend? Will he be to me what Pe

One day he invites me to go for a
him.

As usual, he rides Pasha, and we
different to me; excited, eyes shining, h
questions. From time to time he gives
suddenly, as we pass through some wo
horse and onto my back.

"What do you think you're doing
irritated.

He laughs and lets out cries of tri
why: three big boys, Pedro's brothers,

"See?" he yells. "See there? Was

Crying, terrified, I rear and whirl
of him. I can't. Accustomed to breakin
Pedro Bento clamps his arms around
me. Finally, I take off for home at a g
scared.

"Stop, Guedali! Stop! Let me do
I don't care. I don't listen. I don'

reac
barn
Pedr
poun
bleed

two
erode
strang
skele
head
clay.
I

I
alway
concre
saying
the co
presen
I
of eve

N
has re
one of
furnitu
photog
drives,
sisters
T
me, da
my son
the neg
note sa
keep th
treatme

Shortly before we set off, the mohel appears. He says nothing, only hands me a prayer book in Hebrew and a richly embroidered prayer shawl, and goes away.

And so we begin our journey.

Of this trip I retain only confused memories: my father's figure sitting on the driver's seat, wrapped in a country farmer's cape, rain running off his hat brim. The wet backs of the draft horses shining in the pallid light of early dawn. The narrow, muddy road. The trees with broken branches. The whitish skull of a steer impaled on a fencepost. Blackbirds perched on the barbed wire.

We advance slowly, stopping often. We cook our own meals and sleep beside the road. At night I stretch my legs, numbed from the prolonged immobility. I trot through the nearby fields, mount a little hill, rear up on my hind legs, pound my closed fists against my chest, let out a savage yell. Bernardo looks reprovingly at me, and my father cries, come back, fool! Do you want them to discover us? I come back at a gallop, stop in front of him and hug him. He is a tall man, but I am even taller due to my long legs, and I have to bend over to whisper into his ear: "I'm happy, Father." (It's true, I am happy.)

We go back to the campfire. My brother quietly prepares rice, his hard face illuminated by the firelight.

Finally we arrive in Pôrto Alegre. My father sighs in relief: here you'll be at peace, my son. Nobody will stare at you. City people don't care about anything.

A HOUSE IN THE TERESÓPOLIS NEIGHBORHOOD, PÔRTO ALEGRE
1947–1953

My PARENTS AND SISTERS STAYED AT A CHEAP HOTEL WHILE THEY looked for a house. I had to stay in the wagon, hidden in the woods outside the city. Bernardo, sheltered by a tent, kept curious people away and prepared our food. He was laconic as ever. But one night he drank an entire bottle of wine and started talking. He talked about everything: his envy of me, the family's protected darling; his anger against our father.

"I wanted to have that Patek Philippe watch that belonged to our grandfather. But oh, no, he couldn't give me that. Yet Deborah had the violin the minute she wanted it—Deborah and you. For me, nothing. For the rest of you, everything."

He talked about his plans: "I want to make lots of money," he said. "I want to go to nightclubs and screw two, three women the same night. Do you believe I've never been to bed with a woman, Guedali?" His voice was full of resentment. "I'm eighteen years old and the old man never gave me money to go to a whorehouse." His voice died away to a mumble and he grew quiet. Then he began to snore.

I took him in my arms and carried him to the tent. The next day he didn't remember anything, and he continued to watch me with disgust.

*   *   *

My parents wanted a house in a neighborhood well outside the city; we couldn't live in Bon Fim, where all the Jewish families knew each other, nor in the center of town, nor in Petrópolis. It had to be a place well removed from any of the bus routes, a place more in the country than in the city.

They bought a house in Teresópolis. It was old, with large rooms and an enormous garden full of great trees. Situated at the top of a hill, it was the only house within a quarter-mile radius. At the edge of our lot a deep gully ran around the house, creating a natural obstacle to the approach of strangers, and there was also a high wall. I would be protected from curious eyes.

The previous owner, a distributor of bottled drinks, had built a large storehouse in the back. There, where he had stored his crates and boxes, would be my bedroom. The first weekend we all dedicated ourselves to fixing it up. Once it was cleaned and its walls painted a light green, the old storage area became very cozy. It was about thirty feet long, which permitted me a small gallop, quickly interrupted when I reached the far wall. However, it was quite narrow. There was no possibility of galloping across it the other way.

Most of my father's savings had gone toward the purchase of the house. With what was left, he acquired a small grocery store near the streetcar terminal. The customers patronized the establishment regularly, mainly because of my pretty sisters, who helped behind the counter. My mother stayed at home, cooking; as for Bernardo, he decided to go to work on his own, selling things on the installment plan, in spite of the opposition of my father, who wanted him to keep the cash register at the shop.

The family spent the evenings together. If the weather was fine, we would eat supper outside, under the rose trellis, and I would trot about the garden a bit. How good it was! I would roll delightedly on the thick, dew-dampened grass and inhale deeply, filling my lungs with the fine night air. Seated on wicker chairs, my parents and sisters would watch me tenderly. My brother, as soon as he finished eating, would

mutter something and go out. (He would come back late at
night, smelling of drink, with lipstick stains on his white linen
jacket, obliging my parents to scold him.)

We would talk. My father would tell stories of the Russian
villages, and of his first years in Brazil. His voice was always
full of respect when he mentioned the sainted Baron Hirsch. My
sisters talked about the customers at the shop, the dances to
which they had been invited. Both already had many suitors.
Choose carefully, my father would say, watch out what kind of
sons-in-law you're going to bring me. We would laugh, and
then fall silent.

We would fall silent, and then my mother would begin to
sing. She had a lovely voice, a bit weak and tremulous, but it
was moving to hear her sing old Jewish melodies. Tears would
come to my eyes. "Well," my father would say as he took his
large chain watch from its pocket in his vest, "it's time we got
to bed. Tomorrow is another day, my dears."

During the day, I had to stay shut up—my father wouldn't
even allow me out on the patio—and I had nothing to do. I
dedicated myself to reading. Little by little my room filled with
books. I read everything, from the stories of Moneiro Lobato
to the Talmud. From 1947 to 1953 I read fiction, poetry,
philosophy, history, science—everything. When it came to
books my parents did not economize. "Read, my son, read," my
mother would say. "The things you learn no one can take
away from you. It doesn't matter that you have a handicap, the
important thing is to educate yourself." At their encouragement,
I took correspondence courses: accounting, preparation of legal
documents, technical design, electronics, English, French,
German. I learned the name of the composer of *Cavalleria
Rusticana* and I discovered, to my enchantment, the curious
philosophical metaphor conceived by Buridan to describe the
union of terms in a syllogism: a bridge destined to let the asses
trot across. (*Ass:* this word didn't bother me; I was even amused
at the asses in fables. *Horse,* however, was another matter. My
ears would grow pink when I came across that word in the text.
If there was an illustration, it was even worse.)

I learned to manipulate logarithmic tables. I did language

exercises. *Write a sentence using the word twilight,* the book would order, and I, obedient: *In the twilight hours, the poor centaur died.* There was a time when studying was my solitary vice.

The line of framed diplomas began to stretch across the wall until one day the mailman, curious, asked my father who Guedali was, causing him enormous panic. So I decided to suspend my correspondence courses. But not my reading.

In my books I began to seek answers to the questions that had always bothered me. I devoured volume after volume, reading far into the night (when Bernardo came in, I would still be awake, and I rose when the roosters of Teresópolis began to crow at dawn.) My eyes would peruse the pages impatiently. I would dismiss entire paragraphs; but words like *tail, gallop,* and principally *centaur* made me catch my breath, and I would read and reread the passage. Nothing. The mysterious origins of young Guedali were not clarified.

Disappointed with contemporary texts, I went backward in time. I studied the history of the Jews.

The Jews, a millennial people. Descendants of Abraham; from whence, said one author, came the expression "bosom of Abraham" to refer to heaven. (The image I had was that of a gigantic old man with a long white beard, suspended among the stars and planets, his half-open tunic showing two enormous nipples between which were nestled thousands, millions of small, diaphanous creatures, the souls of human beings. And centaurs? Were there centaurs in the bosom of Abraham too?) Abraham almost sacrifices his son Isaac. Isaac has two sons, Esau (mess of pottage) and Jacob. Jacob, because of his struggle with an angel, becomes Israel.

The Jews become slaves in Egypt. Led by Moses, they flee, cross the Red Sea and wander in the desert. (And the centaurs?) I imagined these people, the Jews, an immense band moving slowly across the Sinai Desert. Thanks to my powers of imagination, I managed to individualize two men out of the multitude: a father and son, or perhaps two brothers. One, his face dusty and lips cracked, goes in the front, gazing toward the horizon; the other, one hand resting on the first man's shoulder, follows, his shoulders slumped, his head bowed. The feet of both are shod in rough sandals and sink into the sand as they walk. I squeeze my eyes tighter, and the two figures unite. With a little more effort I transform them into a sort of quadruped—but the final result is a donkey, a skinny horse or, the most exotic thing I could manage, a camel. A centaur, no.

I would try again, this time starting with the horse I had already conjured: I would try to make little fingers, and then hands and arms, sprout from its eyes. I would try to make its skull crack in half and reveal a child's head, to tear open the neck and expose the trunk of the baby I imagined hidden within. In short, I tried to destroy the ancient image of the horse and recompose it in the form—the outline, anyway—of a young centaur. But it was no good. Horses, even biblical ones, were horses; you couldn't make them into centaurs.

Very well: the Jewish people in the desert. Moses' receiving the Tablets of the Law, in accordance with my father's stories. The destruction, still by Moses, of the said tablets, because of his indignation with the indifference, insensitivity, foolishness, and greed of the Chosen People. The destruction of the Golden Calf.

The arrival in Canaan. The taking of the land. Judges, Kings, Prophets. (And the centaurs?) The fall of the first temple, the fall of the second temple, Diaspora, Inquisition, pogroms. (And the centaurs?) Baron Hirsch, America, Brazil, Quatro Irmãos. What about the centaurs? In the history of the Jews, no one mentioned them; not one of the authors that I anxiously consulted. One group of people was noted, some czars who lived in the south of Russia and converted to Judaism around the end of the first Christian millennium. My parents, coming from the same region, might perhaps be descendants of these czars, but were the czars centaurs? Regarding this point, silence.

I studied mythology and read about beings that were called centaurs outright. The offspring of Ixion and Nephele, they lived in the mountains of Thessaly and Arcadia. They tried to kidnap Didymeia on the day of her marriage to

Pirithous, king of the Lapiths and son of Ixion; they battled fiercely against the Lapiths.

There are no centaurs, the book said. There are clouds similar to centaurs, there are savage tribes which, when mounted on horseback, seem like centaurs, but real centaurs don't exist.

I looked disconsolately at the drawing of the centaur in my book. The artist had depicted a brutish creature, bearded and hairy, with fierce eyes. I wasn't like that. I had nothing to do with Ixion, Nephele, Thessaly, Arcadia. Clouds? Yes, I liked clouds, although I feared certain figures hidden behind them. But, clouds . . . ? I was after something more concrete.

I read Marx. I became aware that class struggle was a constant throughout history. But I couldn't see what part centaurs might play in it. I was on the side of the serfs and against the rulers, for the proletariat and against the capitalists. But what of it? What was I supposed to do? Kick the reactionaries with my hooves?

I read Freud. The existence of the unconscious, the defense mechanisms, the conflict of emotions, became patently clear to me. I understand perfectly the division of the personality. But what about hooves? And a tail? Where did they come in?

In the line of fiction, I read the stories of Sholem Aleichem. I became acquainted with the picturesque characters in the Jewish villages of Russia. Tevia, the milkman, had a horse—but about centaurs, Sholem Aleichem said nothing at all.

Very late one night, the words were spinning before my eyes and the book kept slipping out of my hand, but I wasn't really asleep, or not quite. I was fighting to orient myself amid the alarming confusion that reigned in my mind; names, dates, and places were all mixed together, and I couldn't keep track of who had said what or why. Freud traded ideas with Marx, Baron Hirsch made speeches to Sholem Aleichem.

"Why do you intend to give me financial backing, Baron Hirsch?" asked Marx, intrigued. "You never know what may happen in the future," replied the baron. "I can't be at the mercy of the forces of the market; thanks to them I grew rich,

but I'm not going to risk bankruptcy on account of them. I
have to diversify my investments, and socialism seems to me a
reasonable option." From Baron Hirsch, Freud learned to
charge his patients; before that he had considered money to be
just a symbol, something on the order of Gothic cathedral
towers. Marx scorned the stories of Sholem Aleichem, classifying
them as opium for the people, but this was only outward
show. Secretly he admired fiction, and spent his afternoons in
the British Museum gaining inspiration from the Elgin
Marbles in order to write fantastic stories (about centaurs?).
"Judaism weighs me down," complained Baron Hirsch. He
was thinking about acquiring the Wailing Wall from the Turks
who dominated Palestine at that time. He would have it
dismantled and brought, stone by stone, to Brazil—to the
remote little municipality of Quatro Irmãos. In the same place,
he would set up a zoo full of biblical animals: camels, for
example. (And centaurs?) Sholem Aleichem considered
writing a musical comedy, the characters being himself, Freud,
Baron Hirsch, and Marx. He would base the plot on one of
Marx's stories, entitled "The Caged Jew of the Czar." An
impressive story: hunch-backed, blind, and mute (his tongue
had been cut out by order of the czar), the Jew spent his days
dozing in a cage, hardly touching the food they brought him.
However, the minute a wave of disquiet ran through the
populace in the streets, he would stand up, sniffing the air,
anguish written on his face. Then he would shake the bars of
his cage, throwing himself from one side to the other like a
man possessed. The czar would thus know that it was time to
send out the Cossacks for a pogrom. Mounted on black horses,
the thugs would invade the Jewish villages, murdering, pillaging,
burning. Who could prevail against them? The centaur? But
where was the centaur on the night of the pogrom? Where?

Psychoanalysis, dialectic materialism, nothing; laws of
supply and demand, nothing, nothing; fiction, nothing. Nothing
seemed applicable to my case. I was a centaur, irremediably a
centaur. And without any plausible explanation.

*   *   *

"We are fortunate to live in Brazil," my father used to say after the Second World War. "In Europe they killed millions of Jews."

He would tell of the experiments that Nazi doctors performed on their prisoners. They chopped off their heads and shrank them, in the manner, as I read later, of the Jivaro Indians. They amputated arms and legs. They made strange transplants, uniting the upper half of a man with the lower half of a woman, or the hindquarters of a goat. Fortunately these atrocious operations caused the death of the patients, who expired as human beings and were not obliged to live as monsters. (By this point my eyes would be brimming over with tears; my father thought I was moved by the description of the Nazi horrors.)

In 1948 Israel was proclaimed a state. My father opened a bottle of wine, the best in his store, and we toasted the event. We stayed close beside the radio, accompanying the war in the Middle East. My father was enthusiastic about the new state: in Israel, he explained, live Jews from all over the world, white Jews from Europe, black Jews from Africa, Jews from India, not to mention the Bedouins with their camels—strange types, Guedali.

Strange types—that gave me an idea.

Why not go to Israel? In a war-torn country among so many strange people, I certainly wouldn't attract much attention. Even less if I were a fighter, amid dust and the smoke from the fires. I saw myself running through the little streets of a village, holding a .38 revolver and shooting without stopping. I saw myself falling, shot down by enemy bullets. That, yes, that was the death my soul longed for, a heroic death, a splendid justification for a miserable life led as a shut-in monster. And if I didn't die, I could live in a kibbutz later on. I would be very useful there, I who knew farm life so well. I would be a dedicated worker, and the other members of the kibbutz would end up accepting me; in a new society there is room for everyone, even someone with horses' hooves.

The problem was how to get to Israel. I formulated a plan. My father would nail me up inside a huge crate, along

with a supply of food and water. Then he would ship me to
Haifa. Somehow I would manage to escape from the port
warehouse and gallop to Jerusalem, where the fighting was
thickest.

But my parents wouldn't hear of the idea. "You're crazy,"
they said, "you must never leave us! Who would take care of
you? Forget these mad ideas!"

I argued, fought, cried. I refused to eat. It was useless; they
were inflexible. Then one day the radio announced that an
armistice had been negotiated between the Jews and the Arabs.
My father was exultant: the plan was no longer valid. And we
dropped the subject of Israel.

At the age of thirteen—my birthday was coming up—I
was to undergo the ceremony of the bar mitzvah.

Impossible, said my mother when my father brought up
the subject. It's not impossible at all, said my father. Didn't I
find a way to have him circumcised. So now we will have the
bar mitzvah. But—said my mother, who was having difficulty
breathing and beginning to feel an attack of nerves coming
on—how can you take Guedali to a synagogue? Who said it
has to be in a synagogue? asked my father. We'll hold the
ceremony right here at home. Just for the family. This sounded
more reasonable, and my mother agreed. Deborah and Mina
were excited about the idea. Bernardo didn't say anything.

For weeks I studied with my father the passage from the
Bible that I was to recite in Hebrew. Two days before the party,
my mother, Deborah, and Mina began to prepare the typical
sweets. Father ordered a new suit made, and the girls were
running to the seamstress's house every other minute.

The night before the party I couldn't sleep, I was so
excited. Early the next morning Deborah and Mina danced
joyfully in. They blindfolded me: it has to be a surprise, they
said. For over an hour I waited, hearing their whispering and
the clinking of glass and silver. Finally they took off the
blindfold.

Oh, it was a beautiful sight. The table was covered with a
white cloth; there were bottles of wine, crystal goblets, and

steaming platters of food—the traditional Jewish dishes. On my bed were the presents: books, a record player and records (*Cavalleria Rusticana* wasn't among them), reproductions of famous paintings, a typewriter. And a violin, almost exactly like the one I had thrown in the river.

I embraced my family, crying, and they wept too, but they tried to contain their emotion: Come on, Guedali, we want to start the party. Father came in, bringing the clothes he had bought me for the occasion, a dark suit coat, white shirt, tie, a skullcap. I dressed and placed the ritual shawl the mohel had given me over my shoulders. Mama came in, wearing a party dress and a new hairdo. She hugged me hard, sobbing, and didn't want to let go of me. You'll wrinkle his new coat, said Papa. Bernardo came in and greeted me sourly.

I read the passage from the Bible without a mistake, my voice firm, the fringe of the talit falling over my haunches and hindquarters, one front hoof pawing the ground—as it always did when I was nervous.

"Now," said my father when I had finished, "you are truly a Jew."

My mother served fish balls and wine. We drank a toast. As I turned around, I knocked over a bottle of wine with my tail. It stained the tablecloth and Bernardo's trousers. It's nothing, my mother quickly said. But it was something, something very large. It was my tail, my hooves; it was an animal that was there. Sobbing, I threw myself to the floor: Oh, Mama. Oh, Papa. I so much want to be a regular person, to be normal. There, there, calm down, said my father, don't despair, God will help you. My sisters turned on the record player and played a Russian dance; the happy melody made me smile. Soon they were all dancing around me and I was clapping my hands, the unfortunate incident forgotten.

But Bernardo didn't forget. He tolerated me less and less. It makes me sick, he would say to my parents, just to think of that monster in the storeroom. What you should do is get rid of him, send him someplace far away; instead, you give little parties for him. It's total madness.

Secretly, he wished I would die; that I would catch a
terrible disease, like the equine fever that raged among the
horses of Rio Grande do Sul. That was his hope. Every time I
had a temperature or caught cold his eyes would shine; when I
recuperated, he would shut himself inside his bitterness once
again. He complained that he could never use the storehouse to
store his merchandise. Moreover, he could never invite a client
to his home, much less a sweetheart or even a friend, all because
of that horrible creature. "Be quiet!" screamed my mother.
"Don't make your brother's life harder than it already is!"

"Brother!" snorted Bernardo. "Brother! That's not my
brother, that thing! Nor your son. That's a monster, Mama!"

One day they had a particularly harsh argument and my
father lost his temper.

"Guedali is my son, just like you!" he shouted. "I will
take care of him as long as I am able. If you're not happy, take
your things and get out of here!"

So Bernardo left. He rented an apartment in the center of
the city, and cut off relations with the family. But he made a
point of going by the shop in his car, with a very heavily
made-up woman beside him—a goy, no doubt.

A little while after this, Deborah went to one of the Jewish
Circle dances, where she met a widower, a lawyer from
Curitiba. They fell in love and decided to be married at once.
Fearing my reaction, she hesitated to tell me this news, and
when she did it was in the most disastrous manner, stuttering
and in the end breaking into convulsions of tears. What's this,
Deborah, I said, don't cry, I'm very happy for you. "But you
won't be able to go to the wedding, Guedali!" she moaned.
"He doesn't know about you, and I didn't have the courage to
tell him." She added that she hadn't brought him to our house
yet precisely on account of me; she didn't want to offend me by
asking me to hide myself. What nonsense, I said, you know
I'm used to that, bring him home. Really? she asked, her eyes
shining. You really don't mind, Guedali? Of course not, I said,
forcing myself to smile. I loved her so much.

The lawyer came and dined with the family. He was a

mature man, friendly, a great talker. He drank a lot of wine
and ended up falling asleep in an armchair.

An idea occurred to Deborah. She came running to my
room. Guedali, do you want to see my fiancé? I didn't
understand, but she insisted, come on, quick, he's fallen asleep.

I followed her to the dining room window and peeped
cautiously in. The lawyer was snoring, his mouth open.
He looks like a good man, I whispered. Yes, doesn't he?
she beamed. How wonderful, Guedali, how wonderful you like
him.

The lawyer stirred in his chair and opened his eyes. I ran
to my room and locked the door, my heart pounding. I heard
the man say, "Deborah, I'm certain I saw a man on horseback!"

"Nonsense," she replied, "you've had too much to drink."

A man on horseback! I couldn't contain myself: I fell
onto my mattress, laughing. A man on horseback, it was too
much! I howled with laughter. Mina heard me and, growing
alarmed, came to ask me to be quiet, but she started laughing
too. I was beside myself; my belly, my great belly, hurt from
so much laughter. I rolled onto the floor, chuckling, as Mina
tried to remember a story from the concentration camps to
make us grow serious. But it was no use. I only stopped
laughing when I was completely out of breath. By that time
Deborah had already left with the lawyer, and she never
brought him home again. The next week they were married
and went to Curitiba.

The house is too big now, complained my mother, who
missed her daughter. Now she blamed my father for having sent
Bernardo away. She grew melancholy, and began to frequent
seances at which she conversed with her old neighbors who had
died in the pogrom in the Russian village. But she continued
to cook and take care of the house, and at night we would sit
under the rose arbor to talk as always. Weeks and months
went by. It seemed that nothing else was ever going to happen,
that life would always be just like that, a succession of days
and nights all exactly alike, with occasional small incidents
breaking the otherwise changeless routine. I became irritated
with myself for desiring something else, I knew not what. What

else could I possibly want, I asked myself, what else could I
hope for, if being alive was a great thing in itself?

It was about then I fell in love.

For years I had forced myself not to think about sex. I felt
desire, of course, but following the advice of certain books, I
tried to sublimate it. Before going to bed at night I would do
dozens of exercises for the waist, legs, and arms. I would lift
enormous weights, flagellate my body with wet towels. I would
lie down exhausted, but even so I didn't manage to get to
sleep; I seemed to hear sighs of pleasure, debauched laughter. I
asked my father to buy me some sleeping pills at the
drugstore. With five of them, I would manage to drop off, but
then my dreams would torment me, dreams populated by
women or mares, and in them I was now a normal man, now a
complete horse, and to top it all off, it wasn't always a man
going to bed with a woman, nor a stallion breeding a mare. I
would wake up exhausted. Disgusted, but relieved, I would
verify that I had ejaculated. Nature had done what it had to,
and I was resigned.

But I ended up falling in love. Quite by chance, as these
things always happen.

When I was twenty-one, my father asked me what I
wanted for my birthday. I was then interested in astronomy,
and I asked for a telescope. I was hoping to make some
observations of the stars and planets.

The telescope arrived, a beautiful instrument with good
lenses. I read the instruction manual and immediately began
to explore the heavens. At night I went from Venus to Saturn,
studying the constellations (the Centaur, for obvious reasons)
with some disappointment, since I saw nothing sensational in
them. (What did I expect to see? Abraham and his bosom?
The winged horse?) In the daytime, the telescope hidden in the
curtains of my bedroom window, I examined the hills round
about. That was how I discovered the girl in the colonial
mansion.

This mansion, a very handsome one, was situated about a

mile and a half from our house, but I could observe it easily.
At first I was amazed at the number of servants, all in white
caps and aprons. After a few days I noted the presence of the
girl with copper-colored hair.

She would come out onto the terrace every morning, take
off her robe and lie down nude, completely nude, in the
sunshine. From a table beside her, she would take a pair of
binoculars and examine the house's deserted surroundings. She
looked through her binoculars, I looked through my telescope.
I couldn't see her face clearly, but I imagined her having a
delicate nose, full lips, and perfect teeth. Her eyes, yes. Her
eyes I saw well, through the lenses of the telescope and
binoculars, and they took my breath away. The right eye was
luminously blue, the left eye even bluer. My heart beat madly.
My hoof pawed the floor more nervously than ever. Never in
any book (and I had many), never in any magazine, had I seen
such a beautiful girl. She fascinated me. I couldn't stop looking
at her.

Could she see me, from her terrace? Could she divine my
face behind the curtains? Would she like to have seen me? I ran
to the mirror. No, I wasn't ugly. Handsome unruly hair,
beautiful eyes, straight nose, well-defined mouth. Only a few
pimples on my forehead. I really was a handsome young man.
But below, centaur, centaur, irremediably centaur.

As a centaur, I must resign myself to looking at her only.
Dreaming of her, sighing for her. But no: soon I was no longer
content merely to gaze at her from afar. I wanted to talk to
her, touch her face, her hands.

(In my dreams I went even further. I dreamed of
galloping up to the mansion, going in through the big front
door and up the steps to the terrace. I would take her in my
arms—"My love," she would murmur, "at last you've come,"
and I would carry her far away into the mountains where we
would live, hidden in a cavern, eating wild fruit, making clay
pots, walking together. She would ride on my back, her soft
arms embracing my chest. In these dreams, she lay down naked
on the ground, holding her arms out to me: Come, my love.
Come, my darling centaur.)

Dreams, naturally. But I wanted to see her, at least once. But how to manage it? How to avoid her noticing my hooves, legs, and tail? How should I proceed so that she wouldn't run away horrified, yelling monster, monster?

What if I wrote her a letter?

Why not? I wrote very well, I had beautiful handwriting, capable of impressing a woman. But I didn't know her address, or even her name. (I imagined it to be Magali, the name of the sensuous heroine of the novel *Vacation in the Caribbean.*) No, I couldn't send a letter through the regular post office. I thought about the Lonely Hearts column in the teenage magazines Mina collected. Impassioned love letters appeared there, signed with pseudonyms such as "Solitary Bird," "Desperate Tiger," "Sad Faun." Among these, "Centaur in Love" wouldn't draw much attention. But how should I address her? "Dear Unknown Girl of the Mansion in Teresópolis, Pôrto Alegre"? Would she recognize herself under this affectionate title? And, cruelest doubt of all, did she even read teenage magazines? From what I had observed, she didn't read anything. She took sunbaths and looked through her binoculars. That was all.

Still, the idea of sending her a letter seemed to me a good one. The problem continued to be getting it into her hands.

Then it occurred to me to use a carrier pigeon. An ingenious idea, except that I didn't have a pigeon. But it wouldn't be impossible to get one.

"I'd like to have a dovecote," I said to my father that night. He didn't understand, a what? A dovecote, I repeated, a little house for doves. He was perplexed: dovecote? But what for, Guedali? I don't have anything to do, I said, and raising doves would be fun. He was reluctant, fearing that a dovecote would attract bad boys like Pedro Bento. My mother appeared on the scene: Do what Guedali wants, Leon!

The next day, he brought some wood and tools. We built the dovecote, following a design in a book on how to raise birds. When it was ready, my father bought six purebred pigeons.

I chose the one that seemed the most intelligent—Columbo,

I called him—and began to train him. First, I taught him to go from one place to another in the garden, which wasn't difficult: some corn at the takeoff point, more corn at the destination. The next step was to make Columbo associate patio and mansion with takeoff and arrival. To do this, I pointed him toward the mansion several times each night (the training always took place after dark). Then I would reward him with some corn.

The training took weeks, and during our long sessions together a warm affection was born in me for the white Columbo. Holding him in my hands, I felt his heart beat; you understand me, little dove, I would murmur, you feel the intensity of my passion. There was no sign of emotion in his little black beady eyes, as hard as stones, but I was sure he understood me, and that he would carry out my mission.

Finally the moment came. Brimming with sentiment, I wrote a note and tied it to Columbo's foot. I had addressed it "To the Adorable, Unknown Girl of the Mansion." I told her of my admiration, and proposed that we correspond so that we might come to know each other better. Pressing reasons, I said, impeded me from revealing my identity, but when the right moment came I would do so. I finished the note by asking that she use the same pigeon to send her reply.

I kissed Columbo's head, and threw him up into the air. He circled above the patio three or four times and then went off. In the opposite direction from the mansion, the idiot, the ungrateful imbecile.

I threw the other pigeons out, knocked over the dovecote, and burned it—to my father's surprise: Wasn't that what you wanted so much, Guedali? I didn't answer. I only looked in silence at the white boards being consumed by the fire.

Never again, I thought. I never want to fall in love again, never, never.

I thought it was the end, but no. After a few days passed, I was taken by a sudden optimism. I would try again, and this time God would help me—I would be successful. I would use a catapult to send the message. Naturally, I would have to try many times before I managed to make the note, wrapped around a stone, fall onto the terrace. But that didn't matter; I had plenty of time.

But I didn't even set up the catapult. There was no need to.

The next morning she was on the terrace, naked as usual, looking through her binoculars, when a man came up, a tall, tanned man, with white hair and dark glasses. It's her father, I thought at first. But he approached her from behind, embraced her and fondled her breasts in his hands—no, no, it wasn't her father. Then he kissed her lingeringly on the neck. She let the binoculars fall to the ground. She didn't place them on the table there on the terrace, no, she let them fall. It mattered little to her if the lenses broke, she was already closing her eyes, her nostrils dilating. She was—I saw everything through the telescope—lying down and pulling the man down on top of her.

I became ill. Whether or not there was any cause-and-effect relationship, the fact remained that I was affected by a mysterious fever. For six days I lay on my mattress, barely eating, only sipping water.

My parents never left my side. Up to then I had never needed a doctor, but now they asked each other if they should take me to the hospital, even if it meant revealing my existence to the world. Better I should live, even pestered by reporters and photographers, than die for lack of care. They discussed these things in hushed voices at my bedside. When I opened my eyes, I saw them staring anxiously at me. What's wrong with you, Guedali? my mother asked. Nothing, Mother, I murmured, it must have been something I ate, I have a bit of a stomachache. She extended a hesitant hand, and touched my belly: poor little hand, lost in the immensity of that belly, between a brown spot and a white one. Which breed of horse do I belong to? I asked myself, half asleep. Palomino? Arabian? Percheron? A mixture?

* * *

On the seventh day the fever went down.

I thought a great deal as I lay on my mattress convalescing. What am I going to do? I asked myself. What am I going to do now?

I decided to go away.

I would go somewhere distant, to the woods, and live near the quail and the anteaters, the satyrs and the spooks, the Indians and the solitary birds.

It pained me to leave my family. But I couldn't go on this way, a prisoner in my room, gradually becoming a toothless old centaur with white hair, and finally dying without even having tried to escape my destiny. Maybe in the woodlands I would discover a way to be happy.

On the evening preceding my departure, I didn't go to bed. I stayed awake, pacing back and forth. In the wee hours of the morning, I wrote a letter to my family. I told them I was leaving, but for them not to worry, I would find my way. Then I went out, peeping cautiously through the window of my parents' bedroom. They were asleep in each others' arms. I wished I could have lain down between them, stayed there in the warmth forever. But a centaur . . . ?

I went into the kitchen and took some money from the can where my mother kept her household savings. What am I going to do with this? I asked myself, looking at the rolled-up bills. But I put the money into my pack and went out onto the patio.

It was cold, and a thick fog obscured the mansion (a relief) and guaranteed me a safe flight. I breathed deeply, gritted my teeth, and started off at a short gallop, getting ready for the prodigious leap. In the fraction of a second that preceded the jump I hesitated, realizing all I was leaving behind: the roof over my head, meals at the proper times, and above all the affection of my loved ones. But by then it was no longer I who decided; my hooves were carrying me along, and I was already in midair, jumping over the wall, my fear mingling with excitement and joy—I was free! I continued galloping, pursued by a dog that barked without letting up. I jumped a fence and found myself in an orchard. Another fence—a chicken yard, hens cackling in alarm and flapping in all directions. Another fence—a woman who was washing clothes screamed and ran. One more fence, and I was on a small dirt road, at the end of which was the forest, the unknown.

Galloping by night and hiding myself by day, I covered enormous distances. I had no clear idea of where I was heading; maybe the border—Uruguay, Argentina. I kept on. The South Pole was my limit.

CIRCUS
1953–1954

(I IMAGINED MYSELF WANDERING, NOT IN THE DESERT LIKE THE
Jews, but on a snow-covered plateau. My hooves would sink
into the snow and my benumbed legs would hardly obey me,
but I pressed forward, head held high, risking everything. I was
victorious: suddenly, the whole hind part of my body came
loose and remained stuck there, the hooves buried in the snow,
while my front half, freed now of its burden, advanced toward
the horizon and disappeared.)

I galloped by night and hid by day. When my packet of
food was gone, I began to steal in order to eat. I would sneak
into gardens and come out with armfuls of lettuce. I took eggs
from chicken coops; in the silence of the night I milked cows
that were running loose. Not a few times I had to confront
fierce watchdogs and kick them with my hooves. On two or
three occasions people shot at me; fortunately they were
terrible marksmen. I spent a whole day submerged in a marsh,
only my head sticking out, while being hunted by farmers who
wanted to lynch me. On another occasion, I climbed up into a
cattle car of a train to escape my pursuers. I hid among the
cattle, doubling up my front legs and bending over from the

waist so that only my hindquarters were visible, trying to look like one of the animals. I had a nasty start when the train began to move: I could see myself being taken off to the slaughterhouse. However, I jumped off in time. By looking at the stars I verified that we had advanced in a southerly direction, the way I wanted to go. I saw many places, many people. Negroes, for example. I had never seen a black person before. I knew they existed from books I had read, but I had no idea what a real Negro would be like, walking, laughing. This curiosity was satisfied: one night I saw four Negroes on the road, walking and laughing. (And Negro centaurs? Did they exist?)

I saw emus out in the country. I saw a house burning down. I saw a nocturnal procession: people praying for rain.

The free, decisive pace of my gallop did me good. I was leaving behind a painful memory—to wit, a frustrated love. But I missed many things: my family, my room, books, records, and even my telescope. During this period I prayed a great deal; as evening fell I would turn to the east, toward distant Jerusalem, and murmur the prayers my father had taught me. I wasn't really praying to Jehovah; it wasn't exactly religion I was practicing, it was more a form of nostalgia. I was echoing my own childhood.

I prayed, and I continued southward.

Very early one morning, fatigue got the better of me. I was in the neighborhood of a small town, and it was a dangerous place to stay, but I couldn't go on: I was dripping with sweat and my legs were buckling under the weight of my body. The worst of it was that the region was totally flat, a treeless plain. But I found a ditch, lay down in it, covered myself with some branches, and fell asleep.

I woke up with a start in the midst of an alarming racket. Drums rolling, the strident tones of a cornet, cries and hammer blows. I leaped up, trembling all over. All around me was incredible confusion: cages with wild animals, trucks, crates, people setting up an enormous tent.

A circus.

Two dwarfs in pajamas were gazing at me with great

interest. Is that the new number? asked one, in a squeaky little voice. I guess so, replied the other. He addressed me: You the new number, pal? Well, we'll have to find out, I answered cautiously, as I asked myself with mingled fear and amusement, Why not? I looked at a passing camel. Why not? The elephant chained to a stake: Why not?

I'd like to talk to the manager, I added. The dwarf shrugged his shoulders. The manager had been hospitalized and his wife, who normally substituted for him, had run off with the tightrope walker. It seemed that the only person of responsibility there was the lion tamer—a woman.

I met her beside the tiger's cage. Wearing a grieved expression, she was looking at the great feline, which was lying down flat in a sickly manner. I'm the new number, I said.

She turned around and looked at me, alarmed and supicious. More suspicious than alarmed; she was probably accustomed to exotic creatures.

"Well, what the devil is this?" she asked.

She was a tall, robust woman of middle age. Still pretty: a face with well-defined features, like Greta Garbo's pictures in one of my books. She wore dark glasses, a shirt with epaulettes, a vest and boots, which accentuated her air of authority. I'm the new number, I repeated, I do a centaur act. She frowned: What kind of act? A centaur, I said, a mythological being, half man, half horse. Oh, yeah, she said, I've heard about them.

She took off her glasses—she had pale, cold eyes—and examined me attentively. She ordered me to walk around in a circle. It's well made, your costume, she observed. Is it leather? Authentic horsehide, I answered, hopeful at her demonstration of interest. She continued to examine me.

"And who's inside?" she asked suddenly.

"My brother," I said, and added quickly, "he doesn't like to be seen. He's a deaf-mute and besides that his face is all burned, a woman threw acid at him." "Is he in any trouble with the police?" she inquired, suspicious. "I don't want any problems around here." "Oh, no," I said, "it's nothing to do with the police. He just doesn't like to be seen, that's all."

She stared at me. The story smelled fishy to her, one

could see. But I stood firm, impassively returning her fixed gaze.

"And what do you and your brother do?" she asked. "We run around the ring," I said, "and jump over obstacles; and I can recite poetry, tell stories, play the violin. But I doubt that that will be necessary. The crowds always die laughing when we come into the ring." "I believe it," she said. "The costume really is a good one."

She took a pack of cigarettes from the pocket of her shirt. "Smoke?"

I had never smoked in my life, but I accepted. I nearly suffocated with the first drag, and I coughed. "I guess centaurs shouldn't smoke," I said. She laughed.

"Okay," she said. "But there's one problem. A serious one. I don't know what your agreement was with the former manager, but the circus is bankrupt. I have no way to pay you."

"That's all right," I said quickly. "I can work in exchange for my meals—at least for a while. Later we'll straighten things out."

"Fine. In that case, you two can start working today. What's your name again?"

"Silva," I told her. "Both my brother and I answer to that name."

She held out her hand to me.

"You're nice, Silva." As we shook hands, hers lingered in mine. "I think we'll get along just fine." She glanced at her watch—a big one, a man's watch. "Well, I have to see how things are coming along. Tonight's opening night. Your number is the second one."

Through a hole in the tattered curtain, I peeked at the crowd that filled the grandstand. Poor people: peons from neighboring ranches, factory workers, soldiers, housemaids. Women with sagging breasts, toothless children. (And Pedro Bento? Might he be there by chance?) Rude peasants. (Peri?)

Strangers, goyim. Some were mean looking, with the appearance of bandits. I felt like running away; I wished I was home with my parents. Which in turn made me angry at

myself. Stay right where you are, I told myself, get hold of
yourself, you coward.

The dwarfs came running out of the ring. "It's your turn,"
said a voice behind me. I turned around: it was the lion tamer,
all dressed up to be ringmistress. Starched shirtfront, frock coat,
a whip in one hand and a cane in the other. She smiled and
winked at me. "Do your best, Silva, I'm cheering for you." The
drum rolled, a cornet sounded an off-key salute. "Good luck,"
she said, adjusting the golden cloth I wore over my hindquarters.
Here I go, I muttered, and went trotting hesitantly into the
ring.

The lights blinded me; the noise that went up was
deafening. Terror took hold of me, and I thought I was going
to faint, but I kept on galloping, my legs carrying me forward
as they had when I was a baby, three, four, five times around
the ring. Finally, as had been arranged, I went to the center of
the ring, reared up on my hind legs, and greeted the public.

"Good evening, ladies and gentlemen!" My voice was
tinny, strange, but they responded with applause. And then to
my own surprise I heard myself saying confidently in a loud
voice: "I didn't hear it! Louder! Good evening, ladies and
gentlemen!"

"Good evening," they roared, and I stood there smiling as
the ringmistress explained who I was, a centaur from the
mountains of Tunisia, the last surviving specimen of an almost
extinct race. She turned to me:

"Centaur, my friend! Show the people what you can do!"

I ran around the ring some more, jumped over obstacles.
And when I danced a polka to the accompaniment of an
accordian, my hooves tripping over one another, it brought
down the house. The people cheered like madmen. I had to
repeat the number twice, three times. Finally, I went out,
dripping wet and exhausted. The lion tamer was waiting for me,
smiling. Didn't I tell you, Silva, that you'd be a hit? The
circus people surrounded me, complimenting me. At last things
will be better, we'll be able to fill our bellies again, said the
dwarfs. They offered to go back in the ring mounted on my
back; the trapeze artist wanted to do a number with me too:

"The Flying Centaur." All these compliments were very nice, but so many hands touching me, patting me, was beginning to make me nervous. What if they realized in the midst of the general rejoicing that I wasn't wearing a costume, that I was real, that inside my hide there was no deaf-mute Silva with a burned face, but the guts, liver, kidneys, intestines of a *horse*? I turned around and addressed my back: Come on, brother, let's go take a shower. They laughed. Shower? Do centaurs take showers? But I was already moving away as quickly as I could.

The circus began to draw large crowds. The tent was always full, and I was the principal attraction. I wasn't satisfied with the success I enjoyed: I introduced variations into my number. I would race with the camel, which made the public delirious. I also learned how to juggle. And I leaped through a ring of flames: applause, applause.

Of course, things didn't always go well. Smart alecks would pull my tail; several times drunks tried to ride on my back. The temptation to kick them was very great. Don't upset yourself, the dwarfs said, these people are rough, country louts.

The circus people liked me very much and the dwarfs in particular hardly let me out of their sight. This worried me; the more I was alone, the better. I asked for a trailer all to myself, and the lion tamer was quick to grant my request. You have no need to ask, you give the orders, she said with a wink.

The trailer was a luxurious one, and a big improvement, though it was for people, not a centaur. I could hardly stand up inside it; besides, there wasn't a large, wide mattress like in my house, but rather two narrow beds—for me and my brother, supposedly. Nevertheless I spent most of my time there, reading. When I went out, I covered my hindquarters with a large canvas, which reached down to the ground. Explaining that I didn't want to spoil the centaur costume, which was very expensive, I was really protecting myself from indiscreet hands.

They left me alone. They found me a little strange, but I certainly wasn't as strange as some there: the knife thrower talked to himself, the clown didn't get along with anyone, and the trapeze artist liked to put spiders and cockroaches in the dwarfs' pockets.

I'm fine, I wrote my parents. I'm eating well, and enjoying myself, I don't have any more fever. For the moment I can't say where I'm living, but don't worry, all is well.

All *was* well, in fact. I even felt happy. I began to think that there was a place for me after all among human beings—hooves or no hooves, tail or no tail. The crowds' laughter and the friendship of the circus people comforted me. And there was the way the lion tamer looked at me.

The dwarfs talked about her with a mixture of admiration and fear: a tyrant, they said, who controlled the circus with an iron hand. And hot-blooded, too: there wasn't a man who could satisfy her. The trapeze artist, the knife thrower, the clown, had all gone to bed with her and she had scornfully rejected each of them for his weak performance. They're not men enough for me, she said. At the moment she had no lover, which made the circus troupe nervous, for during these periods she would become irascible and no one could tolerate her.

She watched me. She watched me a great deal. She would look at me from the lion's cage; lying down beside the great feline, she would embrace it amorously, kissing its mouth. Oh, she would exclaim, how I wish I'd meet a man who was like this lion! And she would wink at me. I would smile and move away, perturbed. But the truth was, all I could think of was her. I couldn't sleep; my enormous penis erect, I would toss and turn on the floor, restless. If she liked lions, why not a centaur?

The girls who came to the circus looked at me with admiration. How handsome he is! They would ask to touch me, which made the lion tamer furious and me more nervous than ever.

A presentiment of what is going to happen comes to me.

*   *   *

One night, I can't sleep. It's hot inside the wagon, a
suffocating, oppressive heat. I plunge my face into a basin of
water, roll myself in wet towels, but it's useless. I end up
going outside.

I walk softly among the wild animals' cages. The animals
stare silently at me, their eyes shining in the dark. The elephant,
standing up, sways from side to side. The poor beasts. I
understand them well. My insides are your insides, although my
destiny is not your destiny.

"Where are you going, fella?"

Startled, I whirl around to face the lion tamer. Leaning
against the tiger's cage, she gazes at me, smiling.

"Out for a walk?"

"Just getting a little fresh air," I say, my voice sounding
strange.

She looks around. There is no one there, everyone's asleep.
Come here, she murmurs. I draw close to her. I see the desire
in her eyes, in her half-open lips. As for me, I have a dry throat
and am afraid, but I can't stand it any more, I embrace her.

"Wait," she says. "Not here."

I take her in my arms. We go into the wagon, and I kiss her
furiously, her mouth, her eyes, her neck. Easy, my love, she says,
let me get undressed. I let go of her. Trembling with desire, I
watch her unbutton her blouse, pull off her boots.

And what about your brother? she asks, won't he get
mad? An idea occurs to her. If you want, you can both come
together. No! I answer, almost yelling, and then in a lower
voice, "Uh, he . . . my brother . . . doesn't go in for things like
that. But he doesn't care . . . uh, what I do."

"Oh, okay," she says. She finishes taking off her clothes—in
the semidarkness I can see she has a beautiful body—and lies
down on the bed.

"Come, my love," she whispers. "Come, my dear centaur."

My legs bent, I lean over her and kiss her, kiss her crazily,
her mouth, her breasts, her thighs. Oh, you drive me wild, she
moans, Wild, wild! Come on, love, come on. Take that costume
off, quick!

And then—an avalanche descending a mountain, a torrent

bursting the floodgates—I throw myself on her and see nothing more. Confusedly, I hear her yelling for help—"Help, he's attacking me, he's a monster!" I stop her, covering her mouth, I try to penetrate her, fail, and ejaculate onto her thighs. Then I fall exhausted to one side. She leaps from the bed and runs, still yelling, "He's a horse! A real horse!"

I get up, dizzy, and go out. Excited voices echo through the night, lights go on. The lions growl, the monkeys chatter. There is no time to lose. I take off at a gallop.

(This gallop. This gallop in the middle of the night, through open fields, through swamps that reflect a pallid moon, this gallop is to stay in my memory for many years. Today I remember with longing the times when I could gallop freely, as on that night, even though at the time I was terrified, squashing frogs under my hooves and scratching myself against the branches of the short pampas trees.

It's good to run. My friends go running every morning. They do at least six laps around the park, claiming it's a good way to avoid strokes. They also say that running clears the mind, that the brain, agitated inside the cranium, releases all its worries and obsessions—you can see a little cloud of vapor going up from the heads of great runners.

But I know these aren't the only reasons they run. They run for the sake of running, because it's good; it it weren't for the limitations of time and space, and their responsibilities, families, and so forth, they would run far away in a straight line to a paradise of laughing joggers, a place always limitless no matter how far you run, a place where everyone jogs all the time—some in navy blue jackets, others in white shorts, some in tennis shoes, others barefoot, some jogging alone, others in a group, running and talking, running and eating sandwiches, running and shitting, running without stopping like I ran that night—but happy, without the fear I felt.)

By morning I am far away. From the position of the sun I confirm that I am going southward, as I always intended. Although I was going in the opposite direction from Thessaly and Arcadia, I had to find the legendary country of the centaurs. Centaur kings, centaur subjects, the centaur farmers, centaur writers. And the centauresses.

Or maybe I will go to the South Pole, to the eternal ice that preserves intact the carcasses of our ancestral quadrupeds.

I gallop during the night, as I did before. I steal fruit and vegetables, like before—and food from trucks parked beside the road. Like before, I sleep during the day—but now only in very safe, well-hidden places.

I travel a great distance.

A RANCH IN RIO GRANDE DO SUL
1954–1959

I HEAD FOR THE ARGENTINE BORDER.

(I must have passed through São Borja about the time they were burying president Getúlio Vargas. Of course at the time I knew nothing at all of these matters. I only galloped on.)

One rainy night I took refuge in an abandoned hut, a tumbledown place situated in the middle of an immense field. The sound of the rain and the croaking of the frogs lulled me to sleep—an animal sleep, originating, I believe, from overtaxed muscles, aching tendons. A mulelike sleep.

The next morning . . .
I awaken with a start, full of strange presentiments.
I stand up and peek through the little window of the hut.

The sky is still overcast although the rain has stopped. Some sheep graze placidly; there is no one in sight. Why was I so startled?

But there is something. I feel it deep inside myself. Within me resound the remote hoofbeats of approaching horses. I squint and divine something on the horizon.

A horseman. No, two horsemen. Running flat out, they approach quickly.

The one in front seems to be a woman ... it is a woman, I can distinguish her long wind-tossed hair. The horse is odd. Where is its head? *The horse's head?*

There is no head. There is no horse. The pursuer, yes, comes on horseback, but the figure in front is woman and horse joined, it's half woman, half horse, it's ... can it be true what I'm seeing? It's a *centauress*.

A centauress! (So I'm not the only one, so there are more of us, maybe many more!) And from where—she's a young girl, and appears very beautiful—had she come? From the Quatro Irmãos district? (Oh, if my parents ...) From Argentina, from the South Pole? (Imagine if Deborah and Mina knew!) But this is no time for questions, the girl, the centauress, is in obvious distress; she is exhausted and terrified, her pursuer—an old man—closes in on her. One must do something, but Lord Jehovah, what? If only I were the winged horse ...

"Stop, you devil! Stop!" yells the old man, possessed.

... I would catch her up off the ground, carry her into the clouds. But I'm not the winged horse, I'm only a frightened, angry centaur, and what am I to do? Come out of my hiding place, attack the old man?

"Stop or I'll shoot you!"

He has a revolver in his hand and is less than a hundred yards from the centauress, taking aim, both of them galloping madly. They are going to pass in front of the hut now, *now*.

I throw myself against the fragile door, knock it down, and rush outside and run toward the man, who reins in his horse, popeyed, and lets out a scream of terror. The horse rears up at the exact moment he fires, and he tumbles off. The horse runs away.

Cautiously I approach. The man has fallen face down and is motionless. I kneel beside him, turn him over. Avoiding the sight of his glazed, wide-open eyes, I place my hand on his chest. His heart isn't beating.

"Is he dead?" It's the girl, the centauress, close by me.

We look at each other.

She is pretty. Not as pretty as the girl from the mansion, but very pretty; her delicate, dark-eyed face shows traces of Indian blood.

"Quite dead," I say, getting up.

She began to cry. She is still upset, one can see. I want to console her, to smooth her long black hair and say that it was nothing, that it's all right now. And that is exactly what I do: I smooth her hair, I say it was nothing, it's all right now. I recognize her as mine; she recognizes me as hers. We are of the same aberrant lineage, her hide even resembles mine a little, it's bay.

(Bitterly, I had once thought, looking at myself in disgust, it's not enough that I was born a centaur, I had to be bay in addition! But now—now I was happy I had a bay hide. It was one more thing we had in common.)

She dries her eyes on the sleeve of her long white tunic and looks at me. Only now that the moment of panic has passed does she seem to realize that I too have hooves, that I too am part equine. Amazement is registered on her face, amazement and fear.

My name is Guedali, I say to calm her. She doesn't understand. What? she asks, frowning with an almost comical expression. Guedali, I repeat. Ah, she says, I am called Tita.

Suddenly I realize that we are in the middle of the fields, completely exposed. I hide the old man's body among some bushes and lead her by the hand inside the hut, where I make her sit down near me. Still sobbing, she tells me the story of the dead man, the rancher named Zeca Fagundes.

Zeca Fagundes was the owner of all the land round about.

He had gone into sheep-raising at a time when the price of wool was reaching its height on the international market, and had grown wealthy.

He lived with his wife, Dona Cotinha, in an enormous house—an imitation of a medieval castle, with a moat and drawbridge, murals, turrets, everything. The bedroom doorways and the ample halls were ornamented by authentic medieval suits of armor, acquired in Pelotas from a respectable antique dealer. The floors were of stone; the small windows were protected by heavy gratings. The lighting was provided by torches. In the cellar there was a dungeon and a torture chamber, from the ceiling of which hung an iron cage containing a headless skeleton. That's what happens to peasants who give themselves airs, said Zeca Fagundes, but they all knew it was a joke. The bones were those of a woodsman, a servant who had died a natural death.

Dona Cotinha, a small, thin, silent woman who always dressed in black, never went out of the house. She was dedicated to the art of weaving. Working with ancient looms that had belonged to her grandmother—also a rancher's wife—she wove the wool from her husband's sheep into tapestries of beautiful design: heraldic symbols, animals of the region (emus were always present) or mythological creatures, like the unicorn or the griffin. There were also figures from the legends of southern Brazil, like Salamanca do Jarau. These tapestries were hung from the damp stone walls by means of hooks; the sight of them helped to cheer Dona Cotinha, a sad and solitary woman. Her only son did not get along with his father; he lived in Pôrto Alegre and studied law—he had been doing so for years, he never finished his courses. Anonymous letters would occasionally arrive saying horrible things about this young man, denouncing him as an alcoholic and moral degenerate, which did nothing to help the poor lady's spirits.

Zeca Fagundes, an irascible man, detested his sheep in spite of the wealth they had brought him, and considered them stupid, cowardly animals. He also detested the peasants on his ranch. Do you think I don't know that you screw the sheep? he would say, his tone both tender and mocking, irritated and sympathetic. Why, Mr. Zeca, sir! the men would reply, sheep! Whoever heard of such a thing?

What Zeca Fagundes really liked were his horses. He didn't have many—his neighbors had dozens more—but they were carefully selected: thoroughbreds, fast runners. Zeca Fagundes treated them with affection, and wouldn't let a single peasant near his stables. He himself fed and groomed each horse.

Sultan, the roan, was his favorite. On his back Zeca
Fagundes went galloping through the fields, his shirt open at the
chest, his white hair flying in the wind. Catching sight of a
flock of sheep, he would ride them down. How he chased them!
He was delighted to see the animals flee, bleating in terror.

Horses. Horses and women. Not Dona Cotinha, who was
ugly and unattractive, although a loyal companion, but others.
He would bring them from Bagé and Alegrete: flashy little
shopgirls, divorcées—whores, too. He would find a way to
install them in the ranch house, some as cooks, others as
housemaids, still others to answer correspondence or do
accounting. They all lived in an enormous room with an arched
ceiling in the cellar of the castle. He would come in at any
hour of the day or night and point to one of them, Come here,
you! and take her to a secret room, a bedroom to which only
he had a key, situated in one of the towers and isolated from
the rest of the house.

The women were not prisoners. They could leave if they
wanted. But they didn't dare. They knew that Zeca Fagundes
would go after them, wherever they hid, and that the punishment
would be terrible—the dungeon was there just next door to
them, and the torture chamber (whips and live coals were
whispered of, not to mention the skeleton in the cage). They
preferred to stay. Besides, they had food, nice dresses and
perfumes, since Zeca Fagundes didn't economize in these
things. I like to see my fillies pretty and smelling good, he
would say. And in bed he kept them all satisfied, in spite of
his age.

(Once, a girl from unknown parts had appeared at the
ranch. She was young, pretty, and blonde—a rarity in that
area—with a São Paulo accent. She claimed to be an admirer
of horses who had come especially to see Zeca Fagundes's
stables. The rancher received her with misgivings; she struck
him as a suspicious figure, this woman wearing a low-cut dress,
heavy makeup, and jewelry. In the course of the conversation
she said that she was separated from her husband and was
disillusioned with city men, who were all weaklings.

Zeca Fagundes regarded her in silence for a few seconds,

then invited her to come up to the tower bedroom. She went.
In bed she proved to be nothing special, but nevertheless he
proposed that she stay at the ranch, perhaps because she was so
different from the other women. She accepted "for a while"
according to what she said, and Zeca Fagundes answered drily
that on his ranch, *he* was the one who arranged dates and
schedules.

It became clear at once that she wasn't like the other girls,
this blonde. She didn't confine herself to the big room in the
cellar, but went all over the house, poking into everything,
asking embarrassing questions, taking notes in a notebook.
And she tried to convince the other women to rebel against
Zeca Fagundes: You're slaves, she would yell, this man
dominates all of you! On a surprise visit, the rancher caught her
taking notes. He confiscated her notebook, and when she
attempted resistance—Give me that, you dirty old man!—he
knocked her over. What he read in the notebook left him even
more furious: This is newspaper stuff here! Newspapers! She's a
journalist, the tramp!

The punishment: he stripped her naked, tied her to a pillar
in the torture chamber, and whipped her in front of all the
other women. Then he threw her onto a horse's back and
dispatched her to the city. "Don't come back here!" he yelled.
"And you can keep the horse too, you tramp!")

In Zeca Fagundes's castle the little centauress is born. Her
mother is Chica, a sullen, ill-favored Indian woman whose
presence in the harem is a mystery. Nobody knows what the
rancher sees in her.

The Indian woman becomes pregnant and doesn't tell
anyone. Either because she disguises her condition, or because
nobody really pays much attention to her, the day of her
delivery comes without anyone having noticed her big belly.

In the middle of the night she goes to the bathroom.
There, squatting in the ancient position Indian women assume
while giving birth, she groans and strains. One of the other
women, hearing the noise, discovers her, and they all begin
running back and forth and shrieking. Finally she begins to

have the baby, the women helping her as best they are able; and out comes a horse's leg—screams of horror—then another, and another, and another, and the centauress is born, some of the women screaming, others fainting, the Indian woman herself seeming not to realize what has happened.

Once they have calmed down, the women examine the creature, which whimpers and wriggles on a sheet. How could such a strange thing have come to be? they ask, and one remembers Chica's passion for Zeca Fagundes's horses. What on earth have you been up to? they ask her. The prostrate Indian woman, her eyes closed, doesn't answer. She remains exactly the same until a fever overtakes her—no doubt caused by the delivery—and then she spends days in delirium. Days when, by coincidence, Zeca Fagundes and his wife are away visiting a spa. The women don't know what to do; they dare not call a doctor, for the rancher will not allow strangers in the house. They treat the Indian woman with herbal teas, which she barely swallows. Finally she dies, leaving them faced with the fact that they will have to take care of the little centauress. It doesn't occur to them to put an end to the creature, as it did to the midwife of Quatro Irmãos. They will take care of it. Just like my parents, they decided to keep its existence a secret. But they need some help, and thus decide to tell Dona Cotinha about what has happened. She has always been hostile toward them, but now, they believe, she will be softened by the sight of the pathetic little creature. And they are correct. In the beginning, Dona Cotinha wants nothing to do with them and refuses to speak of the matter: You commit shameless sins, you give birth to monsters, and then you come to ask for help, but I'll have nothing to do with it, it's because you're all syphilitic. But when they bring the baby for her to see, she changes completely; at first it alarms her, but it soon moves her to the point of tears—she too is a mother. From that time on, a warmth, a sort of unspoken solidarity, is born between the legitimate wife and the concubines.

Upon Dona Cotinha's advice, the women hide the little centauress (Marta is the name they give her—Marta, Martita, Tita) in an old empty woodshed adjacent to the room where

they sleep. They feed the baby with a bottle—and also discover
the trick of putting chopped lettuce in the milk—and the
centauress develops well. Always hidden, but surrounded by the
women's affection. Very intelligent, she learns to talk early,
and begins to ask questions early too. "Mothers" (they are all
mothers to her), "why am I like this? Why do I have these
hooves, this tail? Why aren't I like all of you?" She doesn't ask
about her father, for she doesn't know what a man is, let alone
imagine that there is such a thing.

She can't resign herself to living as a prisoner and only
walking about in the woodshed or at the most trotting through
the big dormitory (and that only when Zeca Fagundes is
absent). She wants sun, fresh air; she wants to know all about
the world outside. No, the women tell her again and again,
you can't go out, it's too dangerous, they will kill you. Day by
day, however, she becomes more and more restless (and, what's
worse, prettier). The women begin to realize they aren't going
to be able to hold on to her much longer.

Sure enough: in the wee hours of the morning, on the day
after her sixteenth birthday, she opens the door and creeps
outside, unnoticed by the women. It's still dark, for it's winter;
she can't see much, but even so the sensation of liberty makes
her heady with delight. She resolves to trot about the neighborhood
a little, what harm would there be in that? It's very early,
everyone is asleep.

She is wrong. Everyone is not asleep: Zeca Fagundes is
already up, saddling a horse. He sees the centauress pass, and
rubs his eyes in amazement: Is it a dream? Or was it a
mixture of woman and horse that he saw? But if such a thing
exists, she must be yours! God sent her to you! He mounts his
horse and gallops as fast as he can after the fantastic vision.

You know the rest, she says, wiping her eyes.
I look at her, she looks at me.
I pull her toward me, embracing her. I feel her breasts
against my bare chest; they are firm beneath her tunic. I kiss
her, we kiss clumsily but eagerly. "What is this, Guedali?"
she askes in a whisper. "What are you doing?" "You don't

need to worry, Tita," I say. "It will be something good, very good."

I want to make love the way people do, the way I've seen illustrated in my books, but it is impossible, there's too much volume, too much weight, too many hooves. I end up mounting her in equine fashion—in this movement I bump my head on the roof of the hut, actually making a hole in the straw thatching—I bend forward, embracing her from behind, take her breasts in my hands, murmur tender words in her ears, and gently penetrate her. "It's good," she moans as our large bodies tremble with pleasure, "it's very good."

When night falls we go out. I put Zeca Fagundes's body on my back. (If he were alive, the rancher would capture me for a slave; I would be superb at a roundup, unbeatable in races, and when I got old, I could pull a wagon with no one needing to drive. The driver's seat would be empty, just like those of the ghost wagons that glide silently through the fog.)

We go in the direction of the ranch. Our arrival provokes a tremendous uproar among the women. A centaur! And Tita back again! And the rancher dead! It's too much for them to take in at once; they scream and faint. Finally Tita manages to calm them enough to tell what has happened.

To the rancher's death they have mixed reactions: sorrow, yes, but happiness too. They are tired of the old man's tyranny, of his manias and perversions—making love with his spurs on being one of the more benign. They console Dona Cotinha, who weeps as she holds her husband's body: What can we do, it was God's will. Thank you, girls, sobs the widow, you are all very good to me, I shan't forget you, you may be sure.

Then the women turn to me. They surround me, examine me with curiosity. Look at that, said one, I thought that Tita was a unique case. What good luck he's so handsome, says another, he and our daughter will make a striking pair. They all agree. What are a centaur and a centauress who meet by chance to do, except live together? (Instinct tells them that something has already taken place between Tita and me; the centauress's expression is already different, her walk has changed and she smiles mysteriously; their little protégée has become a woman. A centauress-woman.) But you two must be married, advises a third woman, we can't have anyone living in sin, you must be married in the church. They laugh, imagining the priest's face. Tita also laughs, and so do I. I can't be married in a Catholic church, I say, I'm Jewish to boot.

They stop laughing and look at one another, suspicious. A Jew? That doesn't sound so good. The Jews killed Christ, the Jews are avaricious—and are they going to give Tita to one of them? But there is one who once had a Jewish lover, a traveling salesman, and she affirms that they're not bad people, it's a matter of knowing how to handle them, like with everybody else. Relieved, they laugh again—this time over my name, which they find amusing. Guedali, is that a real name?

And we talk for the rest of the day and far into the night.

When morning comes, the women remember that they must do something about the funeral, to which the other ranchers of the region should be invited. They must not be seen at the event; the dead man belonged to the widow, and only to her. They pack their things—and even argue over the ownership of dresses and perfumes—and tell us good-bye tearfully. They make me promise to take good care of Tita and Dona Cotinha (I am the man of the house now) and they go.

For a week the widow closes herself into her room with her grief. (She is alone; her son doesn't appear at all.)

The house belongs to us, to Tita and me. We walk through the large rooms, go down to the cellar, go up to the tower (with some difficulty, for the stairs are narrow). We make love there, in the room full of mirrors, and in the dungeon, by torchlight, and in the woodshed, where I share the mattress, very much like the one I used to use, with Tita.

Dona Cotinha reappears, surprisingly well disposed, and takes charge of things with unexpected vigor. The first thing she does is to eliminate all vestiges of her husband's presence: she burns his papers, distributes his clothes among the peasants. She orders the door of the room they used nailed shut, and moves to a smaller one.

And as for us, Tita and I, what plans might she have? She doesn't say anything, and I begin to grow uneasy: maybe she can't tolerate me, maybe she thinks I'm depraved. I resolve to seek her out for a private conversation. Tita and I love each other, I say, we want to live together, and if you are not opposed, we will stay on here. Or, if that doesn't suit, tell us how soon we must leave and we'll go somewhere else.

Absolutely not, she says, surprised. Tita is like a daughter to her, and she is growing fond of me too. I may not show it, she adds, but it's just that I'm a bit reserved; so many years living with that animal . . .

She takes a handkerchief from her sleeve and wipes her eyes. You may use the old dormitory where the women used to sleep, she says, adding: Don't worry about this nonsense of marrying. I was married with a veil and all the trimmings, and look where it got me. Stay, my dears, stay and love each other in the way you wish. Your company is enough for me.

From 1954 to 1959 we live on the ranch with Dona Cotinha. Only she and her foreman—a strange man, silent, but entirely trustworthy—know about us.

It is a happy, carefree existence.

During the day, naturally, we have to stay hidden inside, but there is much to keep us busy. Tita helps Dona Cotinha with the domestic chores or with her weaving; I read or study (business administration is a subject that interests me greatly) or play the violin. (The instrument, which I came across in a wardrobe, used to belong to Dona Cotinha's grandfather. It was a mediocre violin, quite rudimentary, but the melodies I draw from it! Tita and Dona Cotinha are often moved to tears.)

At night—very late, in the midnight hours—we go for walks in the fields, Tita and I. Side by side, holding hands, we gallop, the wind whistling in our ears. We stop, we look at each other, laughing and out of breath. Slowly the smile disappears from her face. I want you, she murmurs. I want you too, I answer.

* * *

Tita and Guedali, Guedali and Tita, the lovers of the pampas. Their hides attract each other, their hair, their very membranes. When they make love, it is like a ballet, their two great bodies elevated in the air, arms and limbs intertwining as they tumble without a sound onto the humid grass.

She is little more than a child, Tita. Only a short while ago she was playing with the dolls the women gave her. But she is intelligent, and wants to know all about me and my family. I tell her with much pleasure, about the ranch in the interior of Quatro Irmãos, about my parents and sisters and brother, about the violin, the little Indian boy Peri, Pedro Bento. I tell her about the house in Teresópolis, and of my passion for the girl in the mansion (which makes her jealous, she grows sulky and I have to console her, telling her it was all a lot of nonsense), about my travels through the fields. But there are things I don't tell her about—the winged horse, for instance, whose wings I haven't heard rustle for a long time. I don't tell her about it, I can't tell her. There are things she doesn't really understand: A Jew, what does it mean to be a Jew? I try to explain, I tell her about Abraham and his bosom, about Moses, about Baron Hirsch. I tell her the stories of Sholem Aleichem, I talk about Israel, Jerusalem, the kibbutzim; Marx and Freud also enter the discussion.

Then I stop. Suddenly I'm homesick. I miss my parents, Deborah, Mina, even Bernardo. I continue to write them long letters, which the foreman takes to the post office in town. I tell them that I'm well, that they need not worry about me. But should I tell them about Tita? I decide that the time isn't right yet.

Dona Cotinha appreciates us more and more. She says we are everything to her ("my sweet pets" is how she addresses us), we are more important to her than her son, who doesn't so much as write her a line. The fact that we are lovers makes her slightly uncomfortable. Although she doesn't say anything, we know that deep down she considers our relationship something grotesque, even sinful. If we exchange a hug in front

of her, she looks away, embarrassed. But apart from this, she is
very affectionate toward us, gives us presents—pullovers for me,
necklaces for Tita—which makes us very happy.

Tita and I were very happy indeed in that period from
1954 to 1959.

We were together every day, every minute of every day.
One learned from the other the meaning of every gesture,
every glance. We began to acquire similar habits and our own
private code: I was now Gue, she Ti. Gue and Ti, Ti and
Gue, we were never apart. I knew she liked me to kiss her
earlobes, she knew I liked her to lay her head against my
chest. But above all we knew when we wanted to make love.
Desire sprang up between us at all hours—at night, in the
middle of the day, in the wee hours of the morning, no matter
if we were working, eating, or sleeping. We would embrace,
trembling with desire. And our lovemaking was always wonderful.

Happy, from 1954 to 1959. To 1959? Well, perhaps not.
Perhaps from 1954 to 1958 or even the end of 1957. What is
definite is that the happy days began to draw to an end. A
certain restlessness began to ferment insidiously in Tita. Perhaps
it came from the ladies' magazines she leafed through or the
programs she listened to on the radio. Why can't we get married
and live in the city? she would ask. Why can't I go to the
supermarket like all the other women? Why can't I buy
vegetables, cheese, eggs, tablecloths, things like that? Why
can't I meet my in-laws and have lunch with them on Sundays?
Why won't you let me have children?

(I used the withdrawal method with her—successfully,
fortunately. What else could I do? A stone in the uterus, in
the manner of the Indian women? Gross. I knew nothing of
birth-control pills, and even if I did, would there be
birth-control pills for centaurs? A condom might work, but
where would I find a gigantic condom?)

Her questions revealed a profound ingenuousness, even a
certain strangeness. (Could she have taken after her mother?)
What she did was to try to conjure away her equine part,

which, in her imagination, was separate from Tita the woman, and could be made to gallop far away and never return.

She forgot that she was a centauress. Why can't I be like other girls? she would insist. Because you simply can't, I should have answered, because you have a tail, haunches, hooves, and even a little bit of mane. But I didn't want to be brutal toward her, I didn't wish to shock or disillusion her. Moreover, her questions touched me, even drew from me furtive tears. I too wanted to lead a normal life, I too would have liked to live in Pôrto Alegre in a three-bedroom apartment, ample living room, garage. I too wanted to have a family. And my business—I couldn't even go to college and study anything. I wanted to have friends with whom I could play soccer on Sunday afternoons. But a quadruped playing soccer? Impossible. Polo, maybe. Soccer, never.

What about trying something, some treatment? Science had made great progress in the last few years. Tita showed me a report in a magazine about a Moroccan surgeon who performed miraculous operations, transforming women into men, and vice versa—so why not, she asked, why not centaurs into normal people?

To me it seemed an impossible undertaking. I didn't believe we could ever survive such an operation. And even supposing that the doctor would operate on us, how could we ever get to Morocco? How could we pay for such surgery, which was doubtless extremely expensive?

These ideas were making me lose sleep. To think there might perhaps be a solution to our case, and to be unable to attain it.

One night Dona Cotinha called me.

"Guedali, I'd like a little private talk with you."

I looked at Tita. She seemed to be absorbed in a particularly intricate piece of knitting. I went with Dona Cotinha to her office. She closed the door and turned to me.

"Tita has told me that there is a doctor in Morocco able to solve the problem you both have. She says it is merely a question of money."

"Well, it isn't quite that simple—" I began, but she interrupted me:

"I want you to know that I will take care of all the expenses." I tried to stop her, but she cut me off with a gesture. "I'm old, I don't need money any more, or this ranch, or anything. You two are young, your life is still ahead of you. Go, my children, go to Morocco. Have the surgery, and come back normal."

Her generosity touched me deeply. You are truly a mother to us, I said. I left her office much moved, and that night I cried a great deal. It was not just homesickness for my parents and sisters, but also on account of Dona Cotinha's immense kindness.

Even so, I still couldn't decide.

It was not just that I was afraid of the surgery. I had the sense of violating a work of nature that perhaps was the result of a superior will—a divine will, who knows. Tita perceived the conflict I was going through. She stopped bringing up the subject and waited for me to take the initiative. I walked through the fields. I thought and thought, still unsure that the operation would be the best thing for us.

Perhaps because of the tension I was under at the time, I fell ill.

It began with a light headache, which grew in intensity until it became a powerful, agonizing hammering that caused my brain to feel like it was splitting. I could hardly see or hear, the pain was so awful. It made me throw up. Tita and Dona Cotinha put me to bed, doing what they could: they applied cold compresses, put slices of raw potato on my forehead.

I spent four days out of touch with everything, possessed by strange hallucinations. Sometimes it seemed that my hooves were changed into human feet; other times they multiplied fantastically and my body stretched out, giving me the look of a centipede-centaur. I walked in a long room, forcing myself, one-two, one-two, to maintain a coherent rhythm among those dozens of feet. The attempt proved futile; new legs and feet kept branching out, ever more grotesque and clumsy. In the end I was kicking myself, wounding myself cruelly. My body

was aching, blood running out of a dozen different cuts, and I
looked in terror at two hooves that exchanged blows in a mortal
fight. Later these visions became mixed, and then went away.
Now I seemed to be in a ship or something similar, on the high
seas, smelling the waves, rocking softly, looking at a calm and
restful landscape. It was the coast of a strange country, with
palm trees and the white houses of a city.

When I felt better, but still very weak, I had made up my
mind.

"We'll go to Morocco," I said.

Tita and Dona Cotinha hugged me, weeping. I knew it,
cried Dona Cotinha, I knew God would inspire you, Guedali!

Two weeks later we left for North Africa.

MOROCCO
JUNE–DECEMBER 1959

WHAT A HORRIBLE EXPERIENCE, THAT JOURNEY TO MOROCCO.

We couldn't go by plane, obviously, nor even on a passenger ship. Dona Cotinha went to Rio Grande and spoke to a distant relative who was the captain of a cargo ship. This fellow, an old sailor, hardly believed her story, and thought it was a joke. Dona Cotinha showed him a picture of us (taken despite my reluctance) precisely to convince him. Much impressed, he agreed to take us, as long as we stayed hidden in the hold of the ship—where he would have a special compartment made—and didn't come out. Dona Cotinha gave him money—a lot of money—and he provided a few comforts, foam-rubber mattresses, fans, a refrigerator, a chemical toilet. Even so, our quarters were far from decent. But we wanted to get to Morocco immediately, for the surgeon was expecting us. We had arranged everything with him by letter.

First, we needed to get to Rio Grande, which was almost two hundred miles away. Dona Cotinha rented a truck intended for animal transport; the foreman would drive it. In order to avoid calling attention to us, the truck would also carry the horses that had belonged to Zeca Fagundes. That way I'll get rid of them, said Dona Cotinha, who hated the poor beasts. Everything would be done by night.

We told Dona Cotinha good-bye; she was much moved, and Tita cried. We got into the back of the truck, where the horses had already been loaded. The foreman started the motor, and we were off.

We were tense. It was the first time that Tita had left the ranch, but this was no outing, and it gave her no pleasure. In fact, she was almost in panic, and was controlling herself with effort. The headlights of approaching cars, shining in through the slats of the truck, lighted her pale face and wide-staring eyes.

The horses were quiet. I feared a stampede, the animals throwing themselves from one side to the other, trying to stamp on us. There were reasons for my fear; one of the horses was Sultan, another looked to me like Pasha—older, but still vigorous. Sultan and Pasha, a formidable pair; would we be a match for them? Them and their equine band? Impossible. Fortunately, however, the animals remained calm.

We arrived in Rio Grande in the wee hours of the morning and were smuggled aboard the cargo ship. Only the captain, the first officer, and one sailor ordered to take care of us knew of our presence. As soon as we were settled the ship weighed anchor and sailed.

What a trip. The heat was suffocating, the hold stank; the sea was always tossing. Tita began to be seasick as soon as the ship left port. She had nightmares about sea monsters beating against the hull of the ship. I stayed awake, fighting off the rats that tried to gnaw at our tails. It was an unequal fight; there were many of them, and they were agile, fearless, and cunning after decades of experience at sea. They ran nimbly about the hold, climbed the ropes that hung from the steel girders, and jumped on top of us when we were sleeping or let our attention wander. My hooves were almost powerless against them; but on the rare occasions that I managed to squash one underfoot, I swelled with satisfaction: Gotcha, you pest!

I tried to keep Tita's spirits up. We'll make this trip again, I told her, but by airplane. Or in a first-class luxury liner, with a swimming pool and everything. She would smile weakly: Swimming pool, Guedali? Centaurs in a swimming pool? Very soon we won't be centaurs any more, I would say, trying to believe my own words.

Finally we arrived. From the porthole we could see the African coast: a city of white houses blazing in the sun. What awaited us there?

When night fell we disembarked. We were received by one of the doctor's assistants, a tall man wrapped in a long robe. He led us to a closed black van, disagreeably similar to a hearse. It's so nobody will suspect, said the man in poor Spanish. He let us in through the back. The metal doors closed with a bang and the van took off at top speed. Tita grabbed me around the neck. Half an hour later we arrived at the clinic, which was situated on the outskirts of the city: a group of white buildings ringed about by a high wall and guarded by an armed watchman.

The Moroccan doctor did not inspire much confidence: he was a little brown man of indefinite age and dandified dress, his hair combed carefully back. He wore dark glasses, and had manicured nails and a faintly ironic smile on his full lips. He spoke Spanish and French. Welcome to my hospital, he said, looking at us with interest. Just as I imagined, he added, you are just as I thought you would be ... very, very curious case.

It was late and we were exhausted, but he insisted on examining us: I work better at night, he explained. He took us to a sort of studio, turned on spotlights, got a camera and photographed me in various positions. When it was Tita's turn, he asked her to remove her tunic; she refused, ashamed, but the doctor insisted, saying it was for his files. Do what he says, Tita, I told her.

The photography session over, he took us to our quarters, a small pavilion separated from the other buildings. No one will bother you here, he assured us, opening the door. It was an ample room, almost empty. There were mattresses on the floor and two small wardrobes. There he finished examining us, listening to our breathing and palpating us. Interesting, he kept repeating, extremely interesting; I have observed unusual cases

before, but yours is by far the most exotic I have ever seen. He
said something to his assistant, and then turned to us. I am
going to order a series of X-rays taken, they will be very
important in deciding what kind of surgery is to be done.

He was on his way to the door, and I grabbed his arm.
Will it work, Doctor, the operation? He smiled: Oh, without a
doubt, all my operations are successful. He gave me a little pat
on the hindquarters. A very, very interesting case. Yes, it will
be a success.

I don't like this man, said Tita as soon as we were alone.
And I'm very scared of this operation, Guedali. I tried to calm
her, but in fact I too felt apprehensive. I decided that I would
be the first to undergo surgery. If I died, Tita would go back to
the ranch—still a centauress, but alive.

Death. The idea shouldn't have seemed strange to me.
What was the difference between a half horse and a half man?
But the truth was, I wanted to live. My life was strange and
miserable, but it was mine. And now I had Tita. Looking at
her as she lay asleep on the mattress, the thought came to me
that no, I didn't want to die. Suddenly I was overcome by a
wave of optimism: die? What nonsense was this, to think of
dying? We weren't going to die at all. The operation would be
a success, the doctor would remove those growths—tails,
hooves—as if they were warts, gigantic warts but none the less
removable.

And then I experienced a curious feeling: a tender
melancholy, a sort of advance nostalgia. No, those weren't warts
we had on our bodies. They were extensions of our being; we
are centaurs on the inside, too, I thought, taking my tail in my
hand and letting the hairs slide through my fingers. A
beautiful, thick tail. The use of shampoo had made it soft and
silky. As for my feet, they had never failed me, nor betrayed
me in my galloping. It was true that they ended in hooves, but
what about the knife thrower at the circus, who let the nail on
his little finger grow to a grotesque length? My tail and hooves
were things as much mine as my ego and id. Still, I had made
a decision and wouldn't go back on it: Good-bye, hooves, I

sighed. Good-bye, strong legs, good-bye, beautiful tail. Hide of my belly, lovely in hue, good-bye. Soon none of these things would be part of me any more. The Moroccan doctor had photographed me; the next time I appeared in a photograph I would be wearing trousers, smiling. Before and after, just like the advertisements.

I thought of many other things that night, both sad and happy. The final result, however, was neither sadness nor happiness, despair nor joy, crying nor laughter, nothing. The final result was sleep—a thick, powerful, heavy sleep that engulfed my being like quicksand, hooves, legs, tail, mouth, eyes, everything.

We spent our days in our room at the doctor's recommendation; it's not a good idea for the other patients to see you, he said.

Nor did we see other patients; looking through the little window that gave out onto the gardens—lovely gardens, with banks of rosebushes and a fountain tinkling sweetly—we saw only empty walkways, occasionally a servant with a white apron passing hurriedly by. Important people there, said the doctor's assistant in his rough Spanish, pointing to the other pavilions. Very important people, they can't afford to appear. They didn't.

The examinations went on. Blood and urine tests, electrocardiograms, and principally X-rays. The clinic was fantastically well equipped. They submitted us to a great variety of X-rays. I need to know what I'm going to find inside you, said the doctor. A human liver or a horse's liver? He revealed to us that during the surgery he was counting on the assistance of two veterinarians. French ones, he said proudly. My team is top quality.

At night, exhausted after so much manipulation, we would go back to our room. We would lie down, turn out the light. But sleep wouldn't come. We would hear, almost drowned out by the sound of the water running in the patio fountain, the echo of far-off drums: Africa. Beyond the white walls was the rocky desert: robed, dark-skinned men, running swiftly and

silently on their camels; monkeys in palm trees, sphinxes. The
Zambezi River. Mount Kilimanjaro. The Zulus. Witch doctors
with tribal masks. The night peopled by monsters springing
from the imaginations of poor sleepless centaurs.

I don't remember the night preceding the operation very
well. I know that one of the doctor's assistants came to give
me an injection—to sleep, he explained. Later I realized vaguely
that numerous men were lifting me off the mattress and
putting me on a sort of wagon: the time had come. Tita was
standing up near me. I wanted to say good-bye to her, to tell
her not to worry, that all would be well, but my voice wouldn't
work. She bent over me and kissed me. For a fleeting second I
saw her eye, the sclerotic white of her eye, and then the door
opening to the grayish sky of dawn, a corridor, the operating
room. They laid me on a big table, and secured my arms, legs,
and tail. The light of a strong bulb blinded me. The Moroccan
doctor drew near, already wearing his apron, cap, and mask. He
murmured something. I felt a needle prick my arm, and saw
nothing more.

Then I was in the recovery room, but I still wasn't really
awake. Confused visions: faces that bent over mine; tumultuous
clouds, and among them, the winged horse, beating his wings.
Pain. Horrible, unbelievable pain, the pain of lacerated
flesh. Oh, Mama, oh, Papa, help me, I groaned.
As I lay on my side, my right arm, which was twisted
under my body, hurt me as much as the areas that had
undergone surgery. I tried to call someone, but no sound would
come out of my throat. I stretched out my left arm and
managed to grasp the iron head bars of the bed. With an
enormous effort I turned over. I felt thousands of sharp stabs
up my back—but I realized that at that moment, for the first
time in my life, I was lying *on my back*. On my back. Just like
my parents in their double bed on Saturday mornings. Just like
Deborah, Mina, Bernardo, Pedro Bento, and the girl in the
mansion. Just like the dwarfs, and the lion tamer, and Dona
Cotinha, and everyone else; on my back. I stared at the ceiling,

what a wonderful thing it was to look at that ceiling. It was nothing special, just a white ceiling, but I studied it with great tenderness. I wanted to laugh; of course I couldn't on account of the pain, but I really wanted to laugh for the joy of being alive, at having survived the operation—but especially at being able to lie on my back. I cautiously extended my hand and touched myself. To my displeasure I felt the familiar horsehair of my old legs, but right above, at the end of my thighs, I felt gauze bandages. From my thighs up I was wrapped in gauze, lots of gauze. Gauze, but no hind legs; gauze, but no tail; gauze, but no enormous belly. How nice to be wrapped in gauze, in layers and layers of gauze. I must look like an Egyptian mummy, I thought and once again I wanted to laugh.

"*Buenos Días!*" It was the Moroccan doctor, a smile on his face. He raised the sheet, examined me, and found everything very satisfactory. He described the operation to me, resorting to mimicry when he couldn't find a word, which happened all the time due to his excitement. From what I could understand, he discovered during the surgery that I had double organs—those of a human being and equine ones—so that he was able to remove the entire equine part, except my front legs, without risk.

And what was done with it? I asked.

The question made him uncomfortable. First he answered that he had ordered everything—hooves, tail, hide, innards—thrown into the sea; then he contradicted himself: no, he hadn't ordered them thrown into the sea, he had ordered them burned.

He ended up confessing that he had sold the equine remains to the natives. Horse meat isn't easy to come by here, he said, and you were well nourished. As a matter of fact, he continued, the natives use all the parts of the horse: they make drums from the hide for their ritual dances, fertilizer out of the bones. With the hooves they make ashtrays and other handcrafted objects, and they use the tail to make a sort of flyswatter possessed by the highest dignitaries. I do hope you don't mind, he added. No, I murmured, I don't mind.

There was a small silence. I stared at the ceiling, where a

huge fly was resting against the white surface—a tsetse fly? Ah, said the doctor suddenly, I almost forgot to tell you the most important part!

His face shining, he began to describe the transposition of the penis to the place normal for a human being, between my front legs. It came out beautifully, he exclaimed. He giggled: and what a penis, eh? What a marvelous penis! He winked: I envy you, my friend, I truly envy you.

Then, getting up, he said, "I'll give your, ah, wife the news of the operation. Naturally she can't come in here, but I'll tell her that everything's fine."

That night I couldn't get to sleep. I kept listening to the drums that echoed in the distant desert. Big hands pounded on my stretched-out hide; the hollow sound echoed implacably inside my head. Only when day was breaking did I fall into an exhausted slumber.

Tita's operation, done a few days later, also went very well. By this time I was already sitting in a wheelchair, still in some pain, but much better. The night after Tita's surgery the Moroccan doctor came to my room. I want to show you something, he said. He took me to the clinic's kitchen, deserted at that hour, and opened the doors of the freezer room.

"I had to put this in here, there was no other place."

There were Tita's blood-spattered hindquarters, hanging from a meat hook. From another hook hung the internal organs.

"What should I do with it?" he asked in an unmannerly tone. One could see he was not at all happy at my having expressed disapproval over what he had done with my own equine portion, but nevertheless he recognized my rights over the remains there in the freezer.

I demanded that they be cremated and the ashes sprinkled into the ocean. A procedure that I myself supervised, impassive despite the unkind looks of the doctor's assistant, who performed the task in the silent hours of the night.

The doctor announced that we would be transferred from

the pavilion to one of the rooms in the clinic—we no longer needed to remain hidden.

We made the move that same day in our wheelchairs. The first thing we noticed in our new room was the bed—a wide double bed. It was covered with a quilt in a cheerful design similar to Dona Cotinha's tapestries. We looked at each other, Tita and I, and smiled: it was our very first bed.

With the help of the nurses, we undressed and lay down face to face, gazing into each other's eyes and smiling all the while. Tita said she was sleepy, and turned to the other side. I embraced her from behind, took her breasts in my hands, and kissed the back of her neck.

(Farther down, we still had hooves like a those of a centaur, but the skin-covered area—hands, chest, neck—was now greater than the areas of horsehide. Would skin actually take over the hide someday?)

I sighed. Everything was all right, everything really was all right. The only thing that bothered me was the sound of the drums, but even that was growing more and more distant. As for the rustling of wings, there was none.

Once the scars of the surgery were healed, we were turned over to a team of physiotherapists who were to take charge of training us to walk like normal people.

It was not an easy job. First they made special shoes for us—long-shanked boots with wide soles, able to give us ample stability. Inside them were specially-made supports into which we fit our hooves.

For weeks we exercised, first with parallel bars, then with crutches and canes. We often fell, which discouraged me and made Tita cry. The Moroccan doctor, however, constantly kept our spirits up, and finally the day came when, holding hands, we managed to take our first steps. What a joyful moment! It was surpassed only by our first waltz, which we danced to the applause of the clinic staff.

Seeing me walk more securely every day, the doctor said: you'll soon be a soccer champion back in your own country. He was very curious about Brazil: They say one can make

money there overnight, eh? More or less, I answered, trying to
change the subject, which only increased his interest (and greed,
one could see). One day he took me to his office in the city
and introduced me to various well-dressed gentlemen, some
Moroccan, others European, all in dark glasses. These are some
businessmen, he said, who are interested in Brazil.

They wanted to make investments, to import and export,
and needed information. I told them what I knew, which wasn't
much. For some reason, nevertheless, they were impressed
with me. They gave me their cards, and asked that I write to
them.

In December of 1959 we were ready to go back to Brazil. It
was then that we received a letter from the foreman at the
ranch, saying that Dona Cotinha had suddenly passed away. The
news saddened us deeply, for up to then we had been
corresponding, and had kept her informed as to our progress,
even sending photos of us—in the garden at the clinic, in an
Arabian market, with the doctor. Poor Dona Cotinha, she would
never see us walking like normal people—her greatest wish.
(Later on we were extremely touched to learn that she had left
us a substantial part of her fortune, the rest having gone to her
son, the foreman, the peasants, and the women.)

Our plans had to be altered. To live on the ranch without
Dona Cotinha didn't appeal to us; also, her son had moved back
home. What if we were to go to Pôrto Alegre?

I wrote to my parents for the first time in many years. I
told them about the operation, about Tita, and announced our
willingness to live in Pôrto Alegre. Come, they answered, come
soon, we are awaiting you with open arms.

And so, on Christmas Eve of 1959 we took a plane back to
Brazil. At the airport we drew peoples' attention with our
height and elegance. I was wearing corduroy trousers and a
printed shirt, Tita a silk blouse and jeans, which was to be her
characteristic outfit from then on. And naturally our boots,
which we would have to wear for a long time, perhaps
forever. But who cares? said a beaming Tita, looking through
the window of the plane as it took off.

I leaned back in my chair and closed my eyes. The plane

glided through the clouds; I felt wonderful. Never again would we need to be transported in trucks or wagons. Never again would we have to stay out of sight, in the hold of a ship or anywhere else. Never again would we gallop.

Suddenly my body jerked, startled by a strange sensation. I opened my eyes and peered through the window. No, there was no winged horse flying beside the airplane. Clouds, yes, some of them with strange shapes suggesting animals. But a winged horse, no.

PÔRTO ALEGRE
DECEMBER 25, 1959–SEPTEMBER 25, 1960

BUT LIVING IN PÔRTO ALEGRE DIDN'T WORK OUT FOR US.

My parents received us joyfully, as did Mina, Deborah, and her husband and two daughters, and Bernardo, who after his reconciliation with the family had married a Jewish girl and now had a son. In tears, we all exchanged hugs, stepped back to look at one another, and embraced again.

My parents had aged. My mother's hair was completely white, and my father was no longer the vigorous man he had been, but was stooped at the shoulders. Deborah was a bit matronly but still pretty; her husband, the lawyer from Curitiba, continued jolly. I found Mina somewhat embittered (I'm still an old maid, she whispered as she embraced me. So what, Mina, one day your enchanted prince will appear, I told her.) Bernardo was as reserved as ever; his wife, on the contrary, talked constantly and gave hysterical little shrieks. Their devilish little boy insisted on pulling up my pants legs (I could imagine the conversations he must have overheard), but he didn't get anywhere; our trousers were fastened to our boots on the inside—a precaution against just such situations of this type.

Tita was a bit left out of this whole scene, which was only

natural. But soon the family turned to her, began looking at
her, praising her, telling me how pretty she was. I sensed her
insecurity and tried to encourage her by giving her a hug, but
I realized that she was swaying, and I feared that she might not
be able to stand up. Then suddenly I noticed that my own
foot, the right one, was pawing the ground: the toe of the boot
kicked rhythmically against the polished floor of the airport.
Deborah's husband came to the rescue: Let's be on our way,
folks, he said, our dinner is waiting, and Dona Rosa has
prepared a banquet!

And it was indeed a banquet, food like only Mama knew
how to cook, abundant and delicious: a rich soup, meatballs
and—although it was no longer necessary—an enormous
platter of lettuce and cabbage. Seated between my parents, I told
stories about Morocco, describing the camels and the Arabs
dressed in their flowing robes. Tita, very quiet, hardly touched
her food.

After dinner, we walked through the house. It was the
same old house; very little had changed.

"I've told our parents they should move out of here," said
Deborah in a censorious tone. "They could live in the Bon
Fim neighborhood, in a nice apartment, near Bernardo. But no,
it seems they're rooted to the ground."

"Now, Deborah," said my father, "the house is good, it's
spacious—where would I be able to put you all up—you, your
husband and daughters—when you come to visit us? In an
apartment? Never. I'm very happy here in this house. I am a
country man, I like some space, some trees."

He suggested that we go outside and sit under the rose
trellis like we used to. I shuddered: I didn't want to see the
distant mansion again, nor remember the naked girl or the
traitorous Columbo. It's very cold, Father, I said, let's stay in
here.

"Cold!" scoffed my father. "Eighty-six degrees is cold?
Look at me sweating, Guedali! You think it's cold because
you've just come back from Africa. Come on, come outside."

He took me by the arm and propelled me out. The
mansion, however, was no longer visible, I saw to my melancholy

relief. It was hidden behind a large apartment building.
Indeed, the whole neighborhood was unrecognizable, full of new
houses. The place is very noisy, my mother complained, and
besides, I don't know the neighbors. Deborah is right, we should
go to Bon Fim, nearer our friends. I am a man of the
country, repeated my father. Since I can no longer cultivate the
earth, at least I can take care of the trees in the yard, plant a
little vegetable garden. It's the least I can do to honor the
memory of Baron Hirsch.

I showed Tita my old room, now transformed into a
storeroom for Bernardo's merchandise: boxes of shoes and
shirts were piled up to the ceiling. How's business? I asked
Bernardo. He shrugged his shoulders: bad, of course, inflation
only helps those who can take advantage of it, dopes like me get
burned. And plus, I had to go and get married—you see how
I am. He said good-bye and left with his wife and son, who
made faces at me. Deborah, her husband and daughters made
their way to bed.

Come, said my mother, I have your room ready for you.
It was Bernardo's old room; besides the yellow pine wardrobe
and the single bed, she had had another bed and armchairs
brought in, "So you can really rest," she said. On the table was a
vase of flowers, which she removed, explaining that flowers in
one's room at night are unhealthful. She said good night and
went out.

Tita sat down on the edge of the bed and hid her face in
her hands, sobbing silently. I sat beside her and tried to
comfort her: I know you don't like it here, but it's temporary,
we'll find ourselves a house of our own. She didn't answer,
but dried her eyes and began to undress. I came close to her,
hugged her. Leave me alone, Guedali, she murmured, I'm
tired, I want to go to sleep. All right, I sighed, and took my
clothes off too. We had just finished the complicated process of
removing our hooves from the special supports inside our boots,
and were still naked, when the door opened: it was my
mother. She looked at us, stared at our hooves: sadness and
pain, but curiosity too, was in that look. Excuse me, she said, I
thought I heard you call. She closed the door again.

"Oh, shit, why didn't you lock it?" said Tita. I didn't answer. But it was clear that we could not live there on a permanent basis.

Even so, almost a year passed before we moved away. My father got sick a short time after our arrival; he had a heart attack and spent months in bed. During this time we had to help out. I looked after the store, Tita lent a hand in the kitchen. With the money we had inherited from Dona Cotinha, I could have hired someone to take care of the store, but my father, in his pride, would never have accepted it. "Alms?" he would have said. "Never! Baron Hirsch was against that sort of charity."

My mother didn't get along with Tita.

"She's not one of us," Mama would say to me when we were alone. "I'll never get accustomed to her."

But I'm different too, Mama, I would answer, I am a centaur. With a scornful gesture she would say, Oh, nonsense, Guedali. You *were* different. Now, after the operation, you're just like everybody else. But I have hooves, Mama! I would yell, losing my temper, what could be odder than a man with horses' hooves? And men with wooden legs, she would retort, aren't they people too? Don't give me any excuses, Guedali. You could have found yourself a nice Jewish girl. Hooves or no hooves, you could have found one. Once we reached this point, I would give up; it was useless to try to convince her.

Mina treated Tita better. She invited her to go out, she bought clothes for her. But from time to time Mina went through periods of depression, during which she locked herself in her room and didn't talk to anyone. She was undergoing psychiatric treatment. I need to examine myself on the inside, she would say. Don't count on much from me for about five years. As for Bernardo, he hardly ever appeared; Deborah did what she could to cheer us up when she came from Curitiba, which was rare.

I decided that we would leave Pôrto Alegre as soon as my father was better. I was thinking of São Paulo; I reasoned that in a large city we would hardly be noticed. Besides that, I intended to go into business; with the inheritance money, I could set up an import-export firm, and São Paulo would be the ideal place for an enterprise of that type, about which I was already writing to the businessmen I had met in Morocco. We had agreed on a very advantageous system.

The winter came to an end, and my father was showing some improvement. On my birthday, I gave a party for my family: a splendid dinner, with fine wines served by impeccably uniformed waiters. Beside each person's plate there was a present: a pearl necklace for my mother, a gold pen for my father, earrings for Mina, a bracelet for Deborah, a watch for Bernardo, a wallet for Deborah's husband, a ring for Bernardo's wife (who commented, loud enough for me to hear, that she would like to know where the money had come from for so many presents) and toys for the children—in short, everyone received something.

The next day we were at the airport again, and once more the whole family came, but this time it was to say good-bye. My mother cried, begged us to stay, or at least to come back soon. But I was certain that it was better for everyone that we leave.

The loudspeakers announced our departure. Tita and I took each other's hands and, smiling calmly, went up the steps to board the plane. Wine was served with the flight luncheon, and we toasted our new life. I dropped off to sleep and only woke up as we were landing at Congonhas Airport in São Paulo. Whether or not the winged horse followed us, I don't know. I didn't look out the window even once.

SÃO PAULO
SEPTEMBER 25, 1960–JULY 15, 1968

IN SÃO PAULO, I DECIDED TO DO THINGS SLOWLY AND PRUDENTLY.
The inheritance money would be sufficient to get the firm started and support us comfortably for some time, but I wanted to be prepared for the unforeseen, so we were careful with our money.

I bought a good house, small but comfortable, near Ibirapuera. (I wanted nothing to do with an apartment, with its steps and beehives of neighbors.) I bought a car, too, a Simca. I had learned to drive in Pôrto Alegre, and now I would need to, since getting around was important to make business contacts.

Tita took charge of decorating the house, which she did with extremely good taste—a surprising thing, considering she had never lived anywhere except the ranch. Together we went to look at furniture and home decorations, and she chose everything.

"I want our house to be very pretty," she said, "like the houses in magazines. It's our home, Guedali."

She was happy, and her high spirits were contagious. We made love a lot. More than most people do, I think. Why? Because of our fiery nature? Because of the large penis, the deep vagina? Perhaps. The act of love exhausted us, it was

almost too much pleasure for our now almost-human bodies.
But it was good, so good that it was hard for me to be away
from her. During those first weeks in São Paulo I hardly went
out; I would go downtown to take care of a few items—I was
getting the firm registered and looking for office space to
rent—and come back soon to be close to Tita. We would lie on
the soft rug of the living room in each other's arms, simply
enjoying the satisfaction of being there. When night fell, she
would get dinner while I read the papers and smoked my
pipe. After dinner (always a banquet; she cooked very well) we
would watch TV until bedtime. It was a good life—a calm
life, for two who had spent the midnight hours galloping the
pampas together. It seemed that nothing would disturb our
peace.

Then one night thieves broke into our house.

It was because of Tita's negligence; she had very absent-
mindedly forgotten to lock the back door. When we woke up
in the morning, we realized that the thieves had taken our
watches, the radio, record player, camera, and most of our
clothes.

I decided to go to the police. I put on a shirt and the only
pair of pants I had left—but I couldn't find my boots. Where
are the boots? I asked Tita. She didn't know either. Alarmed,
we searched the bedroom, then tore the whole house apart—
moving with great difficulty, crawling mostly—and finally we
had to accept the fact: the thieves had stolen our boots.

"But why?" screamed Tita, desperate. "What do they
want the boots for, if they're only useful to us? They don't have
hooves, Guedali! Nobody has hooves except us!"

She threw herself on the bed, sobbing. I took her in my
arms and tried to calm her. "Why do we have to suffer so
much, Guedali?" she asked. "Why doesn't God have pity on
us?"

"Calm down, Tita," I told her. "We'll find a solution, don't
make a mountain out of a molehill." Still, it was a mountainous
difficulty. Without our boots we were helpless, as fragile as
newborn babies. Tita sobbed while I tried desperately to think
of a solution. It can't be possible, I repeated to myself, it can't be

possible that everything should fall apart just now, when our life is going so well.

Suddenly an idea occurred to me.

I picked up the phone and asked the operator to put a call through to Morocco, to the clinic. I had good luck: the doctor himself answered. I told him what had happened, and begged that he immediately send us new boots. I'll take care of it, he said, and reminded me that since it was a special rush order, they would cost a lot more. It doesn't matter, I yelled, I'll pay whatever it costs! Okay, he said, as soon as they're ready I'll send them by air freight.

For three days we stayed locked inside the house, almost always sitting or lying down; we could walk only by holding on to the furniture and walls. As for our food, I ordered it from a restaurant which delivered; I would take the tray through a crack in the door so the delivery boy wouldn't see us.

On the third day Tita suddenly began to feel very sick; she complained of an intense headache, so strong that it was driving her mad. Do something, she moaned, call a doctor.

A doctor? No. Out of the question. At least not until I could locate a doctor we could trust, to whom we could tell our story. No. A doctor, no.

I figured out another solution. I took our bed apart and used the slats to make a pair of crutches, rudimentary but strong. Then I wrapped my hooves with layers and layers of gauze, taking care that the shape was like that of feet: small feet, but feet.

Around ten o'clock that night I went out, and made my way to the nearest drugstore. I told the druggist of Tita's headache. Don't worry, he said, I have a medicine that's very good for migraine.

"What happened to your feet?" he asked curiously as he wrapped up the package.

An accident, I replied. I was soaking them in a hot footbath and scalded myself. Footbath, he said, nobody uses them any more. So I discovered, I said, and we both laughed. We laughed and laughed: footbath, he would say, pointing at me, and holding his sides in merriment. Footbath, I would repeat, and laugh some more. Finally, wiping my eyes, I said good-bye and returned home. Tita took the medicine, felt better, and went to sleep.

The next day, very early, someone knocked at the door. I had an intuition it might be the boots and hobbled to the door on my crutches. Sure enough, it was a boy with a big package. Tita tore it open at once. There were the boots, three pairs for each of us. Thank God, she breathed. Thank God.

The boots. They had high tops, not as high as those of farmers' boots, but high enough to cover our fetlocks. Their leather was soft but not too soft; we needed support, not just comfort. They were neutral in color, a discreet beige. Small heels gave them an elegant air, but they weren't so high as to cause us balance problems. (Tita's heels were a little higher—the shoemaker's concession to feminine vanity.) The pointed, false toes were filled with foam rubber. Anyone who purposely stepped on our toes was in for a surprise; he would feel something soft, and would hear no cries of pain or protest.

On the outside, then, the boots looked quite conventional. But on the inside! On the inside they were truly a feat of ingenuity: metal supports, springs, small steel clamps with tension regulated by minuscule screws—in short, a work capable of rivaling a suspension bridge or a space capsule in terms of technological excellence. All conceived by the talent of a Moroccan artisan.

With those boots I was ready to confront the streets of the city. With those boots I was prepared to fight for my life.

A general euphoria was reigning in São Paulo's commercial and industrial world when I first entered it. The economy was almost hyperactive; it was true that inflation was galloping, but—I can't resist the image—that was no problem for someone with hooves.

I opened an office downtown in a good building, traditional, but not archaic. Rather ugly, but very solid. It lacked certain conveniences; it had no reception desk in the lobby, for example. The elevators, which looked like huge cages, were too slow for someone who, like me, was in a hurry to rise. But the other firms in the building enjoyed a good reputation in business circles. True, there were some empty office spaces . . . dark corners . . . and a moldy odor. And once I smashed a big rat with the heel of my boot. Still, for a place to begin, it seemed very good to me. My office was small, but it had a phone. Besides, I didn't intend to stay there all day, waiting for clients. I intended to go out in the streets and get them. In the streets, in offices better or worse than my own. In cafés. In clubs. Wherever men of business were to be found, there I would be, making contacts, offering my products.

I had to walk a great deal, but what was walking through the streets of São Paulo to someone who had galloped across the fields of Rio Grande? For someone who had, besides an immense desire to succeed, a car and a phone to help increase his possibilities? Nevertheless, I soon discovered that making money was not like clearing a fence with a running leap. I came up against obstacles I wasn't accustomed to: the apathy of hired help, the dishonesty of managers, the arrogance of young executives—mudholes, quicksand to slow my pace and make the going harder. I was headstrong, not yet fully tamed. When it came to dealing with the bureaucracy, I would often lose my temper, until—still using equine imagery—I learned to sweeten the bridle-bits with a little sugar. Speed was my concern. I needed to make up for lost time—time on a little farm in Quatro Irmãos, in a circus, on a ranch near the southern border, in a Moroccan clinic; all useful experiences in their own right, but not directly connected with what I was now proposing to do.

Suddenly, amid my comings and goings, an unforeseen danger.

One night I took a taxi home. I gave the driver the address, leaned back against the seat, and took a look at the headlines in the newspaper.

A short while later I had a strange sensation. I looked at the driver's face in the rear-view mirror; it seemed familiar.

That look—unpleasant; that smile—churlish. Why, it was
Pedro Bento! Pedro Bento himself! What was he doing here in
São Paulo behind the wheel of a taxi? What was he doing far
from Pasha, far from Rio Grande do Sul? With distinct
difficulty I managed to hide my alarm, keeping my face
behind the newspaper. What if he recognizes me? I asked
myself. He'll never leave me in peace. He'll blackmail me, he'll
threaten to reveal my story to the papers. He'll make my life
hell.

Looking at the neck that emerged from his dirty shirt, the
idea of killing him occurred to me. I had a weapon in my
briefcase: a long, sharp pair of scissors that Tita had asked me to
buy. Here was my chance: we were passing through a dark,
deserted street. One stab in that neck . . .

"You can let me out here," I said in a monotone that
wasn't my own. "But sir," he said, puzzled, "this isn't the
address you gave me." I didn't care, I was already paying him
and getting out. I disappeared into an alley and leaned against a
wall, still upset and bitter: Haven't you done enough, Lord?
What else is going to happen to me?

I arrived home in a state of depression; I couldn't eat,
and went directly to bed. Tita, worried, asked me what had
happened. Nothing, I answered her, nothing happened,
everything's all right.

The next morning I didn't feel like going out. In the days
that followed, however, I slowly digested the incident. I even
had doubts: Had it really been Pedro Bento I saw? Very
unlikely, I concluded. And I forgot the whole thing. Mainly
because I had other problems: there just wasn't any money
coming in. In the beginning, I had had many buyers interested
in import deals. However, nothing concrete developed, and I
was getting discouraged. At the end of the afternoon I felt worn
out, my mouth full of a bitter taste. My hooves, always
sensitive, now hurt me horribly. Deep inside, in their marrow,
their very nucleus, would come a profound, throbbing pain, as
though their contents would no longer fit into the hoof-walls,
which were restricted in turn by the boots' metal supports. I
began to have headaches, like Tita. It seemed to me that far-off

African drums were pounding inside my head. Along with the drums of the Charrua, Tape, and Tapuia Indians.

It was about then that I made my first sale: a small cargo of Moroccan phosphate. The dealer who bought it, a circumspect German, paid cash on delivery.

That was just the encouragement I had been needing! I felt myself coming to life again. I was so happy that I ordered one of the bills I'd got from the German framed and invited Tita out to dinner. That was when we discovered the Tunisian restaurant, The Garden of Delights. It's not Moroccan, said Tita, but it's close.

The restaurant was in an out-of-the way place, and its decor was Moorish style, with a patio, palm trees, and a fountain—a perfect place. The waiter, wrapped in a burnoose, led us to a table in the open air and showed us the menu. We chose what we would eat, laughing over the strange names, and as the man went off with our order, I took Tita's small, delicate hand between mine and asked her, softly, if she would marry me. She smiled: Oh, come on, Guedali, what's all this? So then I took the ring I had bought that afternoon out of my pocket and slipped it onto her finger. Tears filled her eyes.

"You didn't need to, Guedali," she murmured. "The important thing is our being together."

But it made her happy; she couldn't stop looking at the ring. She remembered Dona Cotinha: I wish she could be here, she said. And the girls from the ranch, my mother ...

She fell silent. It was painful to her, I knew, to talk of her mother. Mother? That brutish, indifferent creature about whom Dona Cotinha had spoken to me, was that any image of a mother? It was: "Mother," Tita would moan in her sleep. And sometimes she called for her father, too. Father? Who was her father? Zeca Fagundes? Or perhaps the foreman? Or maybe the stocky, silent peasant who at times hung about the ranch house.

She dried her tears and managed a brave smile. You grow more beautiful every day, I said, and it was true; she had lost her girlish air and had been transformed into a woman, a lovely woman of exotic beauty. Physically, we were very different.

She shifted her position slightly, and the toe of her boot touched my knee. It was like a message, a warning from the hooves and horses' legs: don't forget us, we're hidden, disguised, but we're still here.

Above the table, Guedali and Tita were dining at a charming restaurant; they conversed, were served by the attentive waiter. Below, the hooves were in command, restless hooves, crazy to gallop, even on the patio of The Garden of Delights, but having to restrict themselves to the meager square yard that was conceded to them for the moment.

On the way home we talked about the wedding. As far as the civil ceremony went, there would be no problem. Naturally, we would have to get her some identity papers; mine I had gotten in order to register the firm. Tita had only her false passport that the Moroccan doctor had procured so we could leave the country.

As for the religious ceremony, I said (choosing my words carefully) it will be a bit harder, because you'll have to convert. She protested, saying she didn't want to become a Jew, that she had no religion at all, she had even forgotten the prayers Dona Cotinha had taught her. But I reasoned that my parents would really accept her only if she became Jewish. It would simplify a lot of things, I said. And besides, it's easy.

All right, she said, taking off her clothes. What do I have to do? I started to explain the conversion process to her, but I interrupted myself. I had been about to tell her about the ritual bath, the mikvah, and now that I saw her naked, the thought dawned on me: How could she go into the mikvah without the other women seeing her hooves?

Leave it to me, I said, I'll solve the problem one way or another.

And I did: I spoke with a rabbi who was leaving the country, after having broken with the Jewish community. He gave Tita a few classes—he charged a lot—and before leaving, furnished me with the certificate of conversion.

We were married in Pôrto Alegre. Only the family and a
few of my parents' friends were present, but it was a very festive
occasion. Tita was beautiful, wearing the bridal dress that had
been Deborah's, and which trailed on the floor, hiding her
boots. My mother and my sisters had offered to help dress and
adorn her, but she had refused out of timidity. She didn't want
them to see her hooves. Where I come from, she said, it's the
custom for the bride to get dressed alone. My mother had
shaken her head in disapproval. Well, do as you like, she said,
and the three had left Tita alone. After the wedding, however,
Mama embraced her, kissed her, and confessed that at first she
hadn't liked the idea of Tita living with her son.

"But now everything's all right," she said. "I am sure you
will be happy."

Back in São Paulo, I resumed my business affairs, which
were now going very well. As for Tita, she spent all day at
home. She took charge of our domestic matters. We didn't
want a maid snooping around, but even so she had a great deal
of free time. She would watch TV, sitting in an armchair with
her boots propped up on a stool and a box of bonbons beside
her (as a result, she was starting to gain weight). She slept
poorly; at night she would pace back and forth, no clothes on,
only her boots. I didn't like to see her that way; her horse's
legs, the enormous scar from the operation. "What's wrong,
Guedali?" she would ask, mockery and bitterness in her voice.
"Have you already forgotten that we used to be centaurs? Only
a little while ago, we used to gallop together."

She would sit down, sigh. "Oh, Guedali, how I miss the
ranch. There, at least, we had room to run and Dona
Cotinha's tapestries for amusement."

I hired a teacher for her. She barely knew how to read and
write, and I wanted her to get some education; later, who
knew, we might go to the university together. Moreover, I was
obliged to refuse invitations for cocktails and dinners because
Tita had nothing to say to people: putting it bluntly, she was a
rough peasant girl. Rough, but intelligent; she made notable
progress in her studies. The teacher, a discreet lady of few

words, showed surprise: Your wife is very capable, Mr.
Guedali.

We began to go to theaters and nightclubs, now that we
had friends: young businessmen and their wives, mostly Jewish.
Just as I had thought, they accepted us without difficulty.
They probably found it strange that we never went to beaches
or swimming pools, and that Tita always wore slacks. But in
our circle there was an Argentine engineer who wrote weird
poems, and an executive from Rio who lived with two women
at the same time. We were not the strangest, by any means.

But Tita still did not feel happy, I could tell. Perhaps you
should consult a psychiatrist, I suggested. The idea only irritated
her: A psychiatrist! What psychiatrist is going to understand
our story? Don't be a pest, Guedali! I would fall silent and go
back to reading the newspaper.

The year 1962 was very eventful: strikes, political speeches,
the dollar skyrocketing. This won't last, Paulo would say,
chewing an olive. An executive at a large company, Paulo was
my best friend. (Peri?) We had gotten into the habit of
meeting after work in a quiet downtown bar. We would have a
beer and talk at length—about business and the situation the
country was in, naturally, but also about other matters. He
would tell me everything: his troubles with his wife, a very
complicated woman, intelligent and beautiful, but full of neurotic
frustrations; and their difficulties with a retarded daughter.
When he asked about my life, I would answer with generalities,
telling him a little about my family, our farm in Quatro
Irmãos, the house in Teresópolis. But I couldn't go much
further without falling into reminiscences of my days as a
centaur. Indeed, even our present level of intimacy was dangerous,
because at times Paulo, remembering a funny anecdote, would
laugh and slap me on the thigh. I don't think he felt horsehide
under the resistant cloth of my trousers, but it was a risk. Only
one risk among many: What if, one day, I had to have an
urgent operation? Or got run over in the street? Or if
someone spied on us inside the house, with binoculars? (As to
that, I had already taken the precaution of buying thick

curtains.) Or what if my pants ripped? Risks. Necessary, if I was to live a normal life.

This baby is going to explode, Paulo was muttering, already half drunk. "This baby" was Brazil. He was certain that a violent revolution was about to occur, with radical changes in government. That guy from Rio Grande, that Brizola, he's crazy, the country isn't ready for socialism. There's going to be fighting, and it's us Jews who will get the dirty end of the stick. I should have gone to Israel, Guedali. I could be in a kibbutz right now, peacefully milking cows. But no, I had to be the smart one, I was determined to make money, then go to Israel when I had plenty.

He drained his beer glass. My own idiocy, Guedali. I'll never go to Israel. You see, my wife is very difficult, a bourgeoise neurotic. All she wants is to live expensively and try my patience.

He stopped for an instant, then returned warmly to his subject. I do everything wrong, Guedali. I believe in socialism when all my classmates were earning good money. Now that I've decided to get rich, a socialist government is about to take over. And I married the wrong woman, and I have a sick child . . . I'm a mess, Guedali.

I tried to console him: Things aren't all that bad, Paulo. I mentioned our friends as examples—Joel, the manager of a chain of stores; Armando, director of the branch office of an American company; Júlio, a big construction financier, all earning good money, unconcerned about the future, satisfied.

In reality, it wasn't all so rosy with them: Joel had ulcers and high blood pressure; Armando panicked every time the American company sent someone down to check on things— what do these gringos want, two of them were here just last month!—Julio was being sued for putting up a building on land that wasn't officially his. But with Paulo drunk and depressed, I couldn't talk about unpleasant things. So I tried to steer the conversation in another direction. We talked about his favorite sport: jogging. Paulo considered himself an excellent long-distance runner, capable of winning marathons. He had discovered this hobby by accident.

"I never was much interested in soccer, volleyball—sports like that."

On the contrary, he had been more the introspective type, and had decided to enter the field of social sciences.

"The dissatisfaction, you know how it is. You have problems, personal ones and others. You can't sleep; you think it's all on account of the social system, and so you decide to study it, thinking that you'll relieve your anxiety that way. Relieve, hell! Does studying medicine keep you from catching diseases? Of course not. And I was going through a difficult time with Fernanda, like I told you ... but I finally got my degree and found a job almost at once, in a government foundation that was set up to develop popular housing. This was right after the diagnosis on our daughter was confirmed, and I threw myself into my work as therapy. Understand, Guedali?"

His companions at the foundation, almost all young leftists, saw in the housing program a real step toward socialism. First a house for everyone, they said, then food for everyone, then transportation for everyone, then the means of production for everyone. That the houses were to be built by private bidders didn't bother them much; the truth would prevail in the dialectic shock between the individual and the collective, between egotism and altruism, between the cost of the houses and the prices charged by the bidders, between the proclaimed top quality of the mortar and the cracks that sooner or later would appear in the walls (enormous cracks, branching out into elaborate drawings: stags' antlers, decision-diagrams, or even letters like those the prophet Daniel interpreted for the king). Moreover, the plan included an idea conceived by the French socialist Louis Blanc (1811–1882). In the public sector of the economy "social workshops" would be created and managed by the workers themselves after company patterns. Part of the profits from these workshops would be distributed among the workers, part set aside for medical and retirement funds, and part reinvested. Workers investing; that was the great thing: the weapons of capitalism being used against capitalism itself!

As for the cracks, nobody in the group—which included architects, sociologists, and economists—had doubts as to their

eventual appearance, and no one questioned their role as
preliminary signs of the advent of socialism; what was in
dispute was merely when they would appear. Some thought it
would happen immediately, others reminded them that the
opposing structure might have unsuspected reserves of power.
Anyway, the maximum time period discussed was a year, a
year and a half. The foundation's internal publication was full of
articles about it. In it one saw caricatures and depictions of
banners with slogans like, "Houses, Bread, and No More
Bosses!"

Paulo was often moved by all this enthusiam. At times he
would even feel goose bumps.

"And what about kibbutzim?" he would holler. "Why
don't we set up a network of kibbutzim?"

Some of his colleagues thought it was a good idea, others
looked on it with suspicion. They had serious reservations as
to Israel and suspected that Jews always harbored Zionist
sympathies.

Paulo's and Fernanda's parents offered another type of
warning. Don't get involved in this, they would say, this isn't
going to turn out well, you can't take risks, Paulo, you have
your family to consider, your daughter is ill.

"But I paid no attention to them. It's just their Jewish
paranoia, I thought. They see Inquisition tribunals and gas
ovens everywhere they look."

Nevertheless, his parents were right. The government
changed, and the foundation came under the directorship of a
man called Honório, a mysterious and intimidating figure.
Impassive, a face carved in stone in which there were no cracks,
only the pockmarks of an old acne. He always wore a gray
suit, a black tie, and old-fashioned metal-rimmed glasses with
dark lenses. One could never be sure just where the man was
looking. Indeed, very little was known about him except that he
was an engineer and a bachelor. And, it was said, he was a
member of an anticommunist organization. In his acceptance-
of-office speech (short and dry) he said that from then on all
employees would have to toe the line, and that he would act
with severest rigor against all opponents of the foundation.

However, he said, his subordinates were not to be worried—he was like a father; just but not cruel. Whoever had a clean record had nothing to fear.

"The question was, who was clean and who wasn't? Nobody felt entirely clean. Even the cleanest could have something, a tiny smudge, in their past—an imprudent remark, a clenched fist, a raised voice. I for one had written an article for the house organ. Now what was that? A little spot? Or mud up to the waist? I had no idea."

The first measure the new chief took was to order all the dividing walls taken out, transforming the floor that the foundation occupied in a downtown São Paulo building into a huge room in which the functionaries' desks were placed in rows, like desks in a schoolroom. For himself, the chief ordered a glassed-in cubicle put up beside the only entrance door. From it he could control all his subordinates.

Next he dispatched a series of memoranda spelling out minutely what was permitted and what was forbidden.

"And all this during a liberal period. It was when Jânio Quadros was president—sure, there were notes and memos, but no institutionalized acts."

Paulo now had very little to do. The construction of the popular housing units had been suspended; at times he received some document or other to evaluate for the foundation— things that had been moving through the official channels for ages. On these occasions he would grow nervous. He would make various rough drafts, choosing his words with care, looking things up repeatedly in the dictionary and asking his colleagues' opinions, although they were of little help.

The director was always present—although not always visible. At times he closed the curtains of his cubicle; other times the smoke from his constant cigarettes made his figure imprecise. When he remained motionless he seemed distant, absent. But then he would move imperceptibly and the light would glance off the metal rims of his glasses. Yes, he was there. Observing and taking note of everything in a notebook with a dark green cover.

About this time Paulo began to notice something strange:

his desk vibrated. At first he thought it must be the heavy traffic down in the streets; then he realized it was he himself who was making the desk shake.

"It was my leg! My leg was trembling from sheer nervousness. I was tied up in knots."

He decided that the time had come to get out of there. Finding another job would be hard, and his expenses with his daughter were large, but he felt he couldn't go on that way.

"I would look out the window and see the kids running in the park. They made me envious. All that freedom, that lack of worry."

One day the errand boy handed him a memorandum from the director. It said he should go to the latter's office that day at three o'clock. Paulo was in a state of panic: that they had discovered something, some sin in his past, something that he might not even remember any more, or that he didn't even know about.

He couldn't even eat lunch. He sat on a bench in the Praça da República thinking about what he should say to the chief in case he should be accused. He decided to deny everything. The others forced me into it, he would say. I became involved against my own will.

At three o'clock sharp he knocked on the plate glass door. The director showed him in, closed the curtains. Sit down, the director said, in a surprisingly genteel tone, and handed Paulo a piece of typewritten paper. I know you're a cultured man, he said. I would like your opinion on this.

It was a sonnet. A horrible sonnet, depicting in impossibly poor rhymes the misfortunes of a wounded bird.

A friend of mine wrote it, said the director, looking hard at Paulo. A very close friend . . . he has many more of this type—he says there are enough for a book. I'm thinking of publishing them, with funds from the foundation. But I want your opinion about it. In writing, naturally. It doesn't have to be right away; you may take ten regular working days to think it over.

Paulo went back to his desk, more anxious and perturbed than ever before. The thing was illegal, of course, the business of publishing the sonnets, but what should he do? Denounce the director? To whom? On the other hand, to go along with it was repugnant to him. Yet he didn't want to lose his job—at least not just then, when he had nothing else to fall back on.

The days went by, and with each one his anxiety grew. He couldn't sleep at night, and he had nobody to whom he could talk. Fernanda was more and more taken up with the little girl. Should he consult a lawyer? Should he run away?

"But then I was saved, Guedali. Saved by the bell, you might say. One afternoon a strange thing happened: the end of the workday came, and the chief still sat in his cubicle. This was odd, because he normally left punctually at six—and naturally we went out a little after he did. But that day, six o'clock came and nothing happened. Six-fifteen, six-thirty—and the man sat there motionless in his high-backed chair. We looked at one another without knowing what to do. Finally the errand boy got his courage up and knocked at the door. The director still didn't move. Then the boy stepped inside and asked very politely if he might be allowed to go home. Nothing. No answer. Are you not feeling well, sir? asked the errand boy. The director was silent. The boy once again got his courage up and touched the man's shoulder. The director fell face-down on his table, stone dead."

Stroke, said the foundation doctor. And he warned us all: This should be a lesson to everyone who leads a sedentary life. I knew this man: he never took any exercise, he smoked too much and worried constantly.

"The next day," Paulo finished up, "I resigned from the foundation. I decided to work for myself; I swore I would never again have a director, nor a boss, nor anything. And I started to learn judo in a health club near where we lived. Later I decided to begin running. To this day I still run. Sometimes I get tired and feel like quitting, but then I remember the director face-down on his desk, dead, and it gives me the resolve to go on running. I would even say, Guedali, that running is the most important thing in my life. After my family, of course. And my friends."

*   *   *

Paulo and Fernanda, Júlio and Bela, Armando and
Beatrice, Joel and Tânia. We would go out to dinner every
weekend. Joel, who knew all the restaurants in São Paulo,
served as our guide. Although he followed a strict diet on
account of his ulcers, he took pleasure in seeing us eat: Isn't
this Hungarian goulash marvelous? he would ask, misty-eyed, as
he sipped his glass of milk.

We would get together in one another's houses. And if it
were Saturday night, we would stay until the wee hours
talking about everything: business, naturally, but also about
children, politics, maids, and cars. And sex education in the
schools. And psychoanalysis. And the latest divorce. And travel.

We would go to the movies and theaters together.
Sometimes we played cards, or even Scrabble or Monopoly.

When carnival time came, we thought up something fun.
Júlio and Bela would dress up in a costume without the others
knowing what it was, and walk a predetermined route in the
center of the city between ten o'clock and midnight. The first
couple to guess who they were would be treated to dinner.

At ten o'clock Tita and I went downtown. Armando,
Beatrice, Joel and Tânia were already there, looking for the
disguised pair. Tita and I, dressed as pirates, moved about amid
the crowds of revelers, many of whom were masked. From
among these harlequins and clowns, we were looking for a
particular pair of harlequins or clowns. Or Arabians? Or
ghosts? We didn't have the faintest idea how Júlio and Bela
might be gotten up. So we searched, Tita and I, laughing at
our own mistakes: I grabbed a werewolf by the arm thinking it
was Júlio, while she yelled at an odalisque, "I've discovered
you, Bela!"—but it wasn't Bela. Then suddenly I saw the
centaur.

It was standing still, this centaur, watching a group of
Indians dance by in the street, but it attracted far more
attention than they. A little crowd was concentrated around it,
laughing and commenting. Some gave it slaps on the
hindquarters, to which it reacted by kicking at random.

Tita grabbed my arm and held me. My first impulse was
to flee from there with her; it was as if they had discovered our

secret, as if they were saying, There's no use in your trying to hide the truth, we know everything, we know what you used to be. And who was saying this? Júlio and Bela? Were they the people inside the centaur costume?

Controlling myself with effort I took Tita's hand and we drew closer to the centaur.

It was a very poorly made costume, of some brown plush material that didn't resemble horsehide at all. The tail was dyed yarn that had been unraveled. The black-celluloid hooves were far too large for the body. As I looked at those hooves an untimely doubt occurred to me: How could the circus people have ever confused a real centaur with a couple dressed up as a centaur? My old hooves, although very large (perhaps due to some Percheron blood in my background) were still much smaller than those false ones. Maybe a person with small feet . . . and walking on tiptoe. . . . Maybe.

There we stood, not knowing what to do. Let's get out of here, whispered Tita. I looked at her. She was pale and terrified—which was what decided me. I resolved to clear up the matter once and for all. If Júlio and Bela were inside that costume, if this masquerade were a message to us, then it was time to lay our cards on the table. Stay here, I said to Tita. Pushing my way through the crowd, I went up to the centaur and placed myself right in front of it.

I couldn't see the man's face; it was hidden inside a paper-bag mask painted to resemble a devil. (Imagine, a centaur with a devil's face!) The hairy chest and paunchy belly could have belonged to Júlio.

"What the hell do you want?" he yelled. "Haven't you ever seen a guy wearing a custome, you clown?"

Pedro Bento!

I drew back, startled and afraid. Yes, it was Pedro Bento. The voice I had heard in the taxi.

"What're you doing, Pedro, starting a fight?" It was a woman's voice coming out of the centaur's belly, and also a voice I knew! The lion tamer from the circus!

Now the two of them were arguing, the woman complaining that she had to stay bent over in an uncomfortable position, sweating inside the host costume.

"And smelling your stinky farts, Pedro! You never stop farting, you bastard! And now you're picking a fight!"

The revelers nearby heard all this and were thoroughly amused. Pedro Bento was now pounding his hindquarters— that is, the woman; and she apparently returned his blows from inside the costume, which finally ripped apart to reveal her, disheveled and surprised. Indeed, it was the lion tamer herself.

Let's go, I told Tita. I put my arm about her waist and led her away to a nearby bar. We sat down, I still very upset, but even more worried by the haggard look on Tita's face. I took her hands in mine; they were icy. I ordered the waiter to bring some cognac and made her drink it. When she was calmer, I told her who the people inside the centaur costume were. She stared at me without a word, and I knew that it wasn't jealousy of the lion tamer she was feeling. It was terror. Fortunately, our friends saw us inside the bar and came to meet us. Let's go eat dinner! shouted Júlio and Bela, delighted that they hadn't been discovered in their astronaut costumes. Tita and I did everything possible to join in the general merriment, but it was an effort. A threat—one more—was now weighing us down. I knew Tita was asking herself the same thing I was: How long could we keep our secret?

The days that followed were nervous ones. I feared from moment to moment that I might again meet up with Pedro Bento. I went around with dark glasses; every time a taxi stopped near me I turned rapidly away. As for the lion tamer . . . yes, I feared meeting her too, but the fear was different, a mixture of alarm and excitement. I imagined myself—after her first surprise had passed—inviting her for a drink, and then taking her to a motel, and then asking her in bed, "So, who was a horse, eh? Who did you call a horse?" and she whispering to me, "You stallion, you. . . ."

As for Tita, she was becoming more and more withdrawn. She quit her studies and didn't even watch TV any more. She spent her days sitting and staring into space.

I thought that it was because of the artificial centaur, the presence of Pedro Bento and the lion tamer in São Paulo. I tried to calm her: Look, Tita, they would never recognize me. The creature they were accustomed to seeing had the body of a horse, hooves and a tail.

The truth was, this didn't bother her. Or rather, it didn't bother her as much. She had something else to think about, something that, if it made her anxious, also made her smile mysteriously at times.

"Whatever's wrong with you?" I would ask, intrigued. She wouldn't answer. One night as we were leaving Julio's house, she told me: she was pregnant.

I refused to believe it. The Moroccan doctor had assured me that, if she took the pill, she would not become pregnant. But it so happens, she said, that I stopped taking the pill several months ago. You are out of your mind, I said. We were sitting in the car, I with my hand paralyzed on the ignition keys. She didn't reply, but lighted a cigarette.

I started the car and drove home at top speed. I went straight to the telephone and put through a call to the Moroccan doctor. He answered but, sleepy or drunk, he didn't understand what I was saying. Finally I managed to make him comprehend that Tita was pregant. He reassured me that she would be all right, she had a normal woman's uterus. But what will come out of it? I shouted. Ah, he said, that I don't know. If you are worried, come over here and if necessary I will perform an abortion.

I hung up. Tita stared at me. I want my child, she said, no matter what it is, human, centaur, horse. I want my child, she repeated.

From that time on I had no rest. In the office, in my car, in my dreams, the same visions persecuted me: monsters with human parts (arms, legs, lips, eyes) and equine parts (legs, tail, mane, penis) all combined in various proportions, and always, always resulting in horrendous figures.

The birth date grew closer, Tita's belly grew alarmingly large, and I implored that we go to Morocco—at least to consult the doctor. Her resolution was unshakable: It isn't necessary, I know everything is all right, she would say calmly, happily even. And what about the delivery? I asked. How will we handle that? It will be however God wills, she answered. I'll have my baby like the Indian women do—ever hear of them needing hospitals, doctors? She sounded crazy to me, stark raving mad.

Sometimes I would wake up before daybreak in a panic. Tita would be sleeping, and I would stare at her belly, outlined by the grayish light of dawn. My predominant feelings: fear, anxiety, and blind revolt—not only against Tita but against my very self, and principally against the divine entity, Jehovah or whatever name you give it, responsible for so much suffering.

Yet at times I managed to reverse these negative expectations, undo the rancor that ticked like a time bomb inside me. The soft light reflected by the taut skin of that belly invaded me, tranquilized me. And if I noticed any movement—no doubt produced by the brusque gesture of a little arm or a tiny head—I would be suddenly moved to feeling, like Schiller, that I could embrace millions. Millions, including at least a few dozen blacks, Indians, Palestinian terrorists, diverse deformed beings (a cyclops with cataracts on its single eye, a troll with its legs curled backward and athlete's foot between its toes, not to mention the hunchbacks and those with their faces burned off by acid), and a baby centaur, if it should be. Yes, I would be capable of loving even a baby centaur, and that sentiment could only have been inspired in me by paternal instinct. So wasn't I afraid then? So was I prepared to run the risk? I didn't know, I really didn't know. At any rate—waves of love rising, tide of hate turning—the final result was a large and deserted beach, a calm landscape which, when I gazed upon it, made me fall into a peaceful sleep. Until the alarm clock woke me. But it wasn't the avenging angel's trumpet, it was only a mechanical device calling me back to a reality that might not be entirely cruel, if I would go and face it.

The first thing to do was to make some preparations so that the delivery could be performed under the proper conditions. But how? I had an inspiration: the midwife who had brought me into the world. Would she still be alive? I called

Mina, praying that I wouldn't find her in one of her periods of depression. Luckily, she sounded euphoric—she had just become engaged to her analyst.

I told her that Tita was pregnant, and she congratulated me, but when I told her of my fears, she got worried and said she was starting to feel her depression coming on. "Oh, no you're not!" I shouted. "You're going to help me!"

She didn't fail me. She got into the car and went off down the dusty country roads of Rio Grande to find the old midwife on a ranch in a very out-of-the-way place, drinking chimmaron tea. She was almost blind, poor thing. Did she remember Guedali? Of course, the little Jewish boy who was half colt. Ah, so he's about to become a father, eh? How time flies, miss.

She was flattered that I had chosen her to perform my wife's delivery. Nevertheless, she didn't want to travel: I'm too old to leave my little house any more, miss. I won't take a step out of here. If they want, they can come here. Mina had a hard time convincing her; she had to promise all sorts of presents: dresses, china, furniture—but in the end she agreed. Mina took her back to Pōrto Alegre and got her on an airplane.

I went to meet her at the airport. The sight of the little old lady, dressed in black and clutching a package (of food, I later learned), perplexed amid the hurrying crowds of São Paulo, sent a pang through my heart. Would she be capable of delivering the baby? Once we got home, however, I had another impression. As soon as I introduced her to Tita, she put down her package, rolled up her sleeves: Take your clothes off, dear, and lie down, she said. Somewhat startled at the hooves ("I'd forgotten what you're like") she examined her with confidence and skill. It's not going to be right away, she told us. It'll be sometime next week. And the child, is it normal? I asked. She didn't reply, pretending not to have heard. God's will be done, I breathed.

Paulo kidded me: There's never been an expectant father as worried as you are, he would say. It was true: I installed the old midwife in the room next to ours, and at the slightest sound

*   *   *

Not completely happy. Right after the twins were born,
but as the months went by, Tita again became distant.
ently this was due to the children: they demanded a lot
e, which took up all her time and energy. She wouldn't
them for a minute. I wanted to hire a nursemaid; we
afford to, for business was going well. But she wouldn't
of it. A cook, yes; and a cleaning woman, a serving maid,
ffeur, a gardener. But she would not even consider hiring
semaid. They don't take good care of children, she
d, they're rough and crude.
The truth was, however, that things had changed between
e hardly talked. At night in bed, when I drew close to her
ouched her, she would jump up: I think the babies are
g! She would run to their room, and come back only after
asleep.

Why do you wear those boots? asked Paulo, curious.
're orthopedic, I answered, I can't walk without them.
He was my friend, he told me everything, but could I tell
about my hooves? Doubtful, I would stay quiet and listen
m instead. He talked a lot, telling me about his days as
anda's sweetheart, which went back almost to their
hood in Bom Retiro. "We were brought up together, we
to the same school, our families were always good
ds—they even came from the same city in Poland. When
nd I were eighteen we decided to leave everything behind
go to Israel together. We wanted to live on a kibbutz, in
ct with nature, running through the fields and planting,
esting, milking cows. Our parents were against it, they
ght we were too young, that we didn't know anything
t life, we had no profession. We rebelled against them, and
away to a friend's home in the country, near Ibiúna, where
lept together for the first time. It wasn't very good, she felt
of pain, and we got this skin rash that made us itch for
. We went home, our parents forgave us, and I studied for
ge entrance exams. We were married before I finished
ol. Our parents gave us an apartment and helped us

from Tita I would run to get her. Be calm, Guedali, the old
woman would tell me sleepily (she slept all the time). It won't
happen right away, I already told you.

One night Tita woke up feeling hard, regular pains. I went
to call the old woman. I found her already up, dressed and
alert. This time you're right, Guedali, the time has come. Let's
go. You are going to help me.

Barely able to curb my anxiety, I saw the child's head
appear; then the body, then the legs. *Normal.* Normal. Is it
normal, Dona Hortênsia, I asked, is the baby normal? Of course
it is, muttered the old lady as she cut the umbilical cord. A
perfectly normal little boy. Why shouldn't he be? Do you think
everyone is born with hooves?

She stopped, looking at me with curiosity. But you used to
have four hooves, Guedali, where are the other two? I had an
operation, I'll tell you about it later, now take care of the child,
for the love of God.

He was a beautiful baby, the child she gave me to hold.
Tita looked at me and smiled, exhausted but joyful. The
midwife looked at her abdomen. It was still large. Hm, she said,
there's still more to come.

More to come? I glanced at her in panic. What more?
What else was coming? Horses' legs? A tail? The body of a
horse?

(The scene: Tita lying on the bed, the sheets bloody, her
hooves wide apart, the midwife palpating her belly, frowning
and murmuring unintelligible things; I, leaning against the
wall, almost fainting.)

I got hold of myself. I took a deep breath. If it's a horse's
body, I thought, I'll mash it to death, even if it shows signs of
life, even if the hooves are moving. I'll mash it with a stick
and burn it afterward.

"Here it comes!" said the midwife.

It was another head that appeared, another body, with arms
and legs. Another child—normal. Another boy—twins!

"You two are prizewinners," said the old lady, but I hardly
heard her. I was already hugging Tita, the two of us in tears.

*   *   *

Those first days were blissful. The children were healthy, two beautiful boys; they nursed well. God has been good to us, Tita would say. He has compensated us for the suffering we went through.

Then a problem arose: she didn't want the boys to be circumcized. Nobody is going to touch my children, she said resolutely. It's enough that I converted, I want nothing more to do with this religious nonsense.

But I was not about to give in. I remembered what my father had told me of his struggle to bring the mohel to the farm; I felt that the children's circumcision was an obligation that I owed him. I explained this again and again, and eventually threatened to go off and take the children with me. Then Tita gave in.

I brought my whole family to São Paulo for the ceremony. The circumcision was performed, all went smoothly, and afterward there were luncheons and dinners at which repeat toasts were drunk. My parents were bursting with joy. You deserve this happiness, my father told me. Nature was unkind to you, but you have struggled and won, and now here you are, the father of a fine family, respected and well off.

After that I no longer went to the bar for a beer with Paulo. At the end of the afternoon I would lock the office and run home to be with my sons. I would sit with the two of them on my lap.

(My horse's legs weren't fond of that contact. They sensed, through the material of my trousers, the children's fine skin; my legs would shift nervously. Quiet, I would snarl under my breath, be quiet. But they couldn't. They obviously felt themselves threatened. Two of them had been amputated; the remaining two were obliged to submit to trousers, boots— and now the babies weighing on them. The heat generated by the two small bodies, persistent and subtly humid, would in the end macerate the horsehide, exposing bone and tendon. They protested; my legs, cramping.

*   *   *

Let them protest.

Those round, cuddly babies were th
When one of them smiled, the house lit
smiled, the world itself glowed.

Adorable children. At times they w
naturally. It was never just one, but both
up, pull on our boots, and go lurching to
into each other. At times we would find
clothes; I would be wearing her negligee
Each of us would pick up a twin, walk u
As we quieted them, Tita would hum Ro
Yiddish melody—strange how the memor
nursery songs came back to me now. At t
by side, Tita and I—a habit from the days
together through the fields?—and at times
opposite directions. When we met I would
did. She was always preoccupied with the
though getting it back to sleep depended on
Tita was an anxious mother, and her anxie
At times I felt like running away, like gall
But I had to control myself, to walk slowly
I was humming.

These were contradictory impulses that
understand, and what was the result? Leg
suffered so badly from leg cramps as during

On account of these cramps, which sug
shape—how long since I had galloped?—an
Paulo complained (You've abandoned me, C
training with him. Once a week we would g
athletic club. Our aim was to do at least six
track. Easy for me, hard for Paulo. He was
with boots on, and with a heavy coat, and yo
tired! People from Rio Grande are like that,
horse, half human.

The two of us would jog regularly, and
panting, about his family problems. You're a
he would say, you have two sons, but you do
what hell marriage can be.

financially and so on, until I graduated and found a job. Our
child was born, and at first we were so happy about her. Then
came the suspicion—and later the despair, when it was confirmed
that she was retarded. And now we're resigned. Resigned, but
not happy, Guedali. We aren't happy. I look at Fernanda, she
looks at me. We don't say anything, but I know what she's
asking herself, because I'm asking myself the same thing:
What became of our dreams? One day not long ago we left the
child with my parents and went to the country house in
Ibiúna, which is now up for sale. We got there, and it was the
same house—old but very handsome, colonial style with a
fireplace and all. We spent the night in the same room where
we had first slept together, in the same bed, but it wasn't the
same, Guedali. Can you believe it? It was so different, there was
no enjoyment in it, you know? Time passes, we stop loving
each other, and start asking ourselves what life is for. For
nothing, it seems. Every afternoon when I close the office, I
think: One more day gone, this day won't be back to bother
me."

It was our sixth lap, and he was quite worn out. Don't you
want to do some calisthenics, some sit-ups? I asked him. No
way, he panted, I'm heading for the shower. I'm dead, Guedali,
dead.

Fernanda. She didn't talk much. But she would look at me,
stare at me intensely. I could see cynicism, bitterness, and
dissatisfaction in that look—but challenge, too. I would turn my
eyes away; Paulo was my friend.

One Saturday they invited us for a little party; it was
Paulo's birthday. Tita didn't want to go. As usual, she gave
various excuses; she was tired, one of the twins had a slight
fever, and so forth. But I insisted: Paulo and Fernanda are so
nice to us, it's not right for us to refuse.

Their house wasn't far from ours: a lovely house of
concrete and glass, with great wooden beams in the ceiling. (Pity
it's rented, Paulo would say.) When we arrived, the group was
already gathered around the fire in the center of the living
room. The fireplace was a great iron basin suspended from the

ceiling by heavy chains hanging at the sides of the chimney—
Fernanda had original ideas. We were greeted with enthusiasm,
as usual. Nobody made any reference to our boots—new, in fact,
having recently arrived from Morocco—but anyone could see
they noticed them. Drink? asked Paulo. Glasses of whiskey in
our hands, we joined in the conversation, which would flow
gently at times, or grow agitated and turbulent; spread out to
include everyone, or divide itself into small groups. Joel and
Armando were discussing the advantages and disadvantages of
the Mustang. Beatrice and Tânia were talking about the
schools of their respective children. Bela commented to Tita on
the scarcity of maids. Júlio asked Beatrice how her analysis
was going. A struggle, breathed Beatrice. Joel, who was in
analysis too, remarked that the process was like diving down
to the bottom of a well and then coming up slowly, clutching at
the sides with your fingernails, suffering, always suffering.
Bela, who still retained traits of her student-leader past, said that
analysis was an elitist amusement for the rich bourgeoisie who
had nothing better to do. That describes you perfectly! exclaimed
Joel, and we all laughed. I don't care if I'm rich or not, said
Beatrice, all I know is I suffer terribly, and I want to be happy,
do you see my point, Bela? Happy!

Her voice was breaking, and we were all embarrassed.
Fernanda had the presence of mind to change the subject,
asking Tânia and Joel about their trip to Israel. It was
wonderful, said Tânia, we saw a lot of people we knew. They
have a hard life over there, said Joel, they work very hard and
don't earn much, their taxes are beyond all reason and they're
always threatened by war. It's a hard life, agreed Paulo, but at
least it has a meaning, while our life here . . . What's wrong
with our life? retorted Júlio. Our life is fine, mine at least is
very good. I don't mean that it isn't, replied Paulo, I know we
have all the comforts, but at times I ask myself if it isn't rather
an empty life, meaningless. Meaningless? scoffed Júlio. What
more meaning do you want? To have a house, food, a good
wife, kids, and some amusing girlfirends once in a while . . .
we all laughed, even Paulo. But he insisted: That may be, but I
still haven't given up the idea of going to Israel. What for?

Júlio was getting irritated. Aren't you doing well here, Paulo? Your business is excellent; you live in a good house; in the end, what are you after? I must say I don't understand you. True, true, said Paulo, but I'm still a Jew, and that's very important to me. Judaism . . .

He stopped. There was an uncomfortable silence. I knew who they were thinking about: Tita, the goy. It was awkward discussing these things in front of her. Once again it was Fernanda who changed the subject; she mentioned that her neighbor had been mugged. It's incredible how much crime we have to live with, said Tânia.

The situation of the nation was discussed. Things can't go on the way they are, said Júlio in disgust, all these strikes, the dollar down, the slogan-wavers bossing everyone around, things are going to blow up. They'll blow up, said Bela, because those in power won't give an inch, they won't make the slightest concession, no matter how small. They won't even stand for a miserable little agrarian reform. What do you know about that, said Julio angrily. I know just as much as you do, screamed Bela, and furthermore I don't handle dirty speculation money! It's money that pays for your designer clothes, said Júlio, laughing. Well, I don't want your damned clothes, shouted Bela. Calm down, said Paulo, you needn't undress, Bela. You know who is getting a divorce? asked Joel, munching cashews. Everybody knows it's Bóris, answered Tânia, but don't eat so much, you'll be farting all night long. You fart too, said Joel. It's true, admitted Tânia, laughing, that's what marriage is, farting together. Joel hugged her and gave her a kiss: I love this woman, folks! I adore this woman!

It was fun to be there, part of that cozy atmosphere. The large panes of glass were fogged over, giving one a sense of isolation; it was as if we were at the bottom of the sea. The conversation was fragmented once again; Bela was telling a long story to Tita, who listened to her very attentively. She was beautiful, Tita. Her strange loveliness set her apart from the other women, who were all good looking but conventional, excessively made-up.

Bring the film projector, Paulo, said Júlio. New films?

asked Joel, a gleam in his eye. Yeah, and what films! said Julio. What films, man!

Paulo set up the projector and screen, turned out the lights. While everyone giggled at the carryings-on of a woman and two dwarves, I got up and went out into the garden behind the house. A beautiful garden, with large trees, shrubs, and planters full of flowers. It reminded me a little of the one behind our house in Pôrto Alegre, though better-kept. There was even a fountain, as in the Moroccan clinic. I sat down on a stone bench and gazed at the view, which was very pretty. The night was cold but I felt good being there.

A hand rested lightly on my shoulder.

"Oh, so there you are, you runaway."

I turned around: Fernanda. We looked at each other for a few seconds. A pretty woman, her tousled hair falling to her shoulders, her semiopen blouse giving me a glimpse of her lovely breasts. She looked at me, her desire for me clear. I began to have an enormous erection, a mounting urge such as I had felt for the lion tamer. I felt myself losing my head. It was madness; I couldn't do this, in Paulo's very house—Paulo, my best friend! Someone might see us; it was a terrible risk. But I could no longer control myself; I pulled her to me, kissed her—and she too was voracious, biting me in her passion. I took her behind the fountain; we lay down, and I lifted her skirt, caressing her thighs. (I trembled; it was skin I was touching, soft skin and not horsehair!) I opened my zipper, removed my penis. Oh, how big you are, she murmured, and I remembered the lion tamer with a pang of fear—what if she started screaming? But no, she didn't scream, she moaned in pleasure, and I did too, the water rippling in the fountain.

I'll go in first, she whispered, putting herself back together. She smiled, kissed me again—calmer now, less urgent—and went.

I sat on the bench, stunned. What had happened? I didn't know. My vision was blurred, my heart was pounding, and my right hoof, I now noticed, was trembling convulsively. I held it down: Stop it, you devil, be still.

I stayed there, waiting for the heat to drain out of my face. When I felt sufficiently calm, I went in.

The films were over, everyone was talking. They looked at me, but nobody said anything. Apparently the only strange thing I had done was not stay to watch the films. You missed some great scenes, said Joel. Oh, I've seen that kind of stuff, I said, my voice almost normal, those films are always the same. Let's go, Guedali, said Tita, it's getting late.

We said good night. Fernanda's hand lingered in mine an instant longer than usual, but only an instant; she didn't seem at all perturbed. Suddenly it occurred to me that I wasn't the first, that other men must have had her behind the fountain. Who? Joel? Júlio? Come on, Tita insisted, the children might be crying.

The Fernanda business didn't continue. For a few days I thought that she might phone to set up a rendezvous. And if she had? I wouldn't have known what to do. Having sex with her had been marvelous, and I wouldn't have minded repeating it. But what if Paulo or Tita should have found out? And what if Fernanda herself should have discovered—ripping off my trousers, let's say, in an excess of passion—my horse's legs?

She didn't call. We met downtown one day by chance, and she was totally natural: How are you, Guedali? How are Tita and the kids? She said she had arranged to meet Paulo in a certain bar, and asked if I'd like to join them. We went to the bar, a luxurious place with low lights. She chose an isolated table, out of the range of indiscreet eyes. We ordered drinks. For a while we said nothing. She seemed absentminded; her gaze wandered from here to there. As for me, I was restless; my stiffened tendons inside their boots sent me constant messages: We're ready to gallop, Guedali, ready to gallop. Once in a while her eyes would meet mine, she would smile. Her fingernails drummed against the table. I asked her how she was feeling.

"Me? Fine."

"Even after that night?"

"Of course, even after that night. Fine."

"No problem?"

She laughed (a bit forcedly, but she laughed nevertheless).

"Oh, come on, Guedali, what problem could there be? We're adults. What happened, happened. It was fun. That's it."

"And Paulo?"

"What about Paulo? Everything's fine with Paulo. You didn't expect me to tell him about it, did you? Even though—I'll be frank with you—I could have. We don't have any sissified little reservations, Paulo and I. I've had other affairs; he knew about them. Nothing happened, no blood was spilled. We're civilized, Guedali. Paulo and I aren't going to kill each other over this. Besides, we have our child to care for."

She drained her glass. And your wife, she asked, did she suspect anything? No, nothing, I answered. She leaned toward me. Don't get me wrong, Guedali, but that Tita of yours is sort of rough, even if you don't see it. She acts like a peasant. I don't think she knows how to appreciate the husband she has ... because you're wonderful, Guedali. You really are a fantastic person. But does your wife know that? I think she does, I said, and got up. I'd best be going, Fernanda. See you around, she said. And smiling, she added, Come over, the garden will always be there—one of these times, who knows ... ?"

I went out. At the street door I stopped, dazzled by the sunlight. Someone grabbed my arm: Paulo. How are you? he asked. Fine, I said, Fernanda is inside waiting for you. I know, he said.

We looked at each other—and everything was all right. Come over, you and Tita, said Paulo. Okay, we will, I answered.

There was one thing Fernanda was wrong about: the garden would not be there much longer. Nor the house. The owner asked Paulo to move out, as he wanted to tear it down and build an apartment building on the lot.

Paulo was depressed over the news. We've lived here for ten years, he said, I never thought of leaving this house; I like it, it's a good place. Fernanda didn't mind as much: Come on, Paulo, living here or someplace else, it's all the same. House or apartment, the important thing is to have plenty of space and be near a drugstore, supermarket, things like that. I can't get used to it, Paulo repeated, I can't get used to it.

Nevertheless, when he called me a few days later his tone of voice was very different: happy—euphoric, even. I've got great news, Guedali! he shouted. Something sensational! I want you and Tita to come over here right now. I'm calling the whole group together!

We had just finished dinner, the twins were asleep, and Tita was watching a serial on TV. Paulo's asking us to come over, I said. You go, she answered without taking her eyes off the screen, I don't feel like it, I'd rather stay here.

(What did all this mean? This apathy? Those dry, laconic answers? What was going on? At times I found her gazing off into space; I heard occasional sighs. I thought it might be nostalgia, or perhaps some illness. I thought about lots of things, but didn't have the courage to ask. She wouldn't have answered me anyway.)

I insisted. Paulo is a good friend, I said, he needs our support, and he asked both of us to come, Without a word she got up and got dressed to go out.

When we arrived, everyone was already there. It was a very hot summer evening. Everyone was discussing the political situation—it was 1964. Júlio believed that Brizola was preparing a coup. He pointed an accusing finger at me: You people from Rio Grande want to tell the whole country what to do. Brizola is right, said Bela, this country has to be overhauled by force! Shut up, said Júlio, what do you know about it? You shut up yourself! screamed Bela. Calm down, said Joel, things aren't that serious. So, Paulo? Guedali's here. What's the big news?

Paulo stood up, a roll of blueprint paper in his hands. He looked at us, smiling enigmatically. Well, tell us, said Beatrice, this reminds me of a detective film.

Paulo told us that he had been looking for a place to live.

"I saw apartments, houses, but nothing was what I wanted. Everything was cramped, small—and the streets noisy and polluted. Then a light bulb flashed on in my head: Why don't we move to the country?"

He unrolled the paper. It was a map of the city of São Paulo, with the neighboring municipalities. There was a region marked out in red. Now this, said Paulo, is a twenty-five acre area with natural woods and a lake—small, but the water is very, very clean. We could divide it up into twenty lots; invite more people we know, and make it into a horizontal condominium. What do you all think?

Everybody began to talk at the same time: It's a kibbutz, a real kibbutz! shouted Bela. A vacation colony, Tânia said. Júlio didn't agree with the idea of the kibbutz; It's totally different, in these condominiums everybody leads his own life. Enthusiastic, Paulo began to explain the details, talking about swimming pools, tennis courts, a little amusement park, paddle boats for the lake, a golf course. Can you imagine, Bela was saying, all of us lying on the grass and listening to the birds sing, looking at the blue sky?

Grinning, Fernanda winked at me. Tita was silent. Paulo was saying that the place could be made very secure, with electric fences, armed guards, an intercom system for emergencies. Beatrice talked of a child-care center with nurses and psychologists.

Tânia wanted to know details about prices, Joel talked about horseback riding: It's always been my dream to own a bay horse, oh, what gorgeous animals! Amazed, Tânia said, I thought you didn't like that kind of thing, Joel. You see, said Joel, you see, there it is, you don't really know me, Tânia. I like horseback riding very much, but I can't do what I like. Because if I could gallop, Tânia, I'm sure that my bad moods would disappear.

He stopped. There was a rather surprised silence in the room, and then he continued: "I've been ugly to our kids, Tânia; I've slapped them, but it's because I've felt so frustrated. I spend my life confined in the office and in our stores, I have hassles all day long, I can't even forget about them at night. When I go to sleep, I dream about televisions—rows and rows of televisions. On the screens of these televisions I see other televisions, and on their screens still other televisions, smaller and smaller ones, twenty-inch, sixteen-inch, eight-inch, five-inch,

three-inch. Swarms of television sets pursue me. At times
like that I would do anything for a horse, Tânia. To gallop off
in the fresh air would do me no end of good. I'm sure that if I
could only go for long rides I could leave the problems behind,
Tânia. I'd come back another man, amiable, good-humored. Our
children would soon adore me, you can bet on it. And they
could even learn to ride too. So could you. You could all take
private riding lessons from a teacher I know. I would buy
horses for everyone—a horse is a lot less expensive than a car,
Tânia. We could all gallop together, you and I in front and
the children behind us, or else Indian file—whatever. The
important thing is, the whole family would be galloping
together."

"That's marvelous," said Tânia, moved. "Really marvelous,
Joel, I had never thought of such a thing." Well, you can start
thinking, said Joel, because my mind is made up. I'm with
you, darling, said Tânia, because I have plans too.

She was thinking about a small open-air theater rather
like the ancient Greek ones, for shows and concerts. And I'll be
the one to inaugurate it, she said, her eyes shining, with a
violin recital. A surprise: no one knew she played the violin. I
don't, she said, but I can buy a violin and learn, can't I? I've
always dreamed of wandering through the fields playing the
violin. Or the flute—but I really prefer the violin. And I'll use
your amphitheater too! said Bela. To present a musical show in
the American style, with me singing and tap dancing. Because
I can sing pretty well, and I can learn tap dancing. Isn't Tânia
going to learn to play the violin?

She spoke of how delightful it was to tap-dance, the sound
of the metal cleats against wood or stone. Something in the
Fred Astaire genre, she said, that's what I want to do. She
sighed. "I'm tired of being so wrathful, of spilling my poison
on other people. You can't imagine how bad it's gotten. A few
days ago, at a charity tea given by the school, I told the
headmistress that she was feeding her face while the poor were
dying of hunger. And what's worse, I threw a plate of petits
fours on the floor. Fortunately, not many people saw it; it would
have been a scandal."

She dried her eyes.

"But who am I, after all? Tell me, friends, who am I? A fanatic? A terrorist? A feminine version of the prophet Jeremiah? A Trotskyist? Tell me, is that what I am? No, my dears, I'm not. At bottom, I'm just a normal person, and I want to smile, to sow happiness around me. And I want to make love with you, Júlio!"

Júlio got up and embraced her. They kissed lengthily as we all applauded. And now Armando had taken the floor, and was talking about the cultivation of flowers—begonias were his favorite—and about keeping birds ("I'm crazy about Belgian canaries") and raising white rabbits ("Friends, there's nothing prettier than a little Angora rabbit, all white . . ."). His voice was thick, his eyes damp. But these things aren't just pastimes, he added, I've thought too about intensive fish farming, which could give us a good profit, maybe even pay the condominium expenses. The only thing we lack is . . .

He interrupted himself, fell silent.

There was a long, tense silence. Nobody looked at anybody else. Finally Júlio spoke. "It's good business," he said in a heavy, tremulous voice. "I've dealt in real estate for years and I know this is a sound investment. But it's not for the business value that we should build this horizontal condominum, friends. It's because it represents life for us, a new and better way of life. Do you all see that?"

He looked at us, swallowed, and continued: "I know you think I'm ambitious, that I live only for business. It isn't like that, I swear. I used to build shoddy buildings, today I build luxury apartments, but what I'd like to do, the dream I've always had, is to build an entire city, well planned and functional, a city something like Brasília, but better than Brasília, using the experience of those who built Brasília. A more humanized Brasília, if you understand what I mean. A smaller Brasília, without so many big avenues, but with lots of trees and parks. It's been my ideal ever since my college days. This condominium—I feel that in this condominium perhaps I can realize that ideal. It will be the masterpiece of my life; it will make people remember me when I'm no longer here."

This time it was Bela's turn to get up, full of emotion: My love, that's how I like to hear you talk, when you talk like that you're a total person! She kissed him. Hooray, yelled Tânia, hear, hear! Perhaps they want to be alone, said Armando. Paulo, show them to the bedroom, this couple can't wait a minute longer, it's now or never.

"Attention, attention here, folks!" yelled Paulo, tapping his pen on the table. "I want you all to study the finance plan and let me know what you think." Everyone started talking at once again, Paulo asking for order. Finally, we decided that we would all give him an answer as soon as possible so that he could enter negotiations with the owner of the land.

Well, what do you think? I asked Tita once we were in the car. I don't think anything, she said. But doesn't it sound like it would be good for the children, for us too? I asked. Maybe so, she answered.

I stopped the car. Tita, what's happening? She stared at me. What do you mean, what's happening? With you, I said, with me, between us. I don't know what you're talking about, she answered, everything's fine with me. Then I'm crazy, I said, I think I'm crazy, Tita, because things don't seem so fine to me, I think we're drifting apart. Tell me, have I done anything to hurt you?

She stared at me again, and I almost hoped to see accusation in her eyes, but there wasn't; there was only melancholy and indifference.

We have to trust each other, Tita, I said. After all ...

She interrupted me: I know, Guedali, I know we have lots of things in common, hooves and horses' legs, but everything's fine. What do you want me to say?

The car was in the middle of the road, and behind us an enormous truck was honking its horn. I shifted into first gear and drove on.

The next day, I phoned Paulo: You can count us in.

Paulo took charge of finding other investors and of purchasing the land for the condominium. Júlio, with his experience in real estate development, helped him. The money was raised quickly. Even so, we couldn't start right away: two days before the actual construction was to begin, President João Goulart was overthrown. Júlio thought it would be better to hold off building until we saw which direction the running of the country would take. ("So they got you gauchos for once!" he told me.) Events convinced him that the investment was a guaranteed success, and that we might even get some breaks: I have friends who are now in positions of influence, he confided to us. But he complained about Bela: She's really getting to be a pain, she says there's no point in staying in Brazil any longer, she wants us to move to Paris, and what's worse, she keeps putting ideas in the other women's heads. But don't worry, I'll get her calmed down.

The design of the houses was entrusted to three architects, partners who had very similar tastes. The plans were different enough to avoid monotony, but they followed a basic pattern so as not to create envy and rivalry. We don't need to argue over a few square meters, Beatrice would say, let's control our greed. Good, balanced Beatrice; she reminded me of Deborah. At my request she had a long talk with Tita, and finally convinced her to have psychotherapy.

With Tita's treatment, and our move to the horizontal condominium, I had hopes that things would improve between us. More than hopes; I had certainty. Besides, strange things were happening: strange, encouraging things.

Perhaps due to the prolonged wearing of heavy trousers, and the abundant use of moisturizing creams, the horsehide on our legs was becoming thinner and thinner, more and more like human skin. This wasn't happening uniformly; there were large smooth patches where the horsehair had fallen out, giving our legs a maplike appearance.

Our hooves were growing longer and narrower too, probably on account of the boots. Eventually it was necessary to take plaster molds of our hooves and send them to Morocco— The doctor there continued to supply us with boots, at ever-higher prices. "Your hooves are becoming more and more like human feet," he wrote to us, and it was true.

*   *   *

My sons. I loved to play with their little feet, rubbing them
to see them grow pink. They seemed to grow stiffer, as
though they contained erectile tissue. What sweet little feet. My
sons would never have to go through the things I did. Now
that they had grown to be toddlers, we would play horseback-ride,
I on all fours with the two of them mounted on my
back. I would gallop about—or rather, I would crawl, more like
a cat hunting a rat. Except I wasn't after a rat at all; the rats
were far away in the dark hold of a cargo ship crossing a
turbulent ocean, while I was safe in my house with my wife
and sons. The atmosphere of warmth that sheltered us began to
thaw glaciers inside me that I had once believed permanently
frozen. A wonderful thing, that. It was true that those two
robust little boys sometimes weighed too much even for an
ex-centaur. But I didn't care. I knew that a father, like Atlas,
carries the weight of the world on his back.

A little before we moved, Paulo and Fernanda separated.
She left the daughter with him and ran off to Rio with an
airplane pilot.

We went to see him, Tita and I, in the apartment where
he was living, temporarily. He seemed very hurt, but planning
to carry his normal life: I'm going to the condominium, I want
to raise my daughter close to nature. If Fernanda comes back,
fine. If not, that's fine too.

His eyes were red. I hugged him. Never mind, Paulo, we'll
still go jogging at the club. Around the park in the condominum,
he corrected me, I've arranged for a track to be put in there.

HORIZONTAL CONDOMINIUM
JUNE 15, 1965–JULY 15, 1972

IT WAS PAULO HIMSELF WHO GAVE THE INAUGURAL BARBECUE, AIDED by the condominium servants. These were a group of Northeasterners that Tânia had discovered, members of a sect that believed in the remission of sins through exhaustive work. These small, dark people, who looked like Peri the Indian or like the Andean Jivaros, moved ceaselessly about, carrying plates and silverware as they murmured prayers.

The sun was shining, and the food was excellent. Tita was happy; the twins scampered about playing ball. "Come play with us, Daddy!" said one, and the other added as I approached them, "But be careful with your boots!"

(They had never seen us undressed. They asked why we always wore boots, and why Tita always wore slacks instead of dresses. Doctor's orders, I answered, with a clear conscience; it was practically the truth.)

Júlio came up, a glass of whiskey in his hand. He was lurching and definitely drunk. I don't like the way these Northeasterners look at our wives, he muttered. But Júlio, I said, they hardly take their eyes off the ground. That's what you think, he said, you're from Rio Grande, you don't know anything about Northeasterners. I've had experience with them.

What's Julio muttering about? asked Bela. Nothing, answered
Júlio, it's no business of yours. I know what it is, said Bela
angrily. You're criticizing the servants, poor things. You're
ungrateful, Júlio, besides being an exploiter and a reactionary.
Here are these people, working hard while you sit and eat,
and you still criticize them. You should be ashamed, Júlio!

She called to one of the servants and told him they
should all help themselves to the barbecue meal. Thank you,
ma'am, the man replied, but we have our own food, don't be
concerned about us. See there? cried Júlio triumphantly. What
did I tell you? You have to know how to handle these people.

As Júlio and Bela argued, Tita and I went to look at our
house, which we were still furnishing. We were the only ones
who hadn't yet moved into the condominium, but we were
planning to do so soon. Our house was elegant, done in
Mediterranean style like the ones in Morocco. On the top floor
were the bedrooms and terrace; below, the living room, dining
room, office, TV room, playroom. There was even a wine cellar
in the basement. It was all costing me a fortune, but I wasn't
worried; business was better than ever.

We moved in, and agreed at once that life in the
horizontal condominium was indeed very good. Everything
functioned beautifully: the nursery school, the little amusement
park, the security service—armed guards wouldn't let anyone in
without authorization, and patrolled the whole area at night.
We bought a van to provide transport back and forth to the city.
Paulo came to introduce the driver to me—a man, he said,
who was completely trustworthy, and could substitute when one
of the guards needed a night off. He's from Rio Grande too,
said Paulo smiling.

It was Pedro Bento. I recognized him immediately. And
this time I had no doubt: it was the taxi driver that I had
managed to forget.

But he didn't recognize me, not even my name. How many
Guedalis could he have met? But he didn't remember.

After he went out, I began thinking. Maybe Pedro Bento
hadn't recognized me, but he might at any moment—a circuit

closing in that brain could trigger his memory of the galloping centaur. It was a risk I couldn't afford to take. But how to avoid it? Get him fired? On what pretext? To Paulo, he was a trustworthy man. What story could I invent?

I decided to make a direct attack. I called the main gate and asked them to send Pedro Bento to my house. A few minutes later he arrived.

"Yes, sir?"

I took him into my office and closed the door. He stood there before me, hat in hand, suspicious but servile. You don't remember me? I asked him. He looked attentively at me: I confess I don't, sir, begging your pardon. Back in Quatro Irmãos, in the country, I said. He studied me again, and his eyes widened: "Why ... you're Leon Tartakovsky's son, the one that had hooves like a horse!"—he contained himself—"Oh, sorry ... I, uh ..."

I reassured him: It's all right, Pedro Bento, don't worry. He still seemed not to believe me. "Excuse me for asking, sir, but what happened to ... ?"

"My hooves?" I said, smiling. "I don't have them any more, I had an operation." I sat down, and indicated a chair to him. No thank you, he said, I'm fine as I am.

He avoided my gaze as I looked at him. Tell me how you came here, I said. He sighed: Oh, you would hardly believe all the things that happened to me, sir. After your family left Quatro Irmãos, I got this girl pregnant. My old man had a fit and kicked me out of the house. I bummed around Pôrto Alegre for a while, got in a fight, and stabbed this guy. He almost died, and I done three years in prison. After I got out, I found a job with a circus, and I had this affair with a lady lion tamer. She talked me into coming to São Paulo—said she was from here and knew lots of people. Said she'd find me a job. Well, she didn't find me a damned thing. We finally broke up. . . . It was actually kind of funny. He laughed:

"It was during carnival, Guedali. She wanted us to dress up like an animal. A centaur. When she asked how the costume should be I said, Hey, I know about those! That's like Guedali! She was real surprised, said she had met a centaur once, and asked if they were very common down in Rio Grande. Well, to make a long story short, we fixed ourselves up in the costume and went through the streets. But we had this fight and I beat her up, so she took off and left me. After that I worked in a lot of different places, but I never did find a steady job." And the taxi? I asked him. "The taxi? I totaled it in a wreck," he answered.

He fell silent. "So you might say," I observed, "that you're not quite as trustworthy as Mr. Paulo thinks." Pedro Bento made an anguished face: Oh, but please don't tell Mr. Paulo about any of this! That depends, I replied.

I could see he was terrified as he stared at me. Do you like this job here? I asked. He smiled nervously. Oh, yes sir, it couldn't be better. I earn plenty and I got good living quarters. Well then, I said, be sure you keep your mouth shut—about that subject back in Quatro Irmãos. Don't worry, sir, I guarantee I'll be quiet as a tomb.

I showed him to the door. Before leaving, he turned around: For the love of God, Mr. Guedali, let me stay here. Don't worry, I said. Just behave yourself and nothing will happen to you.

That was a week full of surprises. Two days later—on a Saturday—the main gate called the house. A man was there wanting to talk to me. He says he's your brother, the guard informed me. But I was suspicious, and didn't want to let him in.

I went out to the gate.

It was really Bernardo. Unrecognizable. He looked like a hippie: long, tangled hair, sleeveless T-shirt, faded jeans, sandals. Hanging on a chain around his neck was a watch: my father's Patek Phillipe. I stole it, Bernardo said as he hugged me effusively, how are you, man? The guards looked at us in surprise. I took Bernardo's arm and led him to our house. Man, I dropped out, he said, sitting cross-legged on the floor of my office. I quit the whole rat race, quit making money, buying a big car, living with my wife—that boring nag!—my kid, everything. I was really sick of it, Guedali, completely sick. I couldn't believe my eyes and ears. But what are you doing now? I asked. He laughed. Doing? Nothing. Does anybody have to do anything, Guedali? I live on the Rio–São Paulo highway, looking for handouts, making a few necklaces and things, living with a woman here or there—living, Guedali. Living. I didn't know what it was to live before. Back in Pôrto Alegre I didn't know what living was, but now I know.

He took a straw cigarette from his pocket and lighted it. Don't get uptight, he said, it's not marijuana, it's just a straw cigarette. I always liked them ever since the days in Quatro Irmãos, except the old man never let me smoke. Now I can smoke as much as I want.

He looked around. You got a nice pad here, Guedali. Good house, good furniture. He made a disgusted face: But why all the guards, all the fences? This is like a prison, man!

He got up, and I did too. He put a hand on my shoulder: I came to bury the hatchet, Guedali. And to invite you to come with me. How about the two of us hitting the road together? It's a great life, brother. Just bumming around, taking it easy. Want to come?

No thanks, I said, I'm fine here, Bernardo, I prefer to stay. He shrugged his shoulders: Okay. At the door, he turned around: Say, since you don't want to come with me, maybe you could spare me some dough? I gave him money, and he hugged me heartily again and went down the gravel walkway. From the main gate, he waved again.

Things were running smoothly in the condominium because Paulo dedicated himself full-time to its administration, as well as caring for his daughter. He had time for nothing else except to jog around the track with me. You need to get married again, I would say, and he wouldn't answer, panting hard. Jogging was getting more difficult for him. One day Fernanda came back, begging his forgiveness. I was a fool, she said. They fell into each other's arms, sobbing. The following night we offered a dinner party in honor of the two of them. Fernanda and Paulo smiled, their arms around each other. How good it is to be back, she said.

Paulo seemed to come back to life: he was once again the talkative, smiling man he had been before. He took the initiative of getting all the men together every afternoon for a drink in the reception room–bar. Sitting in the comfortable stuffed chairs, we would chat about business or soccer. At some point Júlio, Joel, Armando, or even Paulo would lower his voice: Hey, you guys know that woman, that TV announcer? And then would come a story of an afternoon spent in a motel: What a dame, fellows! We would laugh with growing enthusiasm, and one story would lead to another. Sometimes we would get drunk. On one such occasion I told about the lion tamer from the circus. I went on to describe my life as a centaur, and told how I met Tita, even recounted our operation. When I finished, there was silence broken only by the clinking of ice cubes in our glasses.

"I was born with a defect too," said Julio suddenly. "I had a small tail—about twenty centimeters long, if that, but hairy like a monkey's tail. My parents were horrified. But when the mohel performed my circumcision, he cut the thing off."

"And what about me?" said Joel. "Me, I was born covered with scales, just like a fish."

(I looked at him. he really did have a fishlike face; I had never noticed it before, but he closely resembled a haddock.)

"Fortunately," he added, "the scales all fell off of their own accord."

"Without any medical treatment?" asked Júlio.

"Without any medical treatment," Joel replied.

"Not even any cream, nothing?"

"Nothing. They just fell off."

They all stared fixedly at me. Suddenly they started to laugh. They laughed until they choked and had to catch their breath. One would point at me, and they would all roar with laughter again. I gazed somberly at them. Then I bent over, pulled my pants leg out from my boot, and propped my leg up on the table.

"Look here!"

They stopped laughing, dried their eyes. "What is it?" asked Júlio.

"Can't you see anything?" I screamed.

"There's nothing unusual to see," said Joel.

"What about this?"

I pointed. On my leg, near the knee, there was an area about three centimeters in diameter of dark, thick skin from which grew some wiry hairs. It was all that was left of my horsehide.

"Oh, come on, Guedali," said Paulo. "That's just a birthmark. I have one too, Fernanda is always kidding me about it. She says—"

"Fernanda is a great kidder!" I shouted. "Ask her about my prick, Paulo! Ask her if it isn't big, if it isn't a stallion's prick! Ask her, Paulo!"

Outraged, he threw himself at me. "You filthy bastard! You son of a bitch!" We wrestled together; he pushed me down and I rolled over the floor. As drunk as I was, I couldn't even get up. Joel and Armando got me to my feet while Julio held on to Paulo, who was hollering, "I'll kill the bastard! I'll kill him!"

They took me home. Tita asked in alarm what had happened.

"Nothing," said Joel. "Your husband had too much to drink and started talking nonsense."

They put me to bed without undressing me. I fell asleep at once. At two A.M. I awoke, head throbbing, full of remorse. I telephoned Paulo's house. He's out, said Fernanda in an acid voice. (Did she know what had happened?) He couldn't sleep and went for a walk.

I got up dizzily and went out. I knew where to find him. I went to the track and there he was, sitting near the illuminated fountain. He was wearing an undershirt, Bermuda shorts, and tennis shoes, for he had just been jogging. He was still panting. I put a hand on his shoulder. "Forgive me, Paulo," I murmured. "I lost my head, I swear. Forgive me."

He looked at me with expressionless eyes. We stared at each other, I standing before him like a guilty defendant.

"It doesn't matter," he said finally. "It doesn't matter at all, Guedali. In fact, you weren't the only one. She went to bed

with Júlio, too. But what can I do? I still love her in spite of
it. And the child needs a mother, Guedali. Fernanda's the only
one who can manage her, get her to eat. When she left me, I
almost went crazy, remember?"

He sighed, getting up. "Everything's all right, Guedali.
Come on, let's run a little."

I jogged after him. It was a sacrifice. Suddenly, my
hooves hurt me terribly. I could hardly finish my six laps
around the track.

I barely managed to get home. I had to lie down; the pain
was increasing steadily. The sensation was that my hooves
were going to split apart at any minute, like dry lima beans.

(I wasn't afraid of them opening, splitting apart; my fear
was of something else. I was terrified that they might contain,
not embryonic feet with tiny buds promising toes, but rather
more hooves, and then others, and others, and others; like the
Russian dolls my father used to talk about. Finally I would be
unable to walk, and my only consolation would be examining
the microscopic hooves at my extremities with a magnifying
glass as I recalled the days when, aided by boots, I could at least
get around.)

My hooves did split apart a few days after that painful
nocturnal jog. They did not contain more hooves, but rather
feet; small delicate feet like those of a baby. During the first
days they were so sensitive that I couldn't walk. I was already
in bed, and I stayed there, Tita massaging the soles of my feet
with sand to toughen the skin. In fact, her hooves were also
showing cracks. "Sooner or later you'll have new feet too," I
said, moaning in pain as I tried to walk on a soft carpet.
Finally I grew accustomed to walking and was able to go out in
bedroom slippers to buy some shoes. They were very good
ones, made by a specialist who looked at me with curiosity but
never asked me anything. I was moved as I put them on, but
it wasn't the same emotion I experienced when I took my first
steps at the clinic. I even felt a certain indifference as I burned
the boots that night in the fireplace. The moment marked the
end of my dependence on the Moroccan doctor, to whom I

was still nevertheless grateful. I told Tita we ought to pay him a visit.

The twins are delighted to see me wearing shoes. The other children in the condominium couldn't tease them about their weird father any more. "Now you need to start wearing shoes too, Mama," they said in a scolding tone. Tita nodded in silent agreement.

In 1972 we made a trip to Israel and Europe with the other three couples. In Jerusalem I prayed before the Wailing Wall, wearing the prayer shawl the mohel had given me (and which no longer fell over equine hindquarters). We climbed the mountain where the Masada was situated, to see the last stronghold of Jewish resistance against the Romans. We swam in the Dead Sea and the Red Sea—except for Tita, who still couldn't remove her boots. (Why hadn't her hooves fallen off? The delay was making me anxious, but I had learned to be patient. I was sure her feet would appear one day.) We went to the Golan Heights and the Lebanese border, and took pictures in front of bomb shelters and barbed wire barriers. At a kibbutz we played a game of soccer against some Argentines. Their team wore white shirts, ours blue. The four of us advanced against them. It was a real battle, a test to which I hadn't yet put my feet. But they didn't disappoint me: the kicks I gave left their marks on the adversaries' shins, and I made the two goals for our team.

Went to Rome, Paris, London. From Madrid, Tita and I made a side trip, saying good-bye temperarily to our friends. Júlio looked at me suspiciously, for he thought I was taking advantage of a pleasure trip to do business. He was right, but not entirely. I did want to renew contacts with exporters and importers, but my principal intention was to see the Moroccan doctor again. We went to the south of Spain, following a route opposite that of the Moorish invaders of the Iberian peninsula; we crossed the Mediterranean by ship, and one afternoon a taxi took us to the door of the clinic.

The place was decadent looking. The walls needed to be painted, the gate was rusty, and there was not so much as a doorman to open it. The place seemed abandoned; the water no longer running in the fountain. Suddenly we saw the Moroccan doctor.

He had grown much older. His walk was stumbling, his sparse hair gray. He no longer wore his dark glasses. Recognizing us, he hugged us warmly and invited us in. We sat down in his consulting room, now dirty and disorganized. He served us some lukewarm tea from a thermos bottle and asked how we were. Very well, I answered. I told him about our life in the horizontal condominium and about the twins; I ended up taking off my shoes and showing him my feet, which he examined with great interest. It's a miracle, he murmured, a true miracle. And you, madam? he asked, turning to Tita. She still has her hooves, I said, but judging from what happened to me, I think it's only a question of time.

I'm happy to see you doing so well, he sighed. You were my most exciting cases, the high point of my career. Never before or since did I achieve such brilliant results. I even wrote a monograph about the operation.

He rose and went to get the manuscript. The title was "Centaurs: Description and Surgical Treatment in Two Cases." I never published it, he said. Nobody would believe it. We doctors are skeptics. But you were the glory of my career, he repeated.

We were silent. Suddenly he remembered something, and smiled: You know, I was consulted by a young man who had a similar problem. And by coincidence, he was from Brazil too. But he didn't undergo surgery. In fact, he ran away from the clinic.

The doctor sighed again. After you two left, nothing went well. Things began to go from bad to worse.

A series of unsuccessful surgeries and the deaths of various patients—among them an important government figure—led to the police closing the clinic by order of a judge. After several years, during which he spent all he had, they permitted him to reopen it, but it wasn't the same; famous clients no longer came to him, international magazines didn't want to interview him. I was forced to diversify my activities, he said. Now I do abortions

... and take in old Arab sheiks—most of them ruined—as boarders. It's not like in the old days, Mr. Guedali, I can assure you.

Then his face lit up: I just remembered I have a present for you! He got up and ran out of the room, returning with a curious object: a clay drum, artistically decorated. The leather top had several holes.

"This drum," he explained, "was made out of your hide. The natives returned it. They said the leather was not good quality, that it ripped. They gave back the flyswatter too, but I can't remember where I put it. Wouldn't you like to keep this interesting souvenir? For a modest sum it's yours."

I gave him some money, but told him to burn the drum. I don't want anything that reminds me of the past, I explained. I understand, he said.

I reminded him that Tita still needed boots. He reassured me, saying I needn't worry. The shoemaker was very old, almost at death's door, but he knew another artisan perfectly capable of meeting the need. You can go back to Brazil in peace, he finished.

We traveled to Amsterdam and from there returned with the other couples to Brazil. The twins were waiting for us at the airport, each wearing a T-shirt for his favorite soccer team: one International, the other Corinthians.

We found everything going well at the condominium. Things were peaceful, and they were to continue that way until the evening of July 15, 1972.

One night, about a week before, I met with Paulo in the reception lounge of the condominium for a serious conversation. The two of us were planning to form a new company. He wasn't satisfied with his line of business, nor was I with mine. The prospects weren't good. I had reliable information that the government was about to adopt new restrictions on imports— from which I made most of my profits. Paulo was thinking about forming a small consulting firm. We also had had a proposal from Júlio to work with him in real estate development. But being an employee doesn't appeal to me, Paulo said, even

Júlio's employee. Discussing these various questions, we stayed in the lounge until quite late.

When I got home Tita was in bed, reading. I took off my clothes, lay down, and fell asleep almost immediately. I woke up soon after, for Tita was shaking me. What'sa matter, I mumbled, groggy with sleep. I heard a noise downstairs, she whispered. I looked at my watch: 2:15 A.M. It's just your imagination, I said, and turned over. She shook me again: But I'm sure I heard something, Guedali, I think there's someone down there.

This was absurd. Who could be there? The servants were all asleep in their quarters long since, the twins were spending the month of July with their grandparents in Pôrto Alegre, and no thief could ever get past the security system of the condominium. I explained all this to Tita.

Yet she kept insisting: There is somebody downstairs, Guedali, I'm sure of it. Well, too bad, I said impatiently, let them take everything, I don't care! I'm exhausted, I worked all day long, and I want to sleep. Get on the phone and call the guards, then, she said. Are you crazy? I asked her irascibly. Do you really think I'm going to bother the guards, make a big uproar on account of your hallucinations? Then I'll go down myself! she said angrily. Go ahead, I replied. I rolled over and went back to sleep. Awhile later I woke up with a start. Tita wasn't in bed. I called her in alarm.

I'm downstairs, she answered. But what are you doing down there? I asked. I'm just finishing a cigarette, she said, I'll be right up, I don't like to smoke in bed.

During that whole week I met with Paulo. We were both undecided; it seemed to me we were moving in exasperating circles. Finally, on the night of July 15, 1972, I decided to terminate the subject once and for all. Either we would form a new company, go to work for Júlio, or neither one—I wanted a definite decision.

"I'll be at the lounge, talking with Paulo," I told Tita. "Don't wait up, I'll be late."

But when I got to the reception room, no Paulo. The

doorman told he had hadn't been there. That seemed extremely rude of Paulo; disgusted, I went back home.

I opened the door and went in. "I'm back," I called. "Paulo wasn't ..."

I stopped. I could not believe it. What did I see in front of me? It was not on a cinema screen, nor in an illustrated book, nor in my imagination—it was right there in front of me, standing on my living room carpet and looking at me.

A CENTAUR.

A real centaur (A real one, yes, quite real, although the thought flashed through my mind that it was some sort of stuffed doll, a model of a centaur, a statue that Tita had bought to decorate the living room, though it would have been macabre on her part.) with a white coat, very handsome. And very young: muscular chest and arms, but the face of an adolescent; longish hair, blue eyes, a fine-looking lad. He couldn't have been more than twenty.

Beside him was Tita. Actually, they were in each other's arms.

In each other's arms, Tita and *the centaur*. They jumped apart as I came in, but they had been locked in an embrace. For a few seconds we stared at each other without saying a word. The boy stood there silently, his eyes lowered, blushing a bright pink. Tita, smoking, tried to hide her nervousness.

"I don't see any point in trying to hide anything," said Tita. There was a challenging tone in her voice that irritated me, as though she were unquestionably in the right. Who is he? I asked, barely keeping myself under control. A centaur, she said. I can see he's a centaur, I said in an altered voice, I'm not an idiot. I want to know who the centaur gentleman is and what he's doing in my house, grabbing my wife. Well, began Tita, already insecure, he appeared—

I interrupted her.

"Not you. Don't you say a word. He's the one to explain. The centaur. He is going to tell me everything. Absolutely straight, without any lies."

*   *   *

The centaur's story:

He is born in the country like Tita and I, but in a
beautiful house, near an exclusive beach in the state of Santa
Catarina. His parents, a young couple (he was their first child),
are well-off. Both from Curitiba, the father is the son of a
wealthy furniture manufacturer and the mother a rich heiress.
The premature delivery is successfully performed by a doctor
who is a friend of the young couple and who happens to be
spending his vacation at the same beach with them, although
this doctor is horrified at the baby he brings into the world.
Once the initial shock is past, he calls the father aside. It's a
monster, he says, it won't survive, if you want I can give it a
painless ending at once. No, says the man, crying, it's my son, I
don't have the courage, but if my wife wants it that way. . . .
The doctor questions the young mother to no avail; she doesn't
answer, her eyes fixed on the ceiling. (Just like my mother, she
was traumatized by the shock to the point of muteness.)

Three days later they go home. In the car, hidden under
blankets, they take the little centaur baby—who from that time
on they keep hidden. The entire upper floor of their house is
reserved for him; the parents restrict themselves to the lower
floor. The servants know they must not go upstairs under any
circumstances, which gives rise to various speculations in the
neighborhood, some people talking of ghosts and enchantments.
What a surprise these idiots would have if they could see the
forbidden quarters! The centaur wouldn't be the only astonishing
thing. They would be dazzled by an entire magic world.
Thousands of toys and games filled the nursery; there were
colored books, record players, slide projectors, television sets—
everything a child could ever dream of having. In the midst of
it all, the centaur.

He grows up sad, but not rebellious; melancholy, but
polite. He shows gratitude for the efforts his parents have made
to give him a happy life. He has his crises. Often he cries and
kicks the walls with his hooves, but only when he is alone; in
front of his parents he contains himself. They are so good to
him, his parents; their affection makes him forget that he is a
centaur, forget his terrible loneliness. Why do I need friends?

he asks himself (and later, Why do I need a girlfriend?), if I
have a father and mother who are so wonderful. They spend
every evening with him, telling him the little events of the day
and caressing him. I don't mind having hooves and a tail,
he tells them; think of the poor hunchbacks, or those born
without legs or arms, like the thalidomide victims. But
wouldn't you like to go out, to see the world? his father asks
him painfully. You two are my world, he answers, hugging
them.

And then by chance, his mother attends a charity tea
where she meets a pleasant lady whose husband is a lawyer—
Deborah. They become intimate friends, and one night the
poor woman opens her heart, confiding the story of her son.
Deborah, astonished, says she knows of another case exactly
the same. But there is a solution! she exclaims. Write to the clinic
in Morocco—they perform miracles there!
    The parents consult their doctor friend who performed the
delivery and is the only other person to know of the centaur's
existence. I think it's worth the risk, he advises them.
    The young centaur, however, refuses to go to Morocco in
spite of his parents' arguments. He says he will not leave home,
period. But don't you want to have the surgery, don't you
want to be cured? No. He doesn't consider himself sick; he
doesn't need any operation, he is simply different. And as long
as he has his parents' love, everything will be fine. The doctor
intervenes, furious: Oh, no, this is too much! Being born with
a horse's body was horrible, a predestined tragedy. But now,
for him to refuse an operation—how could he? You are going
to Morocco, like it or not!
    His mother begins to sob, his father collapses into an
armchair. In the end, the boy decides: he will go to Morocco,
but he will go alone. Why alone? screams the doctor. I can go
with you! I'm going alone, the boy screams back, or I'm not
going at all!
    In the end they agree. They put him on a ship, in a
compartment in the hold specially equipped with a refrigerator,
a chemical toilet, and so forth. The ship arrives in port, and the

black van is there to meet it. At the clinic, the Moroccan doctor examines him. There's no doubt, he is exactly like the two other patients! The doctor exults: he will have the largest number of centaur operations in the world! (And the money will be welcome; he's in a financial bind.) Let's do the operation at once, he says.

But the young centaur is still reluctant. The idea frightens him; he asks for a few days to think it over.

But nothing helps; he feels himself more and more defenseless, more terrified. He spends his days crying, missing his parents. Yet he is ashamed to go back as a centaur, with his horse's body and horse's tail, not having had the operation; he feels, like the Spartans, that he should return from battle carrying his shield or being carried on it.

And then he begins to think about the centaur couple who had undergone surgery. If he could only talk to them! He feels sure that, like his parents, they would understand him, would help him. His hope is that they will convince him to have the operation. He formulates a desperate plan: he will journey to Brazil, look up the ex-centaurs, and ask for their advice and moral support. When he can muster the necessary courage, he will return to Morocco and undergo the operation.

In the stillness of the night he breaks into the doctor's office. He discovers the centaurs' file in the records. There is an address—to which certain boots are sent—which he writes down. The next day, he tells the doctor that at present he doesn't intend to have surgery; perhaps he will in the future. For now he is going back to Brazil.

Traveling in the same cargo ship that brought him, he gets to the port of Santos. Before the ship docks, he jumps into the water. Desperately kicking his legs—he can't swim—he makes it to shore.

He gallops by night and hides by day. One morning before dawn he imprudently breaks into a house on the outskirts of São Paulo that seems abandoned. A mistake, because the house is *not* abandoned. He wakes up some hours later to find a man staring at him. A middle-aged man with disheveled hair, wearing a T-shirt and—strange detail—a big watch hanging on a chain around his neck. The frightened centaur tries to run away, but the man calms him, asking where he came from. By strange coincidence this man knows another centaur, his brother Guedali. Guedali! says the boy. That's exactly who I'm looking for! The man directs him to the horizontal condominium, which is a few kilometers away. That night he reaches the place. The electric fence is no problem; he clears it with a jump, protected by the dark.

He discovers our house. The back door (Tita's carelessness) is open. He enters and stands there in the dark, not knowing what to do, wavering between waiting or calling somebody, until daybreak. The servants' voices sound in the kitchen. Afraid, he hides in the wine cellar. There he relieves his hunger pangs (he hasn't eaten in days) with some canned goods, and he opens some wine. Soon he falls asleep, slightly drunk.

When it gets dark, he opens the door to the wine cellar and goes upstairs. He gets as far as the living room, undecided as to what to do. Then he hears the sound of feet on the stairs, grows alarmed, and wants to hide, but it's too late—and also there is no reason to flee, for the person coming is Tita, the ex-centauress, now a beautiful woman—as lovely as her photo had shown her. That photo had fascinated him

They face each other. Tita doesn't seem frightened or even surprised; it is as if she were expecting him. She smiles, he smiles back. She takes him by the hand and leads him to the hollow space under the stairway. They stay there talking in whispers for hours, telling each other their stories. Before she leaves him, she gives him a kiss. Only an affectionate kiss on the cheek, but it's love. She is in love with the young centaur.

That afternoon she tells the servants to take the rest of the day off, and goes down to the wine cellar. It is there in the darkness that they make love. Oh, how good it is, she moans, and wants more and more.

Earlier tonight—July 15, 1972, he hears my voice at the door: "Don't wait up, I'll be late." Daringly he comes out of the wine cellar. Darling, you're crazy, crazy! says Tita, embracing him; go back to your hiding place at once.

*   *   *

As he comes to the end of his story he trembles, obviously frightened out of his wits. He is saying that he only wanted to talk with us, to clear up some doubts; but he was going to leave, he hadn't meant to cause any trouble.

But I don't look at him; I look at Tita. There is no doubt: she really has fallen overwhelmingly in love with the young centaur. She has forgotten me, our sons, everything. She has eyes only for him. I realize that I must do something at once, because . . .

The door opens, a group of people burst in, shouting "Happy anniversary, happy anniversary!" Paulo and Fernanda, Júlio and Bela, Armando and Beatrice, Tânia and Joel. Bela is carrying a cake, Armando holds two bottles of wine and Tânia a bouquet. Suddenly I remember: it's the anniversary of the inauguration of the condominium, a date we always celebrate; that was why Paulo wasn't at the lounge, because he had been off calling the others to come to the party.

Bela drops the cake on the floor. Stunned, they all gaze at the centaur. They stand galvanized by that vision. Suddenly, "Call the guards!" screams Tânia hysterically. "For God's sake, call the guards!"

With a fearful cry, the centaur throws himself against the large picture window and disappears amid a shower of broken glass. "Wait!" screams Tita, running. Beatrice tries to hold her, but she pushes Beatrice away and runs out the door with all of us after her, Paulo shouting, "What the hell was that, Guedali? What was it?" Shut up! I scream. Just then we hear dogs barking and shots ringing out, several shots in succession. We run to the park and see the guards from a distance near the fountain—and the centaur, fallen in the midst of a pool of blood.

Tita runs ahead of me, still screaming. Making a desperate effort I catch up with her before she reaches the fountain and grab her by the arm. Let go of me, you animal! she screams, her face distorted with hatred and pain. She resists, scratching my face, pounding my chest with her fists. Finally she weakens and, almost fainting, lets me lead her back to the house. I lay her on the bed. The doorbell is ringing insistently.

I go down and open it. It's Pedro Bento, a revolver still in his hand. He is gray with fright and sweating profusely. Was it your son, Guedali? he asks in a low voice. I don't answer, I just look at him. He continues: Forgive me, Guedali, if that was your son. The other guys got scared and started shooting, when I got to the fountain he was already dying. I only fired a mercy shot in his head so he wouldn't suffer.

Upstairs Tita sobs convulsively. It's all right, I say to Pedro Bento, and close the door.

Strangely, I hardly remember anything of the three days that followed. I know that the morning after the centaur died I went downtown. I didn't go to the office as I normally do, but checked into a small hotel. I remember going to a travel agency and getting my passport in order, as well as taking money out of the bank, selling stocks and bonds, and buying clothes and a suitcase. However, the rest of what happened during the long hours of those days I don't remember. Most of the time I stayed locked in my hotel room watching TV or sleeping (I slept a great deal; when I woke up, I didn't know whether it was night or day). I must have done some thinking. But I have no memory of what I thought about, what plans I made, or why I was proposing to travel. I only know that when the moment came, I went to the airport, arriving just in time to catch the plane. A short time later I was on my way to Morocco.

MOROCCO
JULY 18–SEPTEMBER 15, 1972

I FOUND THE CLINIC IN A DESOLATE STATE. THE WALLS, DIRTY before, were now crumbling; the gate no longer even existed. A stray dog was napping in the sun; when I approached he began to snarl threateningly. I clapped my hands and called out. Finally the doctor's assistant, a sullen old man, showed me in. Answering my questions in monosyllables, he led me through the garden, where a few rosebushes still survived in the midst of a jungle of weeds. Lizards sunbathed on the ruined fountain. I didn't see anyone. Apparently the clinic no longer lodged any patients.

The Moroccan doctor—every much aged, his complete baldness now countered by a straggly gray beard—was amazed to see me. What fair wind has blown you here, Guedali? Is this a business or a pleasure trip? It's sort of a business trip, I said, something I have in mind. He sensed that this wasn't the time to press the subject, and asked after Tita and the boys. We conversed a little, and I told him I was tired, asking if he could arrange a room for me. And I added: I'll pay the daily rate, naturally. His face lit up: But of course, Guedali, with the greatest pleasure! I assume you would prefer one of our first-class rooms. (It was obvious he was in desperate need of money.)

He took me to the room. It was the same one Tita and I had occupied after our surgery. Like the rest of the clinic, it looked totally abandoned: spiderwebs hanging from the ceiling, cracks in the walls, faded curtains. The doctor himself mentioned it: This room needs a good cleaning. My assistant will take care of it. But he'll do it tomorrow—now you must rest.

I spent a sleepless night pacing back and forth, first inside my room and later out in the garden. When dawn came the Moroccan doctor appeared.

"Well then!" In spite of his lighthearted tone, he was apprehensive. But not very: he was an experienced man who knew the risks that threaten us (the rupture of a tiny artery in the brain, for example, can cause death) and perhaps a bit of a fatalist, due to the proximity of fanatical tribes, believers in predetermined destiny. He was a man who wouldn't be surprised at anything I told him, no matter how unusual or dramatic my answer might be.

"I want to have another operation. I want to become a centaur again."

He was not merely surprised. He was dumbfounded. All the marks of astonishment—popping eyes, gaping mouth, pallor (not too perceptible on him because of his dark complexion) were stamped on his face. "But"—he stammered. "But" —he gripped the bedstead for support. He had been unprepared for this.

"You want to do *what*, Guedali?"

"I want to have another operation. I want to be a centaur again."

A surgeon has to recover from shock rapidly. The next instant he was already calm, smiling and normal in color. He gave the situation a quick evaluation and opted to ignore what I had said, at least for the moment.

"Well," he said, "let's have some breakfast. Later we can talk."

Breakfast was served on a little table in the garden. The cups were still porcelain, but chipped; and the linen napkins were yellowed—things that meant nothing to me. I want to be a centaur again, I had said, and having said it I discovered what

had brought me to Morocco. I was surprised in a way, but not
much. I had just put into words a tormenting anxiety, and the
very act of verbalization calmed me in an odd way. Although
I wasn't exactly radiant, I felt at least modestly happy. So this
was what I wanted! To gallop once more through the fields, in
full possession of my four hooves. I no longer wanted Tita, nor
my children, nor my business, nor my friends, nor the
horizontal condominium, nothing. The Moroccan doctor (a true
artist) was chatting nonchalantly about the superiority of
Turkish coffee. It was is if I hadn't said a thing. But I wasn't
interested in coffee.

"Well, Doctor, what do you say?"

He looked at me. Less surprised than before, but more
alarmed. So I had been serious. So what I had said wasn't just
the product of a mind still confused by the journey, by the
time change, by sleeping badly. The word "centaur" wasn't
something left over from the night, it wasn't a nightmare
intruding into the wakeful world. I could see in his eyes that he
felt my determination, perhaps not very firm yet, but growing
firmer as the minutes passed.

"Well?"

"But what are you talking about, Guedali?" He was
frowning now, misery in his face. His lips seemed to tremble.
"What is it you are saying to me?"

"You heard me, Doctor. I want to become a centaur once
again."

Oh, this is very serious, he murmured. Very serious
indeed. He let his napkin fall to one side and leaned back in his
chair.

"I assumed it must be something serious, Guedali. Some
complication that had arisen because of your surgery. But I
never thought it was *this*. I swear I didn't."

"Well, it is."

"And may I know," he asked, his eyes moist, "what it is
that leads you to renounce the human condition, after all the
effort you've made—I've made—to achieve it? May I know,
Guedali, why you come to me with this request? I believe I
have the right to know, my friend. After all—"

"Yes," I interrupted him. "After all, you gave us human form, Tita and I. I am very grateful to you. But ..." I hesitated. "Look here, Doctor, I'd prefer you didn't ask me too many questions. Just please tell me if you are willing to help me or not."

"Of course I am!" he answered, indignant. "You have no right even ask such a question! But what I want to know is what helping you really means. If you wanted to kill yourself, Guedali, I wouldn't provide you with a gun."

"It has nothing to do with suicide. It's ..."

What was it, really? I didn't know. We looked at each other rather stupidly. What were we talking about? Who were we? What did it all mean?

A sudden transformation came over his face. In the twinkling of an eye he became very tranquil; it was as if we were discussing soccer or the weather. He leaned forward.

"It's all right, Guedali. If you don't want to tell me, you don't have to."

Settling back in his chair, he smiled once more. I understood: he had given up trying to question the logic of what I had said. He had incorporated the idea into the context surrounding us, which was, after all, rather absurd: the ruined clinic, the silent assistant who was now removing coffee cups and silverware, the exotic plants in the abandoned garden, the birds that fluttered above our heads. And the Maghrib, the Berbers, the camels and tribal drums.

"I'll only ask you one more time: do you really want to do this?"

"Yes, I do."

"And what if I tell you that it's technically impossible?"

Ah, so that was it. He was attacking another flank. He was giving me the medical reasoning, using the difficulties of the operation as his argument. The part that had been removed no longer existed, and even if it did, even if it had been preserved under special conditions—at extremely low temperatures, like the bodies of American millionaries who hope to be revived someday—there would be the reimplantation, always difficult. Then, there were the transformations undergone by the remaining parts, meaning my present body. I was no longer the front half of a centaur, I was a complete human being.

I answered that I was willing to run all the risks. I would be glad to sign a declaration absolving him of all responsibility for what might occur in consequence of the transplant.

"But the transplant of what, Guedali?"

"Of a horse's body," I said. "The body of a living horse."

This time he really was alarmed. A horse, Guedali? He laughed: It's absurd. Your organism would reject foreign tissue. But he stopped laughing, thought a little, and said hesitantly: "Still, there are cases of pigs' livers being transplanted into human bodies, in Negroes. And monkeys' hearts . . ."

"So?" I said.

He didn't seem convinced. It's terribly risky, Guedali, it's one chance in a million—or less. Besides that, he pondered, there is another problem. He showed me his trembling hands.

"You see? I'm old, Guedali, I haven't performed an operation for ages. I don't know if I'll be able—"

I interrupted him. "That makes absolutely no difference, Doctor. I trust you absolutely."

He stood up. "Is that true, Guedali? Is it true you really trust me?"

I too rose. "Whatever the outcome, Doctor." He couldn't contain himself; he embraced me.

"Thank you, Guedali," he said, wiping his eyes. "It's so long since I've heard those words. I was needing to hear someone say that."

He smiled.

"We can do it, Guedali. Who cares! We'll battle together. I have no idea what your reason is for wanting to be a centaur again, but so what! I'm a doctor, you're my client, and I will carry out your wishes. Furthermore. I will give this operation the best of my abilities, you can be sure. It represents as much to me as it does to you. It is my rehabilitation, Guedali. Can you imagine it? Not only was I the first doctor to transform a centaur into a human being, I shall also be the first doctor to transform a human being back into a centaur! The medical world will reverberate!"

He stopped, recovering from his impulsiveness.

"Sorry, Guedali. I think I got carried away with my own enthusiasm."

Never mind, I said. But he barely paid attention to me; he was already completely absorbed by the idea of the operation. He began walking up and down.

"Wants to be a centaur again ... hm ... wants to be a centaur again. Let me see ..."

He paused, placed a hand on my shoulder.

"It won't be easy, Guedali. A very, very delicate operation. We will have to take every precaution. The horse, for example, must be a well-bred animal, young, healthy. We will prepare him carefully. And you, Guedali, will have to be given rigorous preoperative treatment. You will take drugs to eliminate your antibodies. Your organism must recognize familiar proteins in the horse's tissues, not enemies. This will take time."

He hesitated an instant and then added, "And, I should warn you, it won't be cheap."

I am prepared for any sacrifice, I answered. Money is the very least.

"Wonderful!" he said. "And I know you are a man of substance, Guedali."

He looked at me curiously.

"Pardon me for prying into your personal affairs ... but I must ask you again, why is it you want to go back to being a centaur?"

(Did I really know?)

"I'd prefer not to talk about it," I said. "But I have very serious reasons, very ... profound reasons. Believe me."

He smiled understandingly.

"Of course, Guedali. To gallop through the fields ... I know, it's an ancestral urge. Even I, who only did a little riding when I was young, at times feel this fascination."

He was quiet for a moment, as though thinking. Suddenly, his face lit up.

"I'll make you a proposal. If you advance me a little

money, we can have an excellent dinner tonight. What do you say? A Moroccan couscous and an excellent French wine, eh?"

By all means, I said, taking the money out of my pocket. His eyes shone when he saw the dollars and the Swiss francs. Strong currency, he said, disguising his excitement, that's good, Guedali.

We ate in the clinic's dining room, served by the silent old helper. The couscous was delicious; the wine was strong and made us happy. The doctor told me the story of his life. Born the son of a shoemaker in a small Moroccan village, he had always wanted to become a doctor. By good luck, an old American millionaire took a liking to him and left him enough money to study medicine in Paris. He winked: In exchange for certain favors, naturally.

"I specialized in neurosurgery. Sometime after my graduation I began to be interested in sex-change operations."

He giggled: "In a way, an homage to my patron. But neither he nor I could have guessed that I would end up operating on mythological beings. It's much more interesting than removing brain tumors, I can assure you."

He laughed again as he cleaned his plate, burped (Pardon me, Guedali!), and sighed in satisfaction.

"It's been a long time since I had a good meal, Guedali. A very long time indeed."

We lighted cigars and smoked in silence for a few minutes. He leaned toward me like an accomplice: "Speaking of mythological beings, you have your secret, Guedali, but I have mine also . . . except that I'm not selfish, I want to share mine with you. If you like, that is . . . do you want to know my secret, Guadali?"

I said yes, although I wasn't all that interested in his secrets.

"Then come with me."

We went to one of the rooms, the most isolated one. He opened the door and signaled me to enter. Only then did he turn on the light. What I saw horrified me. There in a heavily barred cage was an amazing creature—amazing even to me, an ex-centaur. It was a woman; or rather, the head and bust were those of a woman, connected to a body that I identified, after a slight hesitation, as that of a lioness. She was lying down, her front legs extended in front of her, and staring fixedly at us. It was a strange emotion I felt, a mixture of tension and repugnance, of pity and disgust. I felt the solidarity that invalids, the deformed, and the sick feel among themselves; but also the anger that invalids, the deformed, and the sick feel toward each other. I felt like laughing and crying all at once. In the end I felt myself blushing. From shame, but what was I ashamed of? As for her, she seemed not to notice our presence

"Meet Lolah," said the doctor, and the tone of pride in his voice made the thing still more absurd. He spoke to her in French: "Say hello to our friend Guedali, Lolah. He is from Brazil."

"Merde!" screamed the creature, and turned her face to the wall.

"But what is it?" I said when I was able to speak. The doctor laughed.

"What is it? Don't you know, Guedali? You, a mythological creature, don't recognize a companion from the collective unconscious? It's a sphinx, Guedali."

Sphinx; Of course. Half woman, half lioness. It hadn't occurred to me before because of the image that I had of the Egyptian sphinx; this was not a gigantic stone statue with a crumbling face. The face was lovely; coppery skin, great green eyes, full lips, tawny hair, shapely breasts. The paws and body of a lioness, tail switching. A sphinx, of course. So sphinxes did exist.

"She is just as real as you are," said the doctor, as if guessing my thoughts. *"N'est-ce pas,* Lolah? And she is very intelligent. Want to see?"

He moved closer to the cage.

"Come on, Lolah. Tell the gentleman here what walks with four legs in the morning, two legs in the afternoon and three legs at night."

The creature didn't answer. She remained facing the wall. The doctor slyly reached through the bars and gave her tail a brusque pull. The sphinx leaped up.

"Merde!" she howled in fury. *"Merde. Merde!"*

She threw herself against the bars, pounding them with incredible blows. I drew back in fear. But the cage was very strong and withstood the attack. The Moroccan doctor laughed at my fright.

"All right, Lolah," he said, "you've impressed our visitor enough. We'll leave you in peace, dear. Good night, sleep tight. You'll forgive us?"

The sphinx didn't answer. Lying down, her head hidden between her front paws, she seemed to be sobbing. The doctor put out the light and we left.

We sat down in the garden. The doctor's assistant appeared and served us wine.

"Where did this creature come from?" I asked, still shaken. A feeble joke: "From Egypt, by chance?"

He chuckled.

"No, not from Egypt. From Tunisia. A friend of mine, another doctor who is fond of big-game hunting, found her. For a long time he had overheard the natives talking about an animal with the body of a lioness and a woman's breasts; and although he had heard of sphinxes, he didn't believe the story. But when they showed him her footprints, he decided to follow them. After a four-day trek they came to a steep canyon between high mountains, a place from which his prey couldn't escape. His helpers blocked one end of the gorge, and he advanced from the other end. When he saw her at last, he became very excited and resolved to take her alive. Lolah tore three dogs and two Tunisians into pieces before they managed to capture her in a net. My friend was entranced by her beauty. Knowing of my experience with the centaur operations, he brought her here in hopes that I could transform her into a normal woman. I think he was in love."

The doctor took a sip of wine. "Good wine, this," he sighed. "It's been years, Guedali, since I drank decent wine."

An airplane flew over the place with a deafening roar.

"The king's airplane," he commented. "It passes over here frequently. Sometimes I think that—"

I interrupted him.

"Yes, and then? What happened?"

"Happened? Oh, yes. Well, I saw at once that it would be impossible to achieve any acceptable results whatsoever. You two, you and Tita, already had almost half of the normal human body, and front legs that could serve as human legs. Lolah's only human parts were her breasts and head. After the surgery, providing it were successful, she would be reduced to an even stranger monster, a dwarf with lion's paws. I told my friend all this. He became so depressed that he decided to go away, and he left the sphinx with me. Only a few days later he died of a heart attack. He was a very impressionable man; he believed in spells and evil curses, which is what probably killed him. And I kept Lolah. In the beginning, she would have nothing to do with me—and she still goes through phases when she attacks me, as you saw. But little by little I managed to gain her trust. I taught her French ... she is very intelligent, learns everything with the greatest ease. She reads a great deal. But she speaks very little. To this day I know practically nothing about her life."

He drained his glass.

"Remarkable, this wine. Simply remarkable ... but, as I was telling you: I concluded that I couldn't operate on the creature. The problem arose of what I was to do with her. I confess to you that the idea of exhibiting her in public crossed my mind. I could charge plenty; by then I was already having financial troubles, and I needed money. With great tact I introduced the subject to her. She became furious, and screamed that she would rather die. I respected her modesty, Guedali. You see, today I'm nothing more than an old, ruined doctor, and my dealings were not always the cleanest, but I still have a little dignity. I keep that room for Lolah, and she lives with all possible comfort; I don't know if you noticed, but I even had a television set put in. As for the cage, it isn't exactly a prison. Its purpose is to contain her during the attacks of fury which, as I told you, are not rare. In the final analysis they are for her own security; she herself recognizes it. Poor Lolah. 'At bottom,' she says, 'I'm a wild beast.' "

He laughed.

"Beast? No, she's not, Guedali. She is a poor girl, nothing more. A solitary, enigmatic creature."

I asked him if I could talk to her. He stared at me; there was a little suspicion, a little jealousy in that stare, although he tried to conceal them.

"Very well, if you like . . . I don't know if she will talk to you. You could try taking her food in tomorrow. If you give me the money I'll send for some roast mutton. It's one of her favorites."

That night, my second at the clinic, was another wakeful night for me. I wandered about the garden, too restless for sleep. Strong emotions simmered inside me. What have I done? I asked myself. Because now I was coming to my senses, blaming myself for having obeyed a wild impulse. For having left my wife, children, and friends behind and hopping on an airplane to Morocco. For finding the doctor and telling him I wanted to be a centaur again. What had set this series of outrages in motion? The sight of Tita and the centaur in each other's arms? His death? True, Tita had been embracing a centaur, the centaur had tried to run away and gotten killed. Wouldn't the normal course of action be to say, Come here, Tita, let's talk this over, let's see what happened, let's identify what's real in this situation and what's imaginary. Wouldn't that be the thing to do? But no, instead of this Guedali turns his back and runs off. To Morocco, just as if he were going out for cigarettes. Couldn't I have at least talked to Paulo?

Reasonable questions for someone coming to his senses. But not having fully come to my senses, being still suspended between sky and earth, like the winged horse, I described circles in the clouds, I flew so high and fast that I became dizzy. I didn't answer my own questions. I preferred to smile like an idiot, or else sob—also like an idiot; I preferred to give myself up to the vertigo that meant not having the slightest idea what was happening or what would happen. Principally, I thought dizzily about Lolah, whose image obscured all others. After seeing what I had seen, I could even ask myself: Did I really live before this? Was that life, or was it a dream? Such was the impression caused by the extraordinary creature, the exquisite sphinx. Before her all else, no matter how important or notable it might have seemed, ceased to exist. Family? Sphinx. Work? Sphinx. Friends? Sphinx. House? Sphinx. Car? Sphinx. House? Sphinx. Clothes? Sphinx. Barbecued ribs? Sphinx. The sphinx surpassed everything in terms of the awesome; in terms of the marvelous. She even overshadowed the image of a centaur galloping on the pampas. Of a centauress galloping on the pampas. Of a centaur and centauress galloping together on the pampas.

Lolah. I walked past the building where her room was. The window had been bricked up, no doubt the doctor's precaution against possible intrusions. But I could sense her inside. First, pacing back and forth in the cage as I walked to and fro in the garden; then standing motionless just as I did, her gaze steady as mine was, thinking of me just as I thought of her.

I could hardly wait for day to come so I could see her again.

The next morning the silent employee brought me a tray of roast mutton. I hurried to take it to Lolah.

I went into her room with great anxiety. How would she react? Would she speak to me? Would she accept food from my hands?

She was lying in the cage belly down, reading a book. At the moment I came in, she was turning a page, and since her paws were too heavy and clumsy for this, she used her tongue. It was pathetic. I was moved.

"*Bonjour,* Lolah."

She looked indifferently at me, and did not answer my greeting. I brought your lunch, Lolah, I said. And I added: It's roast mutton.

She turned around swiftly, her eyes flashing. But immediately she tried to appear indifferent.

"Very well," she said. "Put it inside the cage, please."

I squeezed the tray between the iron bars and handed it to her. She pushed her book aside and began to eat. My presence obviously bothered her, but in truth I was unable to leave. I was fascinated by the lion woman.

With her paws she quickly tore the mutton apart. But to eat it, she had to lean over and grasp the bites with her teeth, a painful thing to see.

"Do you want some help?" I asked.

"It's not necessary," she answered drily, and immediately I saw that my question had been tactless and embarrassing. I watched her in silence.

Now that I was closer to her, I could study her better. Something in that beautiful, well-defined face seemed familiar. Was it her shapely mouth, with its surprisingly small, even teeth? Was it her eyes?

All at once I knew: Lolah reminded me of the lion tamer from the circus. She was much younger, of course, and she didn't have the lion tamer's light complexion, but they were very much alike. The lion tamer. Where might she be? And the girl on the terrace of the mansion?

"You may take the tray," she said. She had finished eating. I came closer, put my hand through the bars, and—how dangerous it was!—caressed her hair with a quick, timid motion. It really was a risk; she could have torn my hand to shreds with one paw-swipe. But she didn't do a thing. She didn't look at me or move, except to hide her face between her paws. I took the tray and went out.

Little by little, I gained her trust.

We talked a great deal. She wasn't laconic as the doctor had said; she liked to talk to me. She told me the story of her life. Different from me, she had not been born of a human mother, but of a lioness. At first she was rejected by the other felines in the lion pride, and treated as a pariah who was only given unwanted scraps from the hunt. At the age of four she was finally accepted by them, after killing her first native. From that time on she had wandered about with the pride through the mountains of North Africa. It was a hard life; pursuing gazelles, attacking herds in the silence of the night, living always under the threat of hunters who, with ever more sophisticated arms, kept eliminating her companions. Besides all this, she was besieged by the lusty young lions who wanted her for a mate.

"But actually," she said, making a face, "I found them repulsive, with their smelly manes and stupid expressions. I didn't let them breed with me, in spite of the desire that often made me run madly across the plateau, searching for a lake where I could refresh my burning face."

Finally her capture, her seclusion in the clinic.

"I like the doctor very much. He treats me well, and I respect him as I would a father. At times he antagonizes me, calling me an animal and so on. But I can't complain. I have my attacks of fury too, and in spite of the dangers I represent—at bottom, I *am* a wild animal—he keeps me safe here, takes care of me, even at his own sacrifice."

Long conversations. I on the outside of the cage, she on the inside, in her favorite position—lying down, her front paws crossed, her head bent slightly, her long hair falling over her breasts, those lovely breasts that trembled when she laughed. She was beautiful.

One day I kissed her. There was something pathetic in that first kiss, with the bars of the cage between us. I held her head between my hands, searching for her mouth with mine. She protested weakly but in the end she returned my kiss passionately.

Why did you do that, Guedali? she murmured, almost complaining. I couldn't answer, because I didn't know what to say. Because she had a beautiful face (and a lioness's body)? Because I hadn't been to bed with a woman for so long? Because of a certain attraction for the grotesque? I didn't know. But the result was her falling in love with me, poor creature. It was instantaneous and violent.

We restricted ourselves to kisses. I kept taking her her food; I would go in to find her walking back and forth in the cage, her tail switching impatiently. The minute she saw me, her face would open into a smile; she didn't care about the food, all she cared about were the kisses. Sometimes if I were delayed for one reason or another, she would be sulky or furious, pounding the bars of the cage with her paws—a sight that made me tremble.

* * *

Soon kisses alone no longer satisfied her. Touch my breasts, she begged me. I would caress her; it made her wild. She herself said it: Oh, Guedali, you drive me wild.

Once, after a prolonged kiss, she looked deep into my eyes.

"I want to ask you something."

She hesitated one instant and then said quickly in a husky voice: "I want you to sleep with me, Guedali."

At first I thought she was kidding. Sleep with her? No, I hadn't thought about that, not even when I myself was most aroused. But make love with *her*? No. For sex, I could have gone to one of the city bars and found a woman. Lolah? No. Kissing her was all right, but to actually . . .

She saw my hesitation.

"Please, Guedali. It's nothing unreasonable I'm asking. You used to be a centaur, you used to make love with a centauress."

I didn't know what to say.

"Don't you love me, Guedali?" she asked, her eyes now full of tears. "Don't you like me?"

"That's not the point," I said. "It's just that . . ."

I deperately searched for some explanation as she stared at me. A sudden inspiration came:

"I can't even get in there, Lolah. The cage is padlocked shut."

Her answer came at once, with a cunning smile, poor thing.

"Just steal the doctor's key, Guedali. It's easy, the old man leaves his key ring all over the place. He even left it here in this room once. I myself, if I had hands . . ."

She stopped and lowered her eyes. The effort had been too much for her. I felt like a worm, a miserable wretch. I took her face between my hands.

"All right, my love. Soon you'll have me at your side."

A strange coincidence: the next day the doctor went to town and left his office door open. As I passed by it I saw the ring of keys on the table.

A slight vacillation. A quick look to one side, then the other. No, the sinister employee wasn't around—I went in. Quickly I identified the key to the cage (it had an "L" engraved on it), took it off the ring and went out as furtively as I had gone in.

Night. I am seated in my room, the key in my hand. Undecided.

Lolah? Yes, her beautiful face, passionate mouth, and full breasts—and I, how long had it been since I had made love to a woman? But the fact remained that she wasn't a woman. A woman's face, a woman's breasts. But the rest of her body was animal. She had hide, fur, a tail. And those padded feet, armed with terrible claws. And the animal scent of her. And fleas, maybe.

Not so different from my old body? No, not so different from the centaur I had been. But now I was no longer a centaur.

As I thought about Lolah, images began to form inside my head. I saw Tita coming to the clinic. (How had she discovered me? Never mind, that was another question.) Tita, and Paulo and Fernanda, and Júlio and Bela, all my friends. The whole group invading the clinic, running through the corridors, opening the doors of all the rooms—and suddenly coming upon me, in the cage with Lolah, on top of Lolah. Now I saw the look of horror on their faces, of terror, of outrage, of nausea, of disgust (Paulo) maybe even of envy (Júlio).

These images made me incredibly excited. Yes, my penis was erect now, not completely, but hardening every second. Yes, I wanted to! I got up, looked at my reflection in the mirror. What I saw there was the face of a satyr, flashing eyes and bared teeth: I did want to.

Stealthy as a thief, I made my way through the darkness to her room.

I went in. By the pallor that filtered through the skylight in the roof I distinguished her figure, her lovely profile, her thrusting breasts.

Once more I hesitated. But I couldn't see her body: it was an amorphous mass hidden in shadow. Besides, I was already here. Why not? I asked myself. Why not?

I went closer. She seemed unaware of my presence; she was lying down, and remained very still. With trembling fingers I opened the door of the cage and went in. I lay down beside her, stroked her face, her breasts. And her body. Her lioness's body. My God, my God, my God!

I had already seen great felines at close quarters when I was in the circus. I had of course held cats on my lap. But I had never touched a lioness. What ... what voluptuous opulence. The great body seemed totally charged with electricity, the soft fur stood up at my touch, powerful masses of muscle rippled beneath the skin like startled little rabbits under a rug. Her tail rolled up, tense and vibrating.

She turned to face me. The desire that rose from that powerful body engulfed her, one could see; she could barely tolerate it. There was anguish in her eyes, passion of course, but anguish too, in her dilated nostrils and glistening teeth.

"Come," she whispered.

I was trembling so hard I could barely get my clothes off. There was a terrible moment of hesitation. She was still lying down: how should I go about it? But I knew, something inside me knew. I mounted her from behind, stroking her breasts, kissing her neck hungrily, and penetrated her as a lion would have. She bit my arms as lionesses do lions. And moaned, and cried out so much that I had to put my hand over her mouth for fear of the doctor hearing us.

The copulation was short, the orgasm, colossal. Mountains of Tunisia! What an orgasm that was! You know nothing, oh mountains, if you have never known an orgasm like that!

When it was over we lay on the floor of the cage, gasping.

Little by little I got myself together, began to emerge from the depths of that dark and turbulent sea. Only then did I realize that something was pinning me down by the neck.

It was her left paw. Cautiously, I lifted it off me with a disagreeable thought: if Lolah were to have one of her temper tantrums just now ...

"Guedali," she murmured. "Guedali, my love. Thank you, Guedali."

I kissed her, went out of the cage, dressed and sneaked back to my room as stealthily as I had come.

I went back on the nights that followed. All the nights, every one.

During the day, we maintained appearances. I continued to take her roast mutton and converse with her. The doctor and his assistant saw only two good friends, two creatures with curious affinities. It's true that Lola would wink at me; it's true that there was complicity in her smile; it's true that, as soon as we were alone she would murmur, "Kiss me, Guedali. Kiss me, now!"

I didn't like that; it was an unnecessary risk. Nor did I like the way she threw herself upon me when I came to the cage at night, often scratching me with her claws. Furthermore, my pent-up hunger for sex had been satisfied—and thus the grotesqueness of the situation became ever plainer to me. Coitus with a sphinx. Tita and the others would probably laugh. Simply laugh: screwing a sphinx, Guedali! Oh, come on, Guedali!

The day of my operation was approaching. The Moroccan doctor had found a donor animal, a handsome Arabian stallion, very young and vigorous.

"Well, Guedali? Didn't I make a good choice? Get acquainted with him; soon he will be part of you."

I looked at the horse in the stable, and the whole thing now seemed very strange to me. Horse? Operation? Centaur? Had I said that? Yes, I had said that, but was I serious? Yes, I was. But had the doctor interpreted my words literally? Hadn't I been speaking in metaphors? Even metaphors could be spoken in a solemn tone. The doctor might well have separated the real from the symbolic. Did he really want to do this? Would it be in his interest? Those questions aside, had he now become so emotionally involved as to want to transform me into a centaur no matter what? And wasn't I going to become a centaur no matter what, at least to keep my word? Or to participate in an experiment? Or to get what I deserved?

It was all very bewildering. In the midst of so much confusion, the affair with Lolah was only making things worse.

She was more and more possessive. She complained about everything: I was late, I didn't show her enough affection. Worst of all, she didn't want me to become a centaur. She wanted me to have an operation; but she demanded that I have the doctor graft me onto the body, not of a horse but of a lion.

A lion man? I would have laughed and laughed, if I hadn't been feeling so bad. Lion man? It was absurd—no, it was the crowning absurdity.

A centaur, with great effort, becomes a man; later, he goes through a crisis and decides to become a centaur again; then he doesn't really know if he wants to be a centaur again or not; meanwhile, he meets a crazy sphinx who wants to transform him into a lion man! Ridiculous. Mythological delirium.

It's impossible, Lolah, I would say. To start with, I don't even know if I could find a lion available for the transplant. Of course you could, she replied, all you have to do is hire some poachers. Or else make contacts with some circus owners. For the love of God, I would say, you don't want to transplant me onto a circus lion's body—old and probably impotent! Besides, I added, it's a difficult operation, very hazardous.

"But wouldn't you do it for me?" she asked, her lips trembling, her eyes full of tears. "Wouldn't you?"

"Myself, yes. But what about the doctor? He'd never consent to do the operation. To turn you over to me afterward? He's too jealous for that, you know it yourself."

"That old fool!" she would roar. "I'll kill that old fool yet! I'll kill all of you yet!"

The blows she unleashed on the bars of the cage convinced me that she meant what she said. I began to think about getting out.

By this time the Moroccan doctor had begun to suspect something.

One afternoon as he was examining me, he asked me about the scratches on my arms.

"Oh, that?" I said, trying to look indifferent. "I don't know. I guess I got scratched when I was working with the roses in the garden."

He looked at me distrustfully.

"Be careful, Guedali. The medication you're taking eliminates the defenses of your organism. Any slight cut could be fatal."

Fatal? So was my life in danger? Besides all the other things that were happening?

It was time to get out of there. Definitely time to take off. I'd wait until later to discover if I did or didn't want to be a centaur again. I decided to leave the next day.

Little did I know what was in store for me.

That night I was awakened by the doctor. He had a syringe in his hand.

"What is it?" I asked, jarred out of sleep. "What's this injection for?"

"It's a sedative," he said. "I'm going to perform your operation tomorrow."

Before I could say anything, he shoved in the needle. Immediately I fell into a deep torpor. I wanted to stay awake, I wanted to call out and tell him that I had changed my mind about the operation, but I couldn't move or talk. In this state, I was placed on a stretcher by the assistant and taken to the operating room. There was the doctor, wearing mask, apron, and gloves. All I could see of him were his eyes looking hard at me. The assistant gave me another shot—this time in a vein—and I saw nothing more.

I woke up very dizzy and weak but—what immediately surprised me—in no pain. And in a bed. A regular bed, narrow. More and more surprised, I touched myself. I didn't find any layers of gauze. More surprising still; I didn't find horsehide or hooves, or a tail, nothing. Down below I still had my own legs. But what had happened? I turned around. The Moroccan doctor was seated beside the bed, smoking and gazing at me.

"It wasn't possible to perform your operation," he said in a

toneless voice. "There was a slight accident. You see, we had
to kill Lolah. My assistant shot her. Fortunately he is always
armed."

I couldn't believe it: Why? What did Lolah do?

"She had one of her attacks of fury. She got out of her
cage, went into the operating room. There was no other way."

From what he told me, I reconstructed the scene.

I am under anesthesia on the operating table. The doctor
begins the transplant, starting with the Arabian horse. It is
harder than he had realized; he has indeed lost his touch. He
fumbles with the instruments, pauses often without knowing
what to do next. The hours go by.

While this is going on, Lolah waits in the cage for me to
bring in her lunch. At first impatient, then hysterical, she begins
to scream for me, for the doctor, but nobody comes.

Then she realizes that the door to the cage is open. She
leaps out and stalks through the deserted corridors of the
clinic, calling for me. All of a sudden she remembers about the
operation. Infuriated, she invades the operating room where
the doctor has finally managed to remove from the horse those
parts that will be grafted onto my body. At the first glimpse of
her he realizes the danger: Lolah is not herself. Go back to your
room, he orders, but she seems not to hear him. Give me my
Guedali, she snarls, advancing slowly toward the doctor. I want
my man, I want him whole. Be careful! the doctor yells,
everything is sterilized here! She leaps upon the horse, or rather
its hindquarters, and destroys it with her claws. The terrified
doctor shrinks into a corner. As she gathers herself for the lethal
blow, the assistant pulls out his revolver and fires six shots into
Lolah's face and neck.

"At first I didn't figure out," he continued, putting out
his cigarette, "how she had managed to get out. It was only later
that I saw how it was."

He got up, completely beside himself: body trembling, eyes
bulging, accusing finger pointed at me.

"You! You were to blame! You opened the door to the

cage, Guedali! You went inside there to abuse the poor little
thing, to satisfy your bestial instincts, you filthy centaur, you
Brazilian savage! That's why you were always scratched, you
scoundrel! You used her, you left her crazy with passion and
then didn't even close the door—knowing how unstable she
was, you bastard! I had to kill my sphinx, my adorable Lolah,
the only creature I ever loved! You miserable Jew! That's
what you always do to us Arabs! You Jews take away everything
we have, our tenderness, our love, everything!"

He threw himself at me. Weak though I was, I managed to
resist him; I pushed him over and he rolled on the floor,
sobbing.

I spent two more days in the clinic. During this time we
didn't speak to each other, the doctor and I. But strangely
enough we continued to walk side by side through the garden.
At times he would sway, and I helped him; other times it was I
who felt dizzy—perhaps an aftereffect of the sedatives—and
then he would take my arm.

I told him I was leaving. He said nothing. I offered him
money. He didn't accept it.

From his pocket he took a small wooden box. I opened it.
Inside was the paw of a lion—of a lioness; Lolah's left paw. I
shuddered, closed the lid, and looked at him. There was no
emotion at all in his face as he extended me his hand in a silent
farewell.

A SMALL FARM IN THE INTERIOR OF QUATRO IRMÃOS, RIO GRANDE DO SUL
OCTOBER 1972–MARCH 1973

I DIDN'T HAVE THE SLIGHTEST DESIRE TO GO BACK TO SÃO PAULO. I stayed there only long enough to change planes and continue to Pôrto Alegre. Once there, I went directly to my parents' house.

I rang the bell. My mother opened the door. When she saw me, she dropped the broom she was holding, brought her hands up to her face and let out a cry. My father came running: What is it, Rosa? What happened? The next instant the two of them were hugging me, slapping me, shouting, crying, laughing; suffocated, I couldn't escape them. Finally they took me inside and made me sit down between them on the sofa. My mother, who had been hugging me and laughing like a madwoman, suddenly became serious.

"It wasn't pretty, what you did, Guedali. To run off from your wife and children! You should be ashamed! I almost renounced you as my son. Tita is desperate, poor thing. She calls here every three days. But I told her, Tita, if he doesn't come back, he is no longer my son. And you can come and live with us if you want.'"

Even if she's a goy? I asked, which was perverse of me. My mother looked at me, hurt and offended: Aren't the

179

Gentiles people too? Why, Guedali! Then she went back to
her subject: But you, you ask me questions? You have no
business asking anything! You'd better tell us where you've
been, you shameless boy! Leave Guedali alone, said my father,
he's tired from his journey. Get his supper ready and make up
a bed. Tomorrow we'll talk.

I had a lot to discuss with my father. Not, as he
supposed, what had happened to me; that would be impossible.
How could I explain my trip to Morocco to him? How could
I tell him about Lolah? Could I show him the poor lion
woman's paw saying 'This, Papa, is all that is left of a
woman who loved me as no other ever did'? He wouldn't
believe it.

Besides, I didn't want to tell him anything. I wanted to
hear. I wanted to find out things. Had Guedali the centaur boy
been happy? Happier than the biped Guedali, or less happy? If
less happy (or more happy), then why my uncontrollable itch to
gallop, why the incessant search for something that I couldn't
even identify? If happier (or less unhappy) what should I do to
reverse the acceleration of my misery, to regain my lost
happiness? And what might be the secret of centaurs' happiness,
if indeed they were happy? That Tita had preferred another
of them to me? (To this last question my father couldn't
respond directly, but he could certainly furnish me elements
from which I could form my own answer.)

To make me understand, my father would have to go far
back in time. He would have to go back to his roots. He would
have to tell of his life in Russia, of the black horses of the
Cossacks, of his coming to Brazil, of his first days in the Jewish
colony, of the night I was born. (Might a winged horse exist or
not?) He would have to recall my first steps.

We would go for long walks, I asking him questions, he
stubbornly refusing to answer. Forget all that, Guedali, everything's
all right now. Yes, you had your problems, but who hasn't?
You are cured now; forget them. But Papa, did I or didn't I
have horses' hooves? That depends, son, on what you call
hooves. But the doctor in Morocco ... Morocco is a long way off,

Guedali, you needn't worry about those things any more. You
need to go back to your family. Forget about Morocco.

He would stop, take me by the arm.

"Go to Patagonia, Guedali. Telephone your wife, ask her to
come to Pôrto Alegre, and sign up for one of those tours. The
two of you could get on a ship, go to Patagonia, to Tierra del
Fuego. It's an excellent opportunity for you to get back
together again; Traveling by ship is relaxing, people have lots of
time to talk, to clear up their problems. Mina has a friend who
decided one day that she was tired of her husband. He took her
on that trip and it was just the thing; they made up. It's the
icebergs, Guedali. The icebergs are beautiful; they say that
people are moved, some actually cry."

He would break off the conversation so as not to lie. Even
worse than lying would have been his answering my questions
with other questions: What is the meaning of existence,
Guedali? Why are we in the world? Is there a God, Guedali?
Yes, it would have been far worse if, as we had our early-
morning tea on the porch, he should have put his hands on his
head and begun to cry, My God, what have I done with my life,
what? Far worse if he had knelt at my feet, taken hold of
where my fetlocks used to be (even fetlocks can't hold up a
father about to collapse), and supplicated: I don't want to die,
my son, I don't want to die! Lift me up on your back, gallop
away with me, save me.

My mother plagued me constantly. She had gotten an idea
into her head: she would organize a huge family reunion. She
would even manage to get Bernardo to come, putting ads in the
papers, calling him through public service announcements on
radio stations, or (her wildest idea) asking the TV comedian
Chacrina to appeal to her son on his nationwide program.

"I'm sure he wouldn't refuse me, Chacrina is a very good
man."

According to Mama, Tita and I would be reconciled during
this reunion. Oh, stop inventing things, I would tell her
irritably, mind your own business.

"But are you or aren't you separated?"

"Yes and no, Mama. It's our problem."

"What do you mean, yes and no? There's no such thing. Yes and no! You're either separated or not. If you are, then do it right, get a divorce, get legal papers, whatever. But if you're not, then make peace! Find each other again, hug, kiss, and you'll see how much you love each other. Think of the children, Guedali! If you and Tita don't want to make up for your own sakes, do it for theirs!"

I avoided my mother. Even Mina looked at me disapprovingly, although she didn't say anything. I preferred to talk to my father. He didn't answer my questions, but neither did he preach at me. And he gave me an important piece of information: he told me who had bought our land back in the colony. It was Pedro Bento's father, who now lived in Pôrto Alegre. I went to look him up and offered to buy the farm back.

This was a project that I had begun to formulate as soon as I had arrived back in Pôrto Alegre, after the first (and disappointing) conversations with my father. I began to think about buying some land, if possible near the place where we had had our farm; the fields where I had been a child, where, as a young centaur, I had been free to gallop. Or almost free: in short, as free as circumstances permitted. To go back to my roots, that was what I wanted. Alone. I needed to be alone so as to intensify the experience and meditate on it. At first I felt any farm of reasonable size would serve my purposes, but our very own farm would be ideal. However, the old farmer didn't agree.

"It's not that I don't want to sell, Guedali. I need the money, I need it a lot. But it's my duty to warn you that you're making a bad deal. The farm is completely abandoned, overgrown with weeds. There isn't even a road leading in there any more."

That was just what I wanted: nobody bothering me. I insisted, I even raised my offer. In the end he agreed, making me several recommendations.

"Machinery, Guedali. Machinery is the principal thing. I'll tell you, I was ruined for lack of machinery. Don't forget: machinery!"

Machinery. I could hardly disguise a smile. That was exactly what I didn't want, machinery. Hands, yes, and feet too. Machinery, never.

What I wanted was contact with the earth—an experience that I considered profound, visceral. I wanted to walk barefoot, I wanted to grow calluses on the soles of my feet, to make them even tougher, ever more like hooves. I wanted real hooves, in short. Hooves of which each layer should be the result of long walks over earth and stones, of meditation on the meaning of life. I intended to walk a great deal. To work, of course, but to walk too. If I grew tired, I would sit down on the ground. I wasn't afraid of my buttocks being pricked by thorns or stung by insects. In fact, that was what I wanted. Let the bites and cuts swell up. Let the swelling increase, let bones develop inside, attached to those of the pelvis, let legs emerge. In short, I wanted what developed to deserve the name "equine." I wanted a tail as well. Four horse's legs, one tail. There: a centaur.

Curious. The image I most frequently recalled of myself, as a centaur, was that of the bar mitzvah party. I saw myself wearing a dark suit, white shirt, tie, and skullcap. I saw the fringes of the prayer shawl falling over my equine haunches.

Yes, I wanted to pray again. One of the things I intended to build on the farm was a prayer house. Not exactly a synagogue, but a place where I could sit by candlelight and turn the pages of my father's old prayer book (a present I was sure he wouldn't refuse me). I wanted to think about God, about the human condition. I felt a need for the wisdom and consolation of religion.

Studying the precepts of the prophets and the Song of Songs, I hoped to ascend little by little into the bosom of Abraham. It wouldn't be easy. In my imagination that bosom became bigger and bigger, a mountain covered with white skin, crisscrossed underneath by channels containing precious milk. I would scale this mountain starting from the plain. As the slope grew steeper I would grasp, one by one, the stiff black hairs of the Levantine Abraham (each hair, a verse). I would ascend, just as I had climbed the mountain of the Masada in

Israel, toward the nipple enveloped by clouds as sweet and
rosy as the cotton candy my sons used to like so much.

My parents reacted with incredulity to my idea of living
on our old farm. Mama, in fact, threw a fit.

"You're crazy, Guedali! Crazy! Who in the world would
leave his wife and children to go off and live in the jungle!
There's nothing there but snakes, Guedali! How can you do
this? You're a refined man, a cultured man. Working the land
is for immigrants, Guedali. You won't go. I won't let you. It
cost us so much to get out of there—and now you want to go
back? No. I won't hear of it!"

Papa intervened: "I don't agree with the idea either, Rosa,
but after all, Guedali is an adult. And if he wants to go to the
country . . ."

(I thought my father would bring up Baron Hirsch, but
he didn't. Actually, as he grew older, his devotion was changing
to resentment and even hatred. Many times when he was
talking to himself, which often happened, he would swear at his
old idol: Stop bothering me, Baron! Get the hell away,
Baron!).

Mina also begged me not to go, but my decision had been
made. One morning I got on the bus and headed for Quatro
Irmãos.

Pedro Bento's father was right. Our old house was practically
in ruins. The door hung precariously by one hinge; the
windowpanes were broken and vines crept in through the
windows. The floorboards were rotten and you could see a
patch of blue sky through a large hole in the roof. I saw I
would have a lot of work to do, but I had no regrets. I hung
the relic of poor Lolah, the mummified paw, on the wall above
the place where my bed would be, and got to work. That very
day I went to town and bought materials to start repairing the
house. One week later it was habitable. The weeds around it
had been mowed and one could get down the little driveway.
Now I could devote myself to the fields. Soybeans and corn
would be my main crops, and I would tend the orchard. I

wanted to raise chickens, pigs, and a couple of milk cows. Only the basic necessities.

For weeks I saw almost no one. A few of the neighboring farmers would come to call, on the pretext of asking if I needed anything. Actually, they wanted to see the crazy fool who had left a good job in the city to come live in the woods. I didn't treat them badly, nor did I encourage them to come back. Soon they grew bored and stopped coming

One afternoon, I was busy weeding in the fields. As I knelt down, I had the sudden awareness that someone was watching me. I turned around and there he was, a peasant of indefinite age, ragged, his toothless mouth open in a smile: Peri.

He didn't recognize me, which wasn't strange, since he would remember me as a centaur. He just stood there gazing at me without a word.

"Are you looking for someone?" I asked.

He said no. He had come to the farm by chance, looking for work.

"I can do about anything," he added in his curious speech. "Mow hay, saw wood, take care of animals. I only want place to sleep and food. I'm hard worker, I guarantee."

All right, I said, you can start right now. He took off his ragged coat, spit on the palms of his hands, grabbed the hoe, and began to chop weeds.

He certainly was a hard worker. He cleared brush, milked the cows, drew water from the well, and even cooked. He spoke very little, barely answering my questions. Not that he was rude; on the contrary, he was well mannered and helpful. But quiet and reserved. I offered him a room in the house, but he preferred to sleep out in the stable.

"There's plenty of room out there. I'll fix up room for me, if you let me."

Yes, I'll let you, I said. But what about the cows? Won't they bother you? He showed his gums in a smile that had nothing innocent about it.

"Oh, I like cows, boss."

*   *   *

A strange man, Peri. Actually that wasn't his name, it was
Remião. But he said, you're the boss-man, you call me what
you like. Although he didn't talk much, he liked to sing, and on
certain nights, often when the moon was full, I would see
him out in the yard, arms raised upward, chanting a strange
melody. Magic prayers, he explained to me once, adding in a
confidential tone, I'm practicing to become medicine man, like
my grandfather.

This was his greatest dream. To cast spells, foretell the
future, things like that. Once he took me to his little room and
showed me his magic objects.

There was the bleached skull of Joaquim, the medicine
man. Peri had various forked sticks for locating wells, giant
snail shells, and crystal balls of different sizes. What most
interested me were stuffed or mummified examples of exotic
creatures: a lamb with two heads, a goat with six horns, a giant
centipede, a sea horse with twelve tiny legs.

"Just look at this one, boss."

I felt a strange emotion. What was the thing he was
showing me now? It looked like a mermaid, a little mummified
mermaid.

I stared at it. What was he trying to say to me, this man?
What was his secret? What was his connection with mythological
beings? With the unicorn, the griffin, the headless mule, the
werewolf? With the sphinx? What did Peri know about the
sphinx? What did he know about Lolah?

But what he held before me wasn't the mummy of a
mermaid. Upon examining it more closely I saw that it was a
gross artifact: the body of a monkey sewed to the lower half of
a large fish.

"An experiment I did, boss."

Going by a picture in an old book, he had tried to produce
a mermaid.

"But it didn't work. It died as soon as I finished the
operation."

He had an explanation for his failure: "I didn't say the
right words over it. If I had prayed the right words, it would

have lived. A spell cast with the right words is the strongest thing that exists."

"So make it rain with your spells," I said jokingly. "We sure do need it, the drought is bad."

He looked at me soberly.

"Don't joke about these things, boss. Don't joke."

Plowing the fields with a horse-drawn plow. Looking at the animal's hindquarters and ruminating on my discontent. Five months after coming to the farm, I was asking myself: What am I doing here? What have I discovered?

I walked through the fields barefoot a great deal. Barefoot. The soles of my feet had coarsened, but naturally they hadn't grown as thick as hooves. They weren't even as rough as the palms of my hands, which were covered with calluses from the hoe handle. I had walked miles, on sunny days and moonlit nights, in the rain and in the wind, but my questions were still unanswered.

Pray I did, every morning. Prayer shawl over my shoulders, book in hand, I would chant my prayers. Without results. Inner peace? None. Even the image of Abraham's bosom was fading in my mind. Indeed, my transcendental questions were subtly giving way to others: Why not rent a tractor? How much was fertilizer costing? What would happen to the soybeans, if we didn't get some rain? Looking at the horse hitched to the plow, I tried to leave these prosaic worries aside. Dammit, where was the centaur in me?

Little by little, I was forgetting Lolah. The mummified paw was still there above my bed, but it was becoming an inconspicuous object, as commonplace to my eyes as the cracks in the walls. Just like them, it had nothing more to say to me. I even had trouble remembering her face.

I had longings, it was true ... for my family. My sons ... I wished they could be here with me, milking cows and helping cultivate the land. It would be good for them. It would be good for me.

I missed Tita too, although I still recalled with bitterness that instant I had surprised her in the young centaur's arms.

That memory pursued me constantly, but at night it would
fade. As I fell asleep, I would touch the empty bed and murmur
her name. Tita. How I missed her mouth, her body. Love?
Yes. Probably. Almost definitely. Yes, it was love.

Why didn't I swallow my pride, then? Why didn't I go
back to Tita, to my children, my friends?

No. That I wouldn't do. Not without first clarifying the
doubts that tormented me. Not without first finding out who I
was: a crippled centaur, deprived of its equine body? A human
being trying to liberate himself from his fantasies?

Sitting at the door of the house one night, and gazing at
the fields bathed in moonlight, I asked myself these questions
one more time.

In front of the barn, his arms raised to the moon, Peri
intoned his chants. I looked at him with envy; there was a
man who had found his way.

Suddenly, I had an idea.

"Peri!"

He came, rather sulky at having been interrupted. I
invited him in. We sat down at the table and I opened a
bottle of cognac. (He refused; he didn't drink when he was
in his prayer phase.) I took a large swig. I need your help,
I said.

"If I can, boss," he said, surprised.

"I have a problem, Peri. A problem that I have to solve. It's
been bothering me for a long time."

And then I began to talk. I talked for hours; I emptied the
bottle of cognac, but I told him everything. My birth, my life
on the farm. I even reminisced over our childhood encounter
(he didn't react, only listened.) I spoke of our going to Pôrto
Alegre, of my flight through the fields, my life in the circus, my
meeting Tita, our trip to Morocco, the operation, the horizontal
condominium, the death of the young centaur, my second trip to
Morocco—everything. He listened, his eyes fixed on me, his
face illumined by the lantern. I told him that I wanted to be a
centaur again—the only way, I thought, of recapturing lost
truths. He, the medicine man (here he interrupted me: I'm not a

medicine man yet, boss, I'm still studying for that), might be able to help me.

"Make my horse's legs grow back, Peri."

"Boss, you're drunk."

"That may be. But I want horse's legs and hooves, Peri. Do you understand? Hooves."

I didn't want permanent hooves, I explained. I wanted deciduous ones, which would last a short time and then dry up and fall off. The important thing was that I should become a centaur for a few days.

I talked and talked, and he never opened his mouth, but only stared at me imperturbably. He really was strange, that peon. If he thought I was crazy, if he felt sorry for me, if he thought everything I said was a joke, he didn't show it. He seemed to be looking at me as though he were evaluating me, like someone who has a secret and hesitates before sharing it. I was irritated.

"Well, Peri? Want to try or not? If not, get your stuff together and leave this farm."

I can try, he said at last. I didn't fail to notice his omission of the word "boss." We were now partners in a new undertaking. By mobilizing the occult energy he received from ancestral gods, he would cause the four quarters of the horse to grow out of my body. I can try, he repeated, eyes gleaming and far away. Already the wheels of his mind were turning, tracing plans, deciding which plants to use, which spells to employ.

Give me some time, he said. He got up and went to the stable. I stayed there drinking. Finally I fell asleep, my head propped on the table.

I gave him plenty of time, mostly because we had a lot to do. The soybeans, our principal crop, were threatened by the drought that had started in December and was now prolonged well into January. The river, normally full, was now so low that in certain places its bed showed. I decided to make a dam and collect the sparse water that was left. The neighbors won't like it, said Peri. To hell with the neighbors, I answered irritably.

We took several days to do this. Finally we finished, and the water started to run through a ditch directly to the soybean field.

"We did it, Peri!" I shouted enthusiastically.

He didn't answer. He was looking at a half-buried object that had appeared in the now-visible streambed. I shut my mouth and looked too. Then I walked slowly over and picked up my old violin.

I hung up the violin—or what was left of it—beside Lolah's paw. That was a sad night. Sitting in my room, looking at the violin and the lioness's paw, I realized I was perhaps finding answers for the questions I had asked myself. I could look at those objects without pain, I realized with excitement and surprise. My excitement grew when, near midnight, I thought I heard the flutter of great wings. I ran outside, my expectations soaring. Dark clouds slid across the sky and from time to time covered the moon, but there was nothing else in sight.

No winged horse (which, according to certain mystics, is a sort of guardian angel of centaurs). I went back inside, disappointed but calm, and went to bed.

I didn't sleep long: I was roused by a loud explosion. I got up and ran outside in alarm. Peri was up and dressed too.

"Down at the river!" he shouted.

We ran to the dam. By the light of dawn we saw that the dam no longer existed; the explosion had destroyed it. The river was running slowly again. My neighbors had done a good job.

Peri turned to me.

"I'm ready, boss."

Ready? Ready for what? At first I didn't realize what he was talking about. Then I remembered: he was ready to turn me into a centaur.

And I, was I ready? I had been more so on other occasions. In reality, I had even forgotten about our conversation. Centaur? I hardly thought about it any more. Peri's reminder struck me as disagreeable, even threatening.

Still, I had to give him an answer. He was watching me, waiting. All of a sudden I felt enthusiastic. For one thing, Peri couldn't turn me into a centaur at all. And even if he did, it would be for a short time; twenty-four hours, maybe. My answer was specific: Yes, I was ready to become a centaur again, but only for a day at most. Was that possible? Of course, he said, you're the boss, you're in charge. I was euphoric now. Centaur for a day, what an experience!

As a precaution, I asked him if he still remembered exactly what a centaur was like (so he wouldn't make horse's legs grow out of my head or back). He said yes, he knew very well what to do.

As evening fell, I went out to the fields. As he had instructed me, I lay down on my back, arms open in a cross. A little while later he appeared, painted and wearing a loincloth like a real Indian medicine man. He didn't say anything, but began to dance around me, chanting a monotonous song.

I looked up at the sky, where black clouds were gathering. All at once the Indian stopped chanting. He drew closer and threw clods of dry earth on my chest, hitting my legs with the staff he was carrying.

The wind began to blow. All at once a heavy rain poured down on us.

"It's the rain!" shouted Peri, excited. "It's the rain! We're saved! My dance worked!"

"Worked!?" I sat up, pulled up one pants leg. Skin, naturally. White skin with dark hairs. "What about my horse's legs, Peri?"

What horse's legs? he said, the important thing is the rain, boss! If it's raining, it means my dance worked!

I stared at him, uncomprehendingly.

"Get up, boss! Let's go home. Boss all soaked, boss get sick. Come on, let's go home."

I got up, disconcerted. And then, my eyes blurred by the rain that pounded in my face, I saw a distant figure galloping toward us. My heart leaped.

"Look there, Peri! Look!"

A centaur? I myself, Guedali the centaur, coming to meet Guedali the biped?

No. It was someone on horseback. It was a woman. It was Tita! She reined in the horse a few yards away from us, jumped off, and ran into my arms. For several minutes we stood there embracing in tears. Let's go home, I said. I put her on the saddle and mounted behind her. Peri watched us in dumb amazement.

"Get up, Peri!" I yelled laughing, as the rain poured down harder and harder. He didn't hesitate; agile as a monkey, he jumped up onto the animal's hindquarters, and home we went.

I carried Tita inside and laid her on the bed. She looked at me, smiling, as I took off her clothes. I lay down beside her, kissing her mouth, her breasts, her belly, her thighs, her feet. How I had missed that body. By Abraham's bosom, how I had missed it!

The best days of our lives? Yes. Almost certainly yes. As good as the days when we used to gallop across the pampas together.

We took walks through the country, Tita and I, looking at the soybean plants, now revived by the rains. Surprisingly, it was she who talked more. She told me of the days that followed my departure, how she had locked herself in the bedroom and refused to see anyone, not even the children. The other wives—Bela, Tânia, Beatrice, Fernanda—would pound on the door, imploring her to let them in. She wouldn't answer, or touch the food they left outside her door.

"But I must confess," she said looking deep into my eyes, "that it wasn't just on account of you that I fell into such a state of depression. There were other reasons. You know—things I saw through psychotherapy."

(Yes. Had she really loved the centaur? She had. Why not? Aren't there women, I asked myself, who suddenly fall in love with a TV actor, or an adolescent they see in the street?)

In the beginning, she hardly cared about my absence. So Guedali had run off? Fine, the hell with him. Little by little, however, she began to realize that she missed me. She too tossed and turned in bed at night, sleepless; she too murmured my name. And then one evening the telephone rang: it was Mina, saying I had gone to the old farm in the Quatro Irmãos district.

"I got on the first plane to Pôrto Alegre," she said, "and after that the bus to Quatro Irmãos. But it was impossible to get a taxi to bring me out here; there was a bridge down on the road. The only way was to rent a horse. Fortunately, I still remember how to gallop," she finished, laughing.

We walked a lot, we talked a lot, we laughed over nothing. At times we were silent, but not for long. Soon we would begin talking again, both at once—we had so much to say. Peri watched us from a distance. Anyone could see that Tita dazzled him. What a beautiful wife you have, boss, he would say with obvious envy and even spite. I would find corncob effigies with nails stuck into them near the house: spells he was casting against me. That peon is really out to win my heart, Tita would say laughingly.

That weekend our sons arrived—and my parents, and my sisters with their families. We're all together again, in the same place we started out, my father said with emotion. We celebrated the reunion with a huge barbecue, Peri showing his talents as a cook. The twins helped him. They hardly left him alone a minute, entranced as they were with the stories the Indian told them.

I took long walks with my father across the farm. Certain trees, certain rocks brought back memories for him. Here I once killed a snake. . . . Mina and Deborah used to play over there. He was excited about the soybeans: They didn't raise these in my day, and I hear it's a profitable crop. Then he would sigh: Ah, if only Baron Hirsch could see your farm, he would be happy. We didn't discuss me; he didn't even ask me how I was. No doubt he feared that I would again start talking about hooves and gallops through the countryside.

The days were bright and sunny, now that the rain had stopped. They were festive days: we would go for picnics in the woods, organize games and tournaments, or swim in the river. My mother seemed rejuvenated, happier than she had ever been. She only lamented the absence of Bernardo, who must be wandering heaven knew where, in some corner of Brazil. Maybe he'll show up yet, said Mina.

Bernardo didn't show up, but Paulo, Fernanda, Júlio, and Bela came to see us. Paulo had good news. He had outlined a plan for us to go into the exporting business, which was now very profitable. We would form a company with offices in São Paulo, Rio, and Pôrto Alegre.

"I was thinking," he said, choosing his words as he studied my face, "that you could take charge of the branch in Rio. Or better yet, Pôrto Alegre, so as to be near your family."

He was afraid, like my parents, sisters, and maybe even Tita and the boys, that I might run away again. But I wasn't offended.

"That's a good idea, Paulo. Very good. I'll think about where we'll settle. But first of all, let me say I accept the offer of partnership."

"Wonderful!" he said with relief, and immediately changed the subject. He spoke of how much he enjoyed being at the farm. You've got so much space to run here, Guedali! he exclaimed with a shade of envy.

"Are you still running?"

"Every night. The guards in the condominium are used to me, they think I'm funny. Speaking of running, I ordered some sensational jogging shoes from the United States. They have arch supports and the soles are hollow, with tiny springs inside. Really well designed, Guedali. You run without even wanting to."

He smiled melancholically.

"I miss you, Guedali. Jogging alone isn't the same. In fact, I know jogging is weird. I really should take up tennis, that's the big thing now, everybody's playing tennis. But I like to run, Guedali. It's one of the things I believe in."

He wasn't very happy with the political situation, he confided, in spite of the prospects for the new company.

"Socialism is coming, Guedali. Sooner or later, you mark

my words. Look at Africa. A day doesn't pass without some country turning socialist. In Asia, the same thing. Here the guys say we have a capitalistic system ... yes, but for how long? There's been so much abuse. A friend of mine has two yachts, another goes to Paris every other month. This situation can't last. One of these days a general or a colonel or even a major, whatever—some military guy will get irritated with the situation and presto, socialism will be proclaimed. And there we'll be, with only so many square yards to live in, only so many cigarettes to smoke per day. Cars won't be for everyone. Trips abroad out of the question. Which means? That we have to learn to enjoy simple things, Guedali. Running, for example."

He had a plan: a gigantic marathon.

"We get guys to sign up, guys we can trust, like us. Maybe a hundred, two hundred runners. We run across Brazil—in stages, naturally. We get to Central America, to the United States, go up to Alaska. We pass through the polar region, through Asia, get to Jerusalem, and enter in triumph through the Lion Gate. We finish our marathon at the Wailing Wall."

His face was shining.

"And there it is; depending on how things are, we don't even come back. We'll stay there in the Old City. Doing what? Whatever we want, making copper bracelets, selling postcards. Anything to earn a little money by day and run at night."

Bela, who had heard part of the conversation, didn't agree.

"Capitalism is consolidated here, Paulo. Do you really think the multinational companies are going to give up their gravy? Have no fear, friend. You can go on exporting by day and running by night with no worries. I've gotten used to the idea. So we've got capitalism? Well, capitalism it is then. Life is too short to be wasted on dramatic gestures. Our protest has to take tolerable forms. We have to base it on the defense of the consumer, the protection of the environment. People are out there dumping poison in the food, killing the wildlife—did you know that the duck-billed platypus no longer exists,

Guedali? Well, it doesn't. I saw a photograph of the last
member of the species. It was an interesting animal, with a
duck's bill and nipples. Yes, nipples! In other words, something
completely unique. Now tell me, Guedali, just because a creature
is different, doesn't it have a right to exist? What right do
people have to liquidate the whales? And another thing we have
to think about is the feminist movement. My God, Guedali,
women make up half of humanity and they're still suffering
unspeakable horrors. It has to stop, Guedali! It's barbarous. It's
not just a matter of competing with men, burning bras doesn't
do any good. It's orgasm that's important, Guedali. We have
to fight for women's orgasm. And you men have to help, you
can't ignore the question. You've behaved like stallions—
you're from the gaucho country, Guedali, you know what I'm
talking about. You men gallop up, have a good screw, and
gallop off again. It won't do, Guedali, let's face it. It won't do!"

It's not quite like that, Paulo began, but just then my
mother came up: Enough idle talk, children! Let's come to the
table, the food is getting cold.

What's this thing? Tita asked me one night, pointing to
Lolah's mummified paw. Nothing, I answered evasively. She
frowned: What do you mean, nothing? This is an animal's paw,
Guedali. It's a sort of amulet, I said, a good-luck charm, Peri
gave it to me.

She wasn't convinced.

"You're hiding something from me, Guedali. Come on, tell
me what this thing is. It's time we stopped lying to each
other."

I hesitated, but in the end gave in. I told her in detail
about my affair with Lolah, leaving nothing out. She listened,
incredulous at first, then crushed. When I finished, she
remained silent, her head bowed. I thought she was jealous,
which irritated me. You were screwing a centaur, I felt like
saying, and me a sphinx, what's the difference? What's the
difference between a horse's penis and a lioness's vagina?
They're both animal!

But she wasn't jealous. It's all right, Guedali, she said as she raised her eyes to me. It's all right. Let's forget everything, let's take a sponge and wipe away the past. Let's live for the future, for our sons.

That night, a hot night, I went outside to walk alone in the fields. In front of the stable, Peri was kneeling, his arms raised to the sky in incantation. Good evening, I said. He didn't answer; he was standoffish toward me these days.

I kept walking down to the river. I sat on a rock and thought for a while. Yes, I was all right now. I no longer felt the desire to gallop, I no longer asked myself questions. One way or the other, I was cured. I got up and ran through the fields toward the house, jumping and rolling on the wet grass as I went. Happy.

When I entered the bedroom, Tita was already asleep. I cautiously drew close to her and lifted the blanket. There were her feet. Feet, not hooves. Small, delicate feet. As on the day of our reunion, I kissed those feet lovingly. It was time to go back to the city.

SÃO PAULO: A TUNISIAN RESTAURANT, THE
GARDEN OF DELIGHTS
SEPTEMBER 21, 1973

OF COURSE, NOW THAT I NO LONGER HAVE HOOVES IT'S IMPOSSIBLE,
but I feel like kicking and stamping on the floor until a waiter
appears. The service in this restaurant is getting steadily worse.
The waiters don't come. The flies, on the other hand, multiply
around my head, their buzzing designed to try my patience.

Across from me, Tita is still talking to the girl in dark
glasses. I know by heart the story she is telling. It's the same
story she tells Bela, for example. What surprises me is that Tita
goes into detail, reveals secrets to this girl, who is practically a
stranger. Why? Is my wife drunk? Or has she found a new soul
sister? It doesn't matter. As far as I'm concerned, she can tell
the story in whatever way she wants. The Guedali she's talking
about is as unreal to me as a centaur would be to anybody
else. The tale that Tita narrates, however, is very credible. There
are no centaurs in the equestrian scenes she describes. There is
a child being born in the muncipality of Quatro Irmãos, Rio
Grande do Sul, but no winged horse hovers over the wooden
house at the moment of birth. It is possible that beforehand,
something had fluttered above that roof, the little soul of the
future child which, according to the Zohar, or Book of
Splendor, is already present when the parents embrace (tenderly

or furiously, desperately or hopefully, apathetically or hungrily) to give the new life beginning. Guedali doesn't know that Tita reads the Zohar, the mystic text that the Jewish Cabalists examined in search of answers for the unknowable things of the universe. That is: Tita thinks that Guedali doesn't know she reads the Zohar; there are secrets between them. But Guedali knows. He knows many things. The wisdom that was in the marrow of his hooves is not lost, in spite of the operation.

Tita tells about the difficult delivery. The fetus Guedali is in breech position in the uterus; instead of his head coming out first, his legs come. (Legs. For Tita, human legs.) The midwife pulls in desperation. Dona Rosa screams, the sisters cry, all in confusion. After the baby is born, the mother has severe depression. For days she lies immobile without speaking to anyone and hardly eating.

As soon as she improves, the father decides to have the circumcision performed. More confusion: the mohel, an old alcoholic, is having frequent hallucinations. Arriving at the house, he sees not a normal child, but a boy with equine legs and body. Terrified, he tries to run away. Leon Tartakovsky doesn't allow him to, and they argue. In the end, seeing Guedali's penis (which looks gigantic to him) the mohel agrees to perform the ritual, apparently fascinated by the opportunity to realize a circumcision such as no one has ever done before.

(The girl laughs, showing strong, perfect teeth. They must have ground a lot of steak, those teeth. They must have bitten many a male shoulder.)

Guedali grows up on a farm. A quiet child, he likes to go for walks, in spite of a birth defect—he has one foot that is slightly equine looking, which makes it necessary that he wear orthopedic shoes. Although he has some trouble walking, he is an excellent horseback rider, and gallops effortlessly over the plains. Leon doesn't like his son to go far away from the house, but Guedali only feels good outdoors. There he can converse with his imaginary friend, the little Indian boy Peri. Indeed, he has no other friend in such a remote place

He likes to ride horseback and to play the violin. At times

he rides playing the violin, a skill that amazes his parents.
They have hopes: can it be their son is a virtuoso? A Mischa
Elman, a Yehudi Menuhin, a Zimbalist? They will never
know: one day, for no apparent reason, Guedali throws the
violin into the muddy waters of the river. That's how he is,
unpredictable. but his parents and sisters love him nonetheless.
Yet his brother Bernardo hates him without reason; he never
loses an opportunity to antagonize him. If that weren't enough,
Guedali has an enemy in Pedro Bento, the son of a neighboring
farmer. This perverse boy forces Guedali to get down on all
fours, and rides him like a horse. A painful episode, which for
Dona Rosa is the last straw. For a long time she has wanted to
leave the farm. This proves that our children can't be brought
up among such brutes, she tells her husband.

They move to Pôrto Alegre, and live in a house in the
Teresópolis neighborhood. Guedali grows to adolescence, still
timid and bashful—to the point that his bar mitzvah is
celebrated at home, with only the family present.

He is most intelligent, but refuses to go to school, to his
parents' despair. They want a better future for him than tending
the counter at the family grocery store. Still, Guedali reads a
lot, takes correspondence courses, and learns various languages
by the Berlitz method. He has an interesting hobby: he likes to
observe the skies through a telescope.

"And because of that, he fell in love for the first time,"
Tita says. "With a neighbor whom he only knew through the
telescope; imagine, he never even spoke to her. The most he
ever did was to send her a love letter by means of a carrier
pigeon named Columbo. Only instead of delivering the
message, Columbo saw his chance and flew away."

The girl smiles. She is lovely, this girl. Actually, she isn't
all that young—it's hard to tell what age she is on account of
the dark glasses. She might even be older than I am; I only
know that she's causing me a hell of an erection. I even imagine
scenes: I pursue her in the mountains of Tunisia, trapping her
in a ravine with no exit. I close in on her, laughing. She laughs
too as she unbuttons her blouse. Then she leaps upon me like

a lioness, mad with desire, and we make love in this ravine in
Tunisia.

Another scene: the two of us cantering side by side on the
pampas, both nude. I jump off my horse and onto hers; we
both fall onto the soft grass, laughing. From then on, everything
happens the same as in the ravine in Tunisia.

A third scene: right here in the restaurant. She notices that
she has left something important in the car, her credit cards,
for example. She asks me to go outside with her and get them; I
agree. A fine rain is falling. Let's run, she says, and we do—I
a little unsteadily because of the wine. Come on, she says, taking
my hand. I put my arm around her waist and we both run to
her car, a Galaxy parked on a hill. She opens the door and slides
behind the wheel. I sit beside her. For a few seconds we pant
from our run, laughing softly and looking at each other. The
headlights from the rare cars that pass light up her face, her
neck, a glimpse of her breast seen through her half open blouse.
The rain grows thicker; now it's a deafening downpour
hammering on the car roof. How will we ever get out of here?
she asks. We won't, I say, we'll wait for the rain to pass. As
she leans over to get her credit cards out of the glove
compartment, her blouse opens and one breast pops out. Then
she is in my arms; we kiss passionately. She lies down on the car
seat and I lie on top of her, the two of us moving with
difficulty because of the narrow space. I raise her skirt, not
heeding her weak protest (what madness, Guedali, what
madness!) and then something unexpected happens that in the
end only serves to make the situation more exciting. By
accident, I bump the gear shift, and the car, which doesn't have
the emergency brake on, begins to roll downhill. But I can't
stop. I'm almost coming as she screams, Guedali! The car's
moving! There, I'm done, I stretch one leg awkwardly and
step on the brake. I look at her. She is pale and wide eyed. Did
you get hurt? I ask her. No, she says, it was just the scare.
And she adds: What a pity, Guedali, I was almost getting there.
Never mind, I say, let's do it again. So we do it again, and this
time she comes. We sit up and look at each other. Then we start
laughing. We roar with laughter, I slapping my hand against

the steering wheel and producing a loud honk, which makes us laugh even harder. Still giggling, we go back to the restaurant.

His passion frustrated, Guedali runs away from home. He wanders about the byways of Rio Grande, often starving. He has to steal to eat. In the end, he gets a job in a circus. Using his fertile imagination to create a comic act, he makes a centaur costume out of a piece of horsehide. The front legs are his own legs, the body and hind legs are stuffed with straw. The public raves with delight when Guedali the centaur appears in the ring.

Then, his second love.

"With a lady lion tamer!" says Tita, and adds with a laugh, "At least it wasn't a lioness!"

The lion tamer: a mysterious, bewitching woman. She is attracted to Guedali. One night she goes to his sleeping quarters. The inexperienced young man throws himself on her, wanting to possess her by force. Scared, the lion tamer screams, A horse! A real horse! Guedali runs away. Once again he takes to the road, and finally ends up at the border. It is here he meets Tita, adopted daughter of the rancher Zeca Fagundes and his wife Dona Cotinha.

"My father was a very difficult man," says Tita, suddenly serious to the point of melancholy. "He tyrannized the peasants on the ranch. And chased women, too—a real degenerate. I even suspect he didn't always think of me as a daughter. He died of a heart attack, poor thing, the day Guedali came to the ranch."

That day: early in the morning Guedali arrives at the ranch. He sees a horse grazing. Missing his home on the farm, he is seized by a desire to go for a horseback ride. He mounts bareback. The horse is a little frisky, but accepts the rider. Spurred on by Guedali's impatient heels, it gallops across the field.

Meanwhile, Tita is also going out for a horseback ride. It's her birthday, and she wants to spend it outdoors.

The rancher sees her riding her bay horse through the light

mist of a winter morning. Hung over as he is (having spent
the night carousing and drinking) he sees not his adopted
daughter, but rather an appetizing female, nude to boot—a
Lady Godiva of the pampas. Quick as a flash he saddles a horse
and chases after her

Guedali, coming from the opposite direction, sees them
approach at a distance. He quickly dismounts, hides himself
and his horse in an abandoned shelter, and observes them
through a crack in the wall. Upon seeing that a defenseless girl
is being pursued by a man, he doesn't hesitate. He mounts again
and rushes out the door. Seeing him, the rancher lets out a
yell and falls from his mount, dead.

Guedali goes to the girl's rescue, for her horse is galloping
out of control. He contains the animal, helps her dismount, and
leads her to the shelter. The poor girl is traumatized and
shaking, her eyes blurred. Guedali tries to calm her. Tita breaks
into convulsive but beneficial sobs. He lets her cry, murmuring
affectionate words, and dries her tears. He kisses her softly. She
hesitates, but returns his kiss. Then he makes love to her, this
time with no clumsiness. On the contrary, guided by a secret
wisdom which surprises even himself, he is an artist with his
caresses, little by little awakening her feminine desire. Trembling
with pleasure, she murmurs, It's good, it's very good.

"But it wasn't love I felt," says Tita to the girl. "Not love
in the true sense of the word, if you understand me. It was
more like passion, and also something symbolic. In a certain
sense Guedali was substituting for my dead father, you see? I
came to realize this afterward, during my analysis."

She puts out her cigarette.

"In fact, the no-good stayed there, taking advantage of my
fantasies. He never even mentioned marriage. You know, my
being a goy, he didn't want to upset his parents. He was afraid
of them."

Dona Cotinha is a true mother to them both. Guedali
and Tita have no worries. They ramble over the pampas, on
foot or on horseback, and make love. They make love
frequently, wherever the desire comes over them. Once, in the

fields, they see Guedali's stallion mount Tita's mare. The scene excites them and, laughing, they tear off their clothes and lie down right there on a hilltop, in broad daylight.

This happiness is interrupted abruptly.

Guedali, up to then a healthy young man, becomes sick. He gets terrible headaches accompanied by strange sensations. It seems to him that his body is growing to an enormous size, and that the skin on his feet is getting thick and hard, like hooves. He exhibits disturbed behavior, getting up at night and running out into the fields. Tita has to go and get him; he doesn't want to come back home. He thinks he is a centaur.

"Centaur!" exclaims the girl incredulously, "Come on!" One can see she wants to laugh, but she contains herself, not knowing if this subject should be viewed as comic, in line with the somewhat playful tone Tita has given the story, or if it is a sign that something serious is about to be revealed. At any rate, she doesn't seem to believe that anyone would get up at night to run through the countryside, believing himself a centaur.

Oh? Doesn't she believe it? What about these legs that stir restlessly during the day and don't let me sleep at night? Why are these legs never still, girl? What inexhaustible energy animates them? Girl, there are nights when I run miles and miles. Not that I want to, but my legs won't stop. Of course, I could cross them, subjugate them one to the other by means of their own weight. Except then I would be running another risk: fusion. Can you imagine my two legs uniting into a single appendage? Can you imagine this new kind of tail growing scales and metamorphosing me into a being even more improbable than a centaur, a male mermaid?

Tita doesn't know what to think, but Dona Cotinha suspects that Guedali's disease is very serious. Doctors are called in; they agree that it's a grave neurological disorder, maybe a brain tumor, but they aren't really certain. Dona Cotinha grows impatient and insists that they make a complete diagnosis, money is no object. The patient is referred to the top specialist in the field, a surgeon who was practicing in Paris but has now moved to Morocco. Not able to charter a private plane, Dona Cotinha rents a ship. The journey is awful, Guedali vomits the whole time, but Tita and he finally arrive. The doctor examines him and decides to operate immediately.

"And it was indeed a brain tumor," says Tita. "Enormous! The doctor said he had never seen such a huge tumor in that exact spot and with such a strange shape."

Tumor. Interesting. *Tumor, How to Generate a:* Imagine a centaur. Imagine him immobile, poised to gallop, head thrust forward, fists clenched, tendons stretched. This figure, although imaginary, naturally generates tremendous energy, which invades your dilated pupils, flows down the optic nerve to the brain, and collects there like water in a dam. The eventual overflow causes an extraordinary activation of cells theretofore quiet, resulting in their wild proliferation à la underprivileged peoples. Soon you have a nodule, which grows and develops appendages that look like horses' legs, a human trunk, human arms and head—and there you have it. A miniature model of a centaur right there in the cerebral mass. It will of course be upside down, having been produced by specular means, but it will be the same in every way to the image which produced it. Except that it's real, very real, at least for Tita, who even has X-rays to document growths of this type.

Guedali is still unconscious in the recovery room when an unfortunate accident befalls Tita. She is run over by a van that is entering the clinic at high speed—the driver's imprudence. Thrown a great distance, she has exposed fractures in the pelvis and legs. The Moroccan doctor performs emergency surgery.

"And so we were both hospitalized. Side by side, me with half my body in a cast. It would have been comic, if it hadn't been for the pain we both went through."

*   *   *

Guedali recovers quickly, Tita more slowly. Everything seems fine, but they are soon faced with another trial: the news of Dona Cotinha's death, which saddens them greatly.

The day of their departure comes. As the clinic staff watches, they dance a farewell waltz. They return to Brazil, not to the ranch, which no longer means anything to them, but to São Paulo. With the money from the inheritance, they buy a house and Guedali sets up a wholesale-distributing firm. In the beginning things are hard. Guedali still has occasional headaches and hallucinations; Tita walks with some difficulty and, like him, must wear orthopedic boots. Because of these problems, Guedali doesn't want to have children. He does agree to formalize their marriage, however. The event takes place in Pôrto Alegre, to the family's general delight, although Guedali's mother still doesn't trust her daughter-in-law.

When Tita announces that she is pregnant, Guedali has a fit. In the end he resigns himself, but he demands that the delivery be performed by the old midwife who brought him into the world. The woman, now very aged, has to be located and brought to São Paulo by plane. All goes well, and soon Guedali becomes the father of two beautiful boys.

"He didn't want to assume the burden of fatherhood," said Tita jokingly, "and as a punishment, he had twins."

They began to have more friends. Before, they were considered a strange couple. They never went to the beach because Tita was very timid and didn't like to be seen in a bathing suit, especially now with the scars from the operation. Besides, on account of her orthopedic boots, she always wears slacks. Nevertheless, their friends learn to like them as they are. Slacks and boots are becoming fashionable, and Tita is even admired for her elegance.

In this amiable climate, the idea of forming a horizontal condominium with their friends is only natural. A new life begins, a happy and peaceful life. There is one problem when they move: Guedali meets Pedro Bento, his old enemy, now the chief guard. Guedali might have had a crisis, but he

remembers the words of Jehovah: vengeance is mine. He
wants to reconcile himself to the past and no mere Pedro Bento
will stop him.

About then Guedali begins to have attacks of jealousy. (He
who everyone knew was having an affair with Fernanda!) He
suspects every telephone call Tita makes, suspects her silences.
Later his jealousy would be shown to be unfounded, sick. But
in the meantime, weeks and months go by. A trying situation,
which the Ricardo episode only aggravates.

Tita tells the story of Ricardo. For her, he is not a centaur.
He is a young man who was killed at the condominium on
July 15, 1972. Centaur? No, not a centaur

He is born, this Ricardo, in a beach house in Santa
Catarina where his parents, from Curitiba, are spending their
vacation. Just like Guedali, he is circumcised on the eighth day.
Unlike Guedali, however, he is raised with every luxury. His
father, a rich industrialist, doesn't want his son to lack
anything. Like Guedali, Ricardo is timid and prefers to stay at
home, absorbed in his toys and (later on) in his books. It is the
books (as his mother says indignantly) that turn his head: the
novels of Michael Gold, Howard Fast, and Jorge Amado, not
to mention the works of Marx and Engels. He grows angry,
wants to reform the world. Restless, he begins to spend all his
time in the streets, he who before always stayed at home. He
wanders through the bars of Curitiba, takes up with a gang of
young fanatics like himself, and devotes his life to the violent
transformation of society. He becomes an urban terrorist.
Though he barely knows how to handle a revolver, he attempts
with others to assault a bank in São Paulo; this is in 1967. He
is put in prison. He manages to escape from the country secretly
and goes to Algeria. There he lives for a few years, working as
a waiter to support himself. Little by little his revolutionary
fervor gives way to melancholy. He misses Brazil, his friends,
and especially his parents, with whom he has been corresponding
through a relative in France. He wants to go home. But how?
He would be imprisoned as soon as he arrived; the national
security organizations all have his photo and fingerprints. An

English forger whom he gets to know at the restaurant
suggests a plan. He should change his face and fingerprints by
means of plastic surgery. But who could do it? asks Ricardo,
finding the idea rather farfetched but willing to try anything,
desperate as he is. The Englishman gives him the name of a
Moroccan doctor, an able surgeon who will do anything for
the right price paid in strong currency.

Ricardo writes to his parents, who send him money. He
goes to Morocco. He has the worst possible impression of the
clinic and the doctor, a shifty-eyed old character with trembling
hands. The doctor hardly manages to conceal his greed; he is
proud of having done the most bizarre operations.

For several days the young man stays at the clinic,
undecided. In truth, he is afraid. He had been afraid before, at
the time of the bank robbery, for instance; but when the actual
moment came, he was very calm and professional, forcing the
functionaries into the bathroom at gunpoint and locking the
door. But now, the idea of being anesthetized and waking up
with his face scored by disastrous incisions leaves him absolutely
terrified. The Moroccan doctor doesn't seem to perceive his
dilemma, but insists that the operation be done as soon as
possible, alleging reasons of security. But Ricardo thinks all he
wants is money; there are no other patients in the clinic, and
the doctor is obviously short of cash. Under one pretext or
another, he keeps putting off the surgery. He doesn't admit he
is afraid; he tries to convince himself that he is only being
prudent. He needs to know more about the doctor: mightn't
he be an informer? So one afternoon when Ricardo is alone in
the clinic, he goes into the doctor's office and examines his
files. He comes across the name of one Guedali, a Brazilian
from São Paulo, and writes down the address: it might be
useful.

That night the doctor announces that he will perform the
operation the next day no matter what. This game isn't funny
any more, he says irritably, and Ricardo sees that he is in
earnest. It's time to get out of here, he thinks. That very night
he packs his few possessions and flees. A Berber gives him a

ride on a camel to the city. He goes directly to the port, discovers a ship bound for Brazil, and bribes the first mate to let him on board. The man accepts the money but tells him he must jump ship near Santos, before the vessel docks. That is what he does. He swims to the beach. Hiding by day and walking at night, he comes to the outskirts of São Paulo. He takes shelter in an abandoned house and there meets an outlandish fellow, a middle-aged hippie, who wears a big watch hanging around his neck. They converse; Ricardo shows him the address of the condominium and asks if he knows how to get there. When he sees Guedali's name, the man exclaims: Why, he's my brother! He insists that Ricardo look him up: Guedali will help you get to Curitiba and out of danger, he guarantees.

Ricardo gets to the condominium. As a precaution, he decides to avoid the guards at the main gate. The fence is high, but it's no problem for him; in his training as a terrorist he learned to get over far more difficult obstacles. That night, using a bamboo pole cut from a nearby thicket, he vaults over the fence with ease.

Hiding himself in the bushes and trees, he identifies Guedali's house by its name plaque. He goes in the back way. But instead of meeting Guedali, he meets Tita.

They look at each other. Tita doesn't seem frightened nor even surprised; it's as if she has been expecting him. She smiles, he smiles too. She takes him by the hand, leads him to the empty space beneath the stairway. There they converse for hours in whispers, telling each other their stories. Tita listens to the young man with fascination; she admires his courage, his altruism. Transforming society is something she has never even thought of. Guedali comes home. She is so perturbed that she hardly is able to speak. What's wrong with you? he asks suspiciously. Nothing, she answers, just a slight headache. She knows Guedali has been disturbed lately; she even fears for his emotional balance. He goes to bed, apparently not noticing anything

The next morning after Guedali leaves, she gives the servants a day off, and feels calmer. Her sons are down south with their grandparents. She prepares some sandwiches and takes them to the young man. Once again they converse at length. In the end he confesses: he is in love with her. It was sudden but unmistakable; he is sure of it. He proposes they run away together. They will live in the interior, maybe in Rio Grande do Sul, raising cattle and planting just enough to get along, for he doesn't want to accumulate wealth. Most important, they will make love. They will make love constantly there in the country, upon the greensward, beside the brooks.

Now it's Tita who is disturbed. She doesn't know what to say. She is afraid of hurting the young man, who has already suffered so much. She is afraid of committing herself. She is especially afraid of her own feelings. She asks for time to think it over. Ricardo insists on an answer, but Tita smilingly evades him. It's nightfall, Guedali will be coming home.

Ricardo wants nothing to do with Guedali. He doesn't even want to meet him. He only hears his voice once, on the evening of July 15, 1972: "Don't wait up, I'll be late." Ricardo comes boldly out of the wine cellar; he wants Tita's answer. You're crazy, she says. Go back to your hiding place at once! But he throws prudence to the winds and embraces her there in the living room.

The door opens. It's Guedali. "I'm back," he says, "Paulo—"

He stops short. He can't believe his eyes. I think there's no point in trying to hide anything, says Tita. There is a challenging note in her voice that irks Guedali still further: it's as if she were unquestionably in the right. Who's he? he asks, controlling himself with difficulty, and what's he doing in my house? Well, begins Tita, already insecure, he turned up here—

Guedali interrupts her. "Not you. Don't you say a word. He's the one to explain. He'll tell me everything, absolutely straight, without any lies."

Ricardo tells his story. He is trembling, obviously frightened out of his wits. He says that he only wanted to ask for Guedali's help to return home to his parents.

Guedali is no longer interested in what he is saying. He is

looking at Tita. He has no doubt: she has fallen overwhelmingly
in love with Ricardo. She has eyes only for him. Guedali sees
he has to do something quickly, because ...

The door opens and a group of people burst in, shouting,
"Happy anniversary! Happy anniversary!" Paulo and Fernanda,
Júlio and Bela, Armando and Beatrice, Tânia and Joel. Bela is
carrying a cake, Armando holds two bottles of wine, and Tânia
a bouquet. Suddenly Guedali remembers: it's the anniversary
of the condominium's inauguration, a date they always celebrate.
That is why he didn't find Paulo, whom he went to see.

Everyone stands stock-still in surprise. All at once, Tânia
becomes hysterical: It's a thief! she screams, call the guards!
For God's sake, call the guards!

With a fearful cry, Ricardo throws himself against the
enormous picture window, and disappears in a shower of broken
glass. Wait! cries Tita. Beatrice tries to hold her but she
pushes her away and runs out the door with the others after
her. Paulo screams, Who is he, Guedali, who is he? Shut up,
shouts Guedali, and at that moment they hear dogs barking and
gunshots, many shots in rapid succession. They run to the park
and from a distance see the guards surrounding the fountain—
and the boy, fallen face down in a pool of blood.

Tita runs ahead of the others, still screaming. By making a
desperate effort Guedali catches up with her before she gets to
the fountain and grabs her by the arm. Let go of me, you
animal! she screams, her face twisted with hatred and pain.
He doesn't let her go, but holds her firmly, pulling her toward
him. She resists, scratching his face and pounding his chest
with her fists. In the end she weakens and, half swooning,
allows her husband to lead her home and lay her on the bed.

The doorbell rings insistently. Guedali answers it. It's Pedro
Bento, revolver still in hand. He is gray with fright and
sweating profusely. Was that your relative, Guedali? he asks
in a whisper. Your friend? Guedali doesn't answer, he only
stares at him. Pedro Bento continues: Forgive me, Guedali, if it
was a relative or friend of yours. The guys got scared and
started shooting; when I got to the fountain he was already dying,
I only fired a mercy shot in his head so that he wouldn't suffer.

Above, Tita sobs convulsively. Everything is all right, says
Guedali to Pedro Bento, closing the door

In the days that follow, Tita stays locked in her room,
unable to see anyone. Finally she permits Bela to go in. Only
to Bela does she confide the story of the young terrorist, her
lover. To the others, Bela and Guedali say that he was merely
a thief that Tita surprised breaking into the house.

The necessary measures are taken. The police inquiry and
the short article in the newspapers: "Young Mugger Shot
Breaking into Condominium." An incident all too common to
arouse any attention. In a few days even the children forget what
happened, absorbed in the bang-bang films on TV.

Lies. Layers of lies, one superimposed on the other. One
needs to be an archeologist to sift out the truth from these
imaginings, if any truth there be.

Guedali runs off. He leaves Tita and the boys and heads
for Morocco. He looks up the doctor, which is not surprising,
since he is someone Guedali trusts absolutely. At this point he
is definitely disturbed. He wants to have an operation—wants,
as he says, to be a centaur again. The doctor suspects that this
bizarre conduct might be due to a recurrence of the cancer; he
decides to run a series of exams once more. During this time
Guedali gets involved with a nurse from the clinic, a mysterious
Tunisian woman named Lolah. From her Guedali receives an
amulet, the mummified paw of a lion.

The doctor, who feels a Platonic love for the nurse,
doesn't want the two to see each other, and actually locks her in
her room. The thing almost ends in tragedy. The nurse
invades the room where Guedali is having X-rays taken under
general anesthesia, and tries to attack the doctor. In the end
she is shot by the assistant and moved to another hospital, where
she recovers by the skin of her teeth.

As for Guedali, he wakes up from the anesthesia cured: he
no longer wants to have an operation, he wants to go back to
Brazil. He is in such a hurry that he would have even forgotten
the lion's paw if the doctor hadn't reminded him of it.

*   *   *

"Lion's paw!" the girl exclaims. "That's something I'd really like to have. I'm crazy about good luck charms." Ask him, says Tita, maybe he'll give it to you. He wouldn't let me have it. Will you give me your lion's paw, Guedali? the girl asks me, holding my arm. I'll have to think about it, I reply with a grin.

"So then," says Tita, "Guedali came back from Morocco. Still stubborn: he didn't want to go back home. He bought a farm in Quatro Irmãos that used to belong to his father, and stayed there working the land, helped by a peasant man from the region. At night, the two of them would cast spells, repeat incantations. Guedali likes that kind of thing, you know? And the Indian had a true arsenal of charms and amulets. But then my mother-in-law told me that he was at the farm and I decided to go there. You see, it was only then—and mind you, we'd been married for so many years—only then that I realized I actually did love Guedali. We made up, and now we're living in Pôrto Alegre, where he takes care of the branch office of the firm he set up with Paulo."

She speaks of the house we built on the south side of Pôrto Alegre. A beautiful house in the Moorish style, something quite unusual in the city. Enthusiastically she describes the garden, small but in very good taste. "Now there's a garden that really could be called The Garden of Delights," she exclaims, alluding to the restaurant's name. She speaks of the fountain bubbling in the moonlight, of the planters with their exotic flowers, of the breeze that stirs the branches of the dwarf palm trees, of the graveled walks.

Of course she doesn't mention the hoofprints in the black soil of the flowerbeds. She knows that these marks exist; she attributes them, however, to the wandering horses still sometimes seen in our neighborhood, which isn't yet fully urbanized.

These horses come from São Paulo. The use of the combustion engine for transportation and farm work has made them dispensable as beasts of burden. Confined in narrow

corrals, they are doomed to the inglorious death of the
slaughterhouse. Their instinct saves them from such a destiny.
Guided by some obscure tropism, they go south toward Rio
Grande. They pass through Pôrto Alegre (and it's at this point,
according to Tita's theory, that they invade our garden) and
get to the borderlands where once they galloped, some once
ridden by dapper horsemen and horsewomen. In this country,
however, they are now no longer welcome because they are old
and toothless. Therefore they continue their long forced march.
Passing through the Patagonian plains, exhausted and dying,
they finally reach the region of the eternal glaciers. In a last
effort, they manage to climb a lonely mountain, and there they
die, jaws open in an enigmatic smile.

Very pretty, Tita. But is it really the truth? Are those
really the hoofprints of horses, those marks in the soil of the
garden? Couldn't they be the footprints of someone who runs
through it in the dead of night? I'm speaking of someone with
a human body, and even human legs and feet, but with a
peculiar way of stepping that imprints in the soil the unequivocal
mark of a horse's hoof. I'm talking about a centaur, or about
what's left of him. I'm talking about Guedali, Tita.

But Tita's no longer talking about Guedali. She's telling the
girl how remarkable our children are. One's a champion
athlete who swims like a fish, the other is the best student in his
class and studies the violin. We live in comfort, she finishes.
We lack nothing; everything turned out happily.

It's like the end of a TV serial, says the girl. And she's
right. The story is as ingeniously woven as a soap opera. With
one single objective: to convince me that I never was a
centaur. And they're doing it, at least in part. I still see myself as
a centaur, but a centaur growing constantly smaller, a miniature
centaur, a microcentaur. Even this naughty creature runs away
from me, wants to gallop I don't know where. Maybe it would
be better to let him go, to accept this reality they want to impose
on me: that I am a human being, that the mythological
creatures that so marked my life don't exist, neither centaurs,
nor sphinxes, nor winged horses.

"I like Rio Grande very much," the girl was saying. "As a matter of fact, I have a sister who lives there. Now there's an adventurous soul, just like you, Guedali. She went there as a journalist, to do an article about the ranches on the southern frontier. She ended up joining a circus. Who knows but what she was the lion tamer you fell in love with?"

The two burst into giggles. I laugh too. Why shouldn't I?

"As a matter of fact," she continues, "there's another coincidence. For a time I lived in the house of an old friend of mine, near your Teresópolis neighborhood. Couldn't I be the girl you saw through the telescope, Guedali?"

I laugh again, and she winks at me. I'm sure she winks at me, in spite of her dark glasses.

The other day I saw a poor man in the street. He was begging for alms, showing one stump of leg. I gave him some money, no doubt because of the feeling of guilt inspired by the impulse (aborted) to tell him: You have only one leg? That's nothing, friend. That doesn't hinder you from working. You're looking at somebody who used to have horse's hooves, know that? Someone who struggled and succeeded nevertheless. Follow my example, friend, and fight the battle. Believe me, having horse's hooves is far worse than being without a leg.

Just then a doubt occurs to me. Whose bare feet are these that I've been caressing under the table with my own feet, also bare? They could be Tita's as easily as they could be the girl's. The expression on their faces doesn't help me solve the puzzle: both are smiling with an air of complicity. From the softness of the skin, I would think they were Tita's, but who's to say the blonde doesn't use moisturizing creams too? What's certain is that our feet search for each other, caress each other: erogenous feet, they are.

The girl lifts her glass of wine in a toast. To freedom, as would be expected.

"To freedom!" I say, lifting my glass, and in that instant I realize: one of the feet is Tita's, the other is the girl's. Of course! Why hadn't I realized it sooner? There are people with oddly shaped feet, there are even centaurs' hooves, but feet with the big toe on the outside don't exist. One foot belongs to one, the other to the other.

The discovery causes me an attack of laughter. They look at me in surprise, and laugh with me. In fact, everybody laughs: the twins, Paulo, Fernanda, Júlio, Bela, everybody. Even the Tunisian waiters laugh. They laugh without knowing why, but they laugh delightedly, in ringing peals. One actually doubles up from merriment.

Still laughing, the girl leans over to get her purse. At that moment, her half-open blouse reveals a glimpse of her shapely breast. From her necklaces dangle myriad charms: a Star of David, little Indians. Farther down between her breasts, a small sphinx in bronze, a horse with outspread wings, and a centaur.

She opens her purse. Even before she speaks, before she says she left her credit cards in the car, before she asks me to come outside with her to get them, I am already getting up, I'm standing. Even before Tita, smiling and winking at me, can invite me to go back to our hotel room, I'm getting up, I'm standing.

Like the winged horse, about to take flight toward the mountains of eternal joy, the bosom of Abraham. Like a horse, hooves dancing, ready to gallop across the pampas. Like a centaur in the garden, ready to jump the wall in search of freedom.